"Shannon Sue Dunlap has pe[...]
have ever read before. Set on a[...]
ians, this romantic comedy w[...]
—Sarah Monzon, author o[...]

"A cast of delightfully mischievous women living aboard a cruise ship, who dub themselves the Shippers, bring *Love Overboard* to life. Shannon Sue Dunlap has created a laugh-out-loud romantic comedy with a twist of cozy-mystery intrigue. The story reminded me of the zany, headstrong women in one of my favorite television shows, *The Golden Girls*, so I loved every minute of it. The Shippers are spunky matchmakers determined to bring together Lacey Anderson and hunky Jonathan King. *Love Overboard* has all the ingredients for a great book."
—Sharee Stover, author of *Seeking Justice*

"*Love Overboard* is a laugh-out-loud story of matchmaking and mayhem on the high seas. I loved everything about this book, but the matchmakers were absolutely the best! If you love a cruise with touches of romance and mystery and a generous dash of *Golden Girls*, this is absolutely your book! I can't wait for the next one."
—Kathleen Y'Barbo, *Publishers Weekly* best-selling author of *The Black Midnight* and the Bayou Nouvelle series

"Shannon Sue Dunlap knocks it out of the park with her sweet and funny cruise ship rom-com. The walkie-talkie-wielding group of 'Shippers' absolutely cracked me up. I want to go on a cruise with them. And the romance between Lacey and Jon started with sparks and didn't stop! I can't wait to read more in this perfectly paced, witty series."
—Elly Gilbert, author of *Under the Blue Skies*

"I absolutely adored *Love Overboard*. Whether you enjoy romance, comedy, mystery, or women's fiction, this is the book you're looking for. I laughed aloud, teared up, curled my toes in anticipation, then sighed in satisfaction when I reached the last perfect page. The quirky characters endeared themselves to me, and I look forward to joining them on their next cruise."
—Angela Ruth Strong, author of the Love Off Script series

"Shannon Sue Dunlap takes readers on a laughter-filled voyage on the high seas. This is a cruise you don't want to miss! Filled with meddling matchmakers, a swoony hero, and a heroine you'll root for from the start, *Love Overboard* is a delight from the first page to the last."

—Liz Johnson, best-selling author of *The Red Door Inn*

"They say matches are made in heaven, but Emily Windsor and her gaggle of geriatric girlfriends, known affectionately as 'the Shippers,' don't mind doing the footwork when it comes to matchmaking on their resident cruise liner. On a glamorous ship, the friends finagle every opportunity to bring a couple with a history—guy-shy hostess Lacey Anderson and cruise director Jonathan King—back together. But when high jinks on the high seas threaten to seize the day the wrong way, the girls sail into action. This story hit the high-water mark with romance, adventure, humor, and heartfelt moments that reel in all the right feels. Highly recommend!"

—Linda Kozar, author of *Gimme Some Sugar: Devotions to Sweeten Your Day in a Godly Way*

"Move over, Captain Stubing and Dorothy Zbornak! There's a new love boat and a new set of golden girls that have captured my heart! In *Love Overboard*, Shannon Sue Dunlap has gifted readers with an endearingly quirky group of senior citizen matchmakers who will keep you laughing out loud with delight and wanting to gather them all up in one big group hug. Meanwhile, a swoony romance unfolds despite some choppy seas, and the dash of suspense adds further opportunity for delightful mayhem to ensue. If your heart needs a boost of joy, then *Love Overboard*—with its lovable characters, hilarious antics, sweet romance, and gentle faith message—needs to be your next read!"

—Carrie Schmidt, ReadingIsMySuperPower.org

L♥ve Overboard

A NOVEL

SHANNON SUE DUNLAP

I wish you fair skies and a merry heart!

♡

Shannon Sue

KREGEL
PUBLICATIONS

Love Overboard: A Novel
© 2024 by Shannon Sue Dunlap

Published by Kregel Publications, a division of Kregel Inc., 2450 Oak Industrial Dr. NE, Grand Rapids, MI 49505. www.kregel.com.

Published in association with Books & Such Literary Management, www.books andsuch.com.

The persons and events portrayed in this work are the creations of the author, and any resemblance to persons living or dead is purely coincidental.

Library of Congress Cataloging-in-Publication Data
Name: Dunlap, Shannon S., author.
Title: Love overboard: a novel / Shannon Sue Dunlap.
Description: Grand Rapids, MI: Kregel Publications, a division of Kregel
  Inc., 2024. | Series: Love overboard; book 1
Identifiers: LCCN 2023057371 (print) | LCCN 2023057372 (ebook)
Subjects: LCGFT: Romance fiction. | Christian fiction. | Novels.
Classification: LCC PS3604.U5523 L68 2024 (print) | LCC PS3604.U5523
  (ebook) | DDC 813/.6—dc23/eng/20231215
LC record available at https://lccn.loc.gov/2023057371
LC ebook record available at https://lccn.loc.gov/2023057372

ISBN 978-0-8254-4869-0, print
ISBN 978-0-8254-7435-4, epub
ISBN 978-0-8254-7434-7, Kindle

Printed in the United States of America
24 25 26 27 28 29 30 31 32 33 / 5 4 3 2 1

*To my beautiful mother
who dreamed of cruising,
Billie Sue Dunlap*

CHAPTER 1

WALKIE-TALKIE. BATTLE PLAN. BUTTERSCOTCH candy.

Emily Windsor sifted through the mess in her cavernous purse. Her hand dug until she found a well-worn, faded picture. The cheeky grin of her late husband stared back as he stood resplendent in his dress whites and flashy aviator sunglasses.

How she missed that smile.

"Good morning, love." She smoothed a creased corner on the photo. "Time to launch a new mission. I can imagine the scolding you'd give me. But this match is worth the meddling, Bill. Even you'd agree that sweet girl is worth it.

"Lord"—she pointed her eyes heavenward—"I hope you're taking good care of my man up there."

Emily riffled in a side pocket. She grabbed a small set of opera glasses with the words *Golden Years Tour Company* printed on the side. If her calculations were correct, the target should appear at any moment. She peeked around the corner. Her seventy-eight-year-old spine cracked twice as she bent.

"Mrs. Windsor?"

Her jaw tightened at the squeaky voice. She faced the first mate, Peter. His frowsy white-blond hair and pasty complexion combined with his pristine uniform to give him the appearance of a skinny, befuddled ear swab. Was he going to offer her another lecture on the proper behavior for cruise ship passengers? It would make the second one this week.

His gaze bounced to the binoculars and back again. "Did you lose something?"

"No, dear." She stuffed the equipment in her bag and slid the straps over her wrist. "Just preparing for the voyage."

Three bells sounded on the loudspeaker, followed by an announcement.

Peter pointed at the ceiling. "It's time for muster. Shouldn't you head for your deck?"

"Pish-tosh. The ship won't fall apart if I miss one safety drill."

She tapped an orthopedic sandal against the carpet. His patient expression brought to mind the nurses in the assisted living facility she'd briefly called home when she'd experienced a slight problem with her heart. He raised his voice and spoke in a slow, measured tone as if she was hard of hearing.

"I. Know. You've. Done it. Many. Times. But every. Passenger. Has. To be there."

"I. Un. Der. Stand." Emily pasted on her best doting-Nana impression. She patted his elbow. "Now don't waste your time on me. You have a cruise to launch." One more pat, and she headed for the elevators at the end of the hallway.

Peter called a goodbye at her retreating back and walked in the opposite direction. She waited until he was out of sight, then returned to her post. Nothing and no one would delay her mission of arranging a love match for Lacey Anderson. In the days gone by, when Emily still held out hope for children of her own, she had pictured a daughter just like the hard-shell, soft-center cruise ship hostess.

Lacey had adopted Emily without permission. The young woman always checked if the septuagenarian was eating well, taking her medicine, and getting enough exercise. It was bothersome in the most endearing way. That kind of mothering soul should have kids to love on, and Emily was determined to find the perfect father for those yet-unrealized offspring.

She drew a breath, poked her head around the corner, and jerked back. After Emily raised the walkie-talkie and pressed the side button, static crackled.

"All operatives, take your positions. Operation Ambush is a go."

Lacey froze at the familiar sound. She recognized that voice.

Maybe it was a coincidence. There were lots of people on this deck. Lacey moved again, at a cautious pace this time.

No need to be paranoid. The sweet-but-salty meddler couldn't possibly know where she was. Lacey had avoided Emily Windsor ever since she recognized the gleam in the lady's eye. She used to laugh at the incorrigible woman's matchmaking schemes, but now that they were focused on her, Lacey's stomach quivered like a lifeboat in a hurricane. Romance wasn't on her to-do list. Ever.

Static crackled, and Lacey heard the whispered words she feared.

"Target located."

She fought the urge to run. It wouldn't be dignified for a Monarch Cruises employee. But that didn't mean she couldn't take evasive maneuvers. She swung on her heel and skulked away.

The shiny faux-wood doors of the ship's cabins zoomed by as she hurried through the connecting corridor that led to the parallel hallway. The heels of her navy pumps sank in the carpet and slowed her progress. Lacey glanced over her shoulder and saw a flash of floral print coming into view.

Not today!

She took a right and almost plowed into the noisy group of passengers filling the space. They pounded the back of a large, bearded man with a T-shirt declaring, in lime-green letters, "Walter's 40th Wedding Anniversary." Lacey straightened her white hostess jacket and sidestepped with a smile, her body pressed against the wall. They passed without acknowledging her, as she preferred—part of the invisible but efficient service customers bragged about when they reached home.

Another crackle.

Where were they? Why couldn't she lose them?

Lacey craned her neck to see past the rowdy cruisers and spotted a pint-size head with a mass of frizzy gray curls under Walter's chubby arm as he stretched with a groan. Forget conducting herself with decorum. She bolted like a three-year-old at bath time and rushed down the hall. Taking a hard left, she slammed into something tall and unyielding.

"Whoa," a man said as they collided.

Two large hands grasped her arms as her nose pressed into a broad chest covered in the white Monarch polo. It must belong to the fitness director. He was the only male crew member with such a well-defined torso.

"Sorry, Sven." She ducked behind his muscular physique, hoping her pursuer would pass without discovering her. "The Shippers are after me."

"What's a Shipper?"

Lacey's insides clenched at the voice. It definitely didn't belong to Sven, but she knew that butter-smooth baritone. She just refused to believe what her ears were telling her. The man turned, and she looked up into the symmetrically perfect features of Jonathan King. It was a face she had worked hard to forget. Chocolate-brown hair, dark and twinkling eyes, one straight nose that had never seen a fight, and a pair of lips that were full enough to be kissable yet manly.

"Lace?" His eyes widened as he stared down at her. "Is that you?"

"Hello, Jon." Lacey eased away, but he reached out and pulled her in for a bear hug.

"How long has it been? Two years?"

A riptide of old emotions swept through her as Jon crushed her body against his. Lacey's heart pounded so hard she feared he might feel it. She concentrated on breathing.

In and out.

In and out.

In and in.

No, wait. That wasn't right. How could her brain still be this affected by the man? She stood straight as a broomstick with her hands at her sides and waited for the hug to end.

"Two and a half," she said in a muffled voice from inside his embrace. "But who's counting?"

He was counting. It had been two years and seven months since Lacey Anderson walked out of his life. Correction—she bailed off the boat without so much as a goodbye. Jon held Lacey a few seconds longer than an ex-boyfriend should, enjoying the way she fit against him, her head tucked under his chin. Then he finally noted she wasn't reciprocating and let her go.

She could have posed for a cruise commercial with her shapely figure and spotless uniform. Her honey-blond hair was twisted in a sophisticated knot at the nape of her neck. Was it still as long as he remembered—from when it was normal to give the silky strands a mischievous tug?

"How have you been?"

"Very well, thank you." Her tone stayed in business-friendly mode. "What are you doing here? I thought you were working the Scandinavian route."

"Been keeping tabs on me?" Jon bumped her with his elbow and grinned.

"No." Lacey stepped away—out of bumping distance. "Someone happened to mention it once."

Jon also withdrew a step and studied her like a stranger instead of the woman he still dreamed about from time to time. He'd known she worked on this ship when he took the assignment and had wondered how Lacey would feel when she saw him again. Gazing at the model of politeness in front of him, he still wondered.

"Meet the new cruise director." He gave a slight bow. "The old one backed out at the last minute, and I got a promotion." Technically that was true, if he counted his predecessor floating face down in the Atlantic without a pulse as "backing out." "I was in the right place at the right time."

"I'm sure you'll do fine." Lacey raised her left eyebrow so it pointed in the middle. "You were always good at whatever job you tried."

Jon recognized the look. He'd been the recipient of that snarky eyebrow on more than one occasion. "You say that like it's a bad thing."

"On the contrary, the MS *Buckingham* will benefit greatly from your varied talents. Now, if you'll excuse me, I have to swing by the dining room on the way to my muster station."

She fake-smiled and scooted around him without making physical contact. His old flame was sending signals loud and clear, none of them good, and for the life of him, he didn't know why. Shouldn't he be the one with a grudge?

Two years and seven months ago, they'd finished a long sailing stretch and taken the mandatory vacation period the cruise line required of all the employees. Whenever he'd tried to have a "defining the relationship" conversation in the past, she'd always put him off. But he'd sensed her softening in her unguarded comments about *their* future. He and Lacey had made a dinner date for after she returned from visiting her family. Jon had practiced his speech a dozen times, trying to find the most sincere, nonthreatening, romantic way to say "I love you." But all his preparation had been in vain. She never showed, changed her phone number, and requested a transfer to a different ship. His pulverized heart required months of soul-searching and midnight prayers to recover.

Lacey did the abandoning. He should be the standoffish one. Instead, his rowdy pulse could rival a high school marching band at a homecoming game.

"The dining room?" Jon followed as she strode purposefully away from him. "I was hoping to meet the chef before we sailed. You can introduce me."

Might as well use Lacey to make inroads with the staff. He needed to win people over fast. Then they would let him in on the latest scuttlebutt.

Work.

That was the reason he was tagging along, not because of any residual feelings he still harbored for the beautiful hostess. Jon ignored the frustrated puff of air she blew from her nostrils and kept up a casual stream of conversation as he fell in beside her.

Lacey hurried, but so did Jon. The infuriating man from her past kept pace with her no matter how fast she walked. She bit her tongue to keep from shouting, "Go away already!"

"How have you been?" he said.

"You already asked me that."

"Did I? Has the answer changed in the last two minutes?"

One thing hadn't changed. He could still charm a fish out of the ocean and straight into his net. His presence filled the space around them as the hallway seemed to shrink. Lacey scanned the passage for an escape route, but reason reasserted itself. They were stuck together on this boat, and her contract had three months remaining before she could request a new station. Perhaps cruise ships appeared massive to the passengers, but they were claustrophobic to the employees who lived with each other day and night. Crew members might as well be attached at the hip.

Jon chatted, and Lacey grunted in response until they reached the elevators. The area was empty except for an older woman in white polyester slacks and a long-sleeved paisley blouse, carrying an ancient black handbag. She ran unsteady fingers over her disheveled mass of silver-gray curls.

"Mrs. Windsor?" Lacey stared at the short lady. There was the same floral print she'd spied underneath Walter's arm as she'd fled down the hall. How had this frail woman beaten her here?

"Hello, Lacey." The woman's voice sounded a bit breathless as she greeted her. "So nice . . . to see you. And who . . . is this fine young man?"

"Jonathan King, ma'am." He straightened tall and gave her a salute. "I'm the MS *Buckingham*'s new cruise director, at your service."

"How wonderful." The pocket-size woman with the poofy mop of hair beamed at him. "I'm Emily Windsor. Tell me, Jonathan—"

"Please, call me Jon."

"And you must call me Emily. Tell me, Jon, are you married?"

"No, ma'am. Are you?"

"My wonderful husband, Bill, went to be with the Lord. He was a navy captain, and we had fifty-one years of traveling the world together."

"You must have led an exciting life."

"I did. But it wouldn't have been half as much fun without Bill. Trust me, Jon, marriage is a risk worth taking."

Lacey cleared her throat as she reached to press the call button. "It's only fair to warn you, Jon. You're speaking with the ship's most notorious matchmaker. She lives on board year-round, and no one is safe from her machinations."

"Machinations!" Emily placed her small, wrinkled hands over her chest. "You make love sound like a trip to the dentist, Lacey."

"I think I'd prefer the dentist. At least they give you anesthesia."

Emily's lips pinched in a sad little line. "You can't run forever, dear."

"But I can try." Lacey winked at her sweet stalker. "Have you taken your medicine today?"

"Oh, pish-tosh." Emily flicked a wrist. "The bracing sea air is all the medicine I require."

"Not according to the doctor."

Emily focused her light-blue eyes on Jon, who was looking bemused and a little startled, and pointed a finger at Lacey. "Don't let her gruff exterior fool you. This one will take care of everyone else before herself."

He grinned. "I'm well aware of her softer side."

The bell dinged as the elevator doors slid open. Lacey leaned inside and pressed the button for the seventh floor, placed a gentle palm on Emily's back, and pushed her in. "I'm sure I heard the muster announcement. You'd better get going. Promise me you'll take your medicine before dinner."

Emily clicked her tongue. "Very well, dear. If it will make you happy."

The doors closed, and Lacey turned to Jon and his ever-present smile. "No time for the dining room." She dashed toward the stairs before he could respond. "I have to tell Chef about a VIP passenger's special cake request after we finish the drill. Nice to see you."

"Cake? I love cake. What kind did they order?"

Jon caught up in two strides, and Lacey finally halted in defeat. No sense wearing herself out if he refused to take a hint. She didn't remember him being this slow on the uptake. Perhaps she should be more direct about her desire to be left alone.

She opened her mouth. "Listen, Jon—"

A text alert dinged.

Jon pulled his phone from his pocket. His shoulders straightened as he scanned the screen. "Sorry, Lace. We'll have to continue our conversation later."

He sprinted past her, taking the stairs three at a time. His attractive form disappeared in a matter of seconds, and Lacey's lips twisted.

"Same old Jon."

Nice of him to remind her why it hadn't worked the first time around. The flighty charmer was always racing away without warning or explanation. And she was a girl who needed explanations. She wanted stability. Craved it. And Jon represented a pulse-racing jump off the cliff of uncertainty. No matter how gorgeous the man was, he couldn't be trusted. Not with her heart or anything else.

Like someone else she knew.

CHAPTER 2

"Rendezvous at HQ in one hour for new intel."

Emily Windsor grasped her walkie-talkie while the elevator ascended. Wouldn't the girls be excited to hear her news? She hummed an old love song from the days of crinolines and corsages as she raised her eyes upward.

"This is an interesting development, Lord." She chuckled. "The air was hot as jalapeños with those two. Did you have me witness their reunion on purpose? I sense a little heavenly intervention. If so, who am I to argue with the Ultimate Matchmaker?"

The car stopped at several floors for other passengers, and Emily tapped her foot with each interruption. The digital display took pity on her, and the number seven lit. She made a token appearance at the safety drill, then inspected the latest group of merry vacationers before heading to her cabin. The most punctual Shipper, Geraldine Paroo, stood waiting in the hall, her lengthy spine as rigid as the book she was carrying.

"Where are the others, Gerry?" Emily unlocked the door, walked in, and dropped her walkie-talkie in the charger on the desk. She smoothed a pucker from the colorful crocheted afghan at the end of her bed.

"I haven't talked to Daisy since breakfast." Gerry stepped around Emily to settle on the short loveseat by the wall. "And I remember Althea saying something about bingo. If the game has started, we may not see her for a while."

Emily straightened the silver-framed photo of her late husband and propped her hands on her hips. "I gave them a whole hour."

"They're from Louisiana. The clocks move slower down there." Gerry lifted the cat-eye spectacles hanging from the chain around her neck, placed them on her thin nose, and opened her book.

Emily snorted as she pulled out the desk chair opposite Gerry and sat. Five seconds later, she was up again, pacing in the tiny pathway from the door to the bed. The timer was ticking, and she was missing half her team. What could possibly be more important? Didn't they realize it was duty first?

"I can text Althea, but Daisy doesn't own a cell phone," Emily grumbled.

"You know why." Gerry didn't bother to look up. "She says there's no one she wants to talk to that much."

"But it would make everything so much easier. Then we wouldn't have to use these antiquated contraptions."

She reached for her walkie-talkie to summon the AWOL members but stopped when someone knocked. She opened the door to find the always-put-together Daisy Randolph Masterson standing in a black linen jumpsuit with matching floppy sun hat.

"I tried to hurry." Her unhurried Southern drawl contradicted the words. "Did I miss anything?"

"Yes!" said Emily.

"No," said Gerry.

The delicate Daisy floated into the room on a cloud of magnolia perfume and lowered her dainty self to the couch. "I was in the middle of a manicure when you radioed. Magda can't be rushed. She's such a perfectionist. That's what makes her the best." She held up her freshly polished nails and waggled them.

"If we can get Althea here." Emily grabbed the walkie-talkie and raised it to her mouth. "Althea Jones, report to headquarters ASAP. Right now!"

Twenty long minutes later, Althea's voice sang out in the corridor. Emily opened the door and waited with pursed lips as the substantial girth of the sassy seventy-two-year-old New Orleans native entered the cabin.

"*Gonna lay down my burrrrr-dens,*" Althea crooned.

"Your chronic tardiness is a burden," Emily said.

"I take it you won today." Gerry slipped off her reading glasses and closed her book.

"Two hundred smackers." Althea waved the crisp twenties like a fan. "I cinched the deal with two fat ladies."

"I hope you didn't call them obese to their face," Daisy said.

"It's not a 'them.' It's bingo slang. Number eighty-eight. We call that 'two fat ladies.' I'm hardly qualified to fuss about weight."

Daisy changed her spot to the chair in front of the desk, and Althea settled on the loveseat. She folded her winnings and stuck them in the tight pocket stretched across one of her wide, beignet-loving hips.

"Can we please get started?" Emily struggled to keep her tone even.

"Emily, baby." Althea took out a compact and powdered her nose. Her bronzed Creole skin contained fewer wrinkles than a woman half her age. "What's the commotion? You sound like someone set your Spanx on fire."

"I already burned that elastic torture device years ago."

"Ladies." Daisy withdrew a handkerchief from her purse and touched it to both nostrils. "Can we please refrain from public discussions of *underwear*?" She whispered the last word and shook her refined head, her chin-length hair swinging in disapproval.

Gerry readjusted her lanky frame in the narrow sitting area. "It would have been better if you used the term *knickers*, Althea."

Emily poured herself a glass of water, trying to calm her impatience. They were just warming up, and there was no way to focus the girls until they finished clowning around.

Althea laughed and slapped her knee. "Since you were a librarian all those years, I bet you memorized a ton of words we could use."

"Yes, indeed." Gerry nodded as she pushed an errant bobby pin into the salt-and-pepper bun on the top of her head. "Lingerie, drawers, un-mentionables, skivvies."

With each new synonym, Althea chortled, and Daisy reared back as if she might faint. Gerry paused between undergarments to take a breath.

Emily clunked the glass down and interrupted the laundry list. "We don't have time for your ribbing, Gerry. There's a breakthrough in the Lacey case."

The unmentionables chatter came to an abrupt halt.

"Do tell." Daisy sat straighter. "Are things finally rolling with her and Ricardo?"

"Forget him." Emily paced in the cramped space between their legs with her hands clasped behind her. "We need to recalibrate our sights to Jonathan King, the new cruise director."

"What happened to the old one?" Gerry dropped her book on the side table.

"Irrelevant. Let's find out everything we can about Jon. All I gathered is his name and that he worked with Lacey a few years ago. This will mean a whole new round of research—his background, likes and dislikes, temperament, spiritual status, the works."

Daisy's nose scrunched at the whiff of more paperwork. "We agreed to match Lacey with Ricardo, the pastry chef. Can't we stick with him? Why is the cruise director a better choice?"

Emily walked to a long piece of paper stretched from one end of the cabin wall to the other and then motioned to the index of every male crew member on the MS *Buckingham*. The other three stared at the chart with the pluses or minuses next to each name.

"Lacey is our most unwilling client to date. She's sharp as a tack and evades every attempt to match her. We spent an entire Caribbean cruise choosing a man to set her up with."

"Yes, so why rock the boat now?" Gerry asked.

"I still say that surgeon from N'Orlins was a good option." Althea moved to the empty chair closest to the list and squinted. No matter how nearsighted she got, she refused to wear glasses.

"She's not allowed to date passengers." Gerry returned her spectacles to their skinny perch. "How many times must I remind you?"

"Phooey." Althea rolled her eyes. "Don't be such a stickler. A cruise line can't dictate who to love. If she fell for him, she could get a new job."

Daisy placed a gentle hand on Gerry's arm before the two could get into another verbal skirmish. "But Lacey takes longer than most to warm up. She has a better chance of forming an attachment with a man she already knows. Wouldn't you agree, Althea?" She gestured for her roommate to answer.

Althea shrugged and crossed her arms. "I suppose." She turned to Emily. "Daisy brings up a good point. Lacey already knows Ricardo. Why are you in such an all-fired hurry to switch him with a stranger?"

"We know Ricardo was raised Catholic, but I'm not sure he still attends church. If Jon has a closer relationship with the Almighty, I'd prefer a man like that for my girl." Emily tapped the chart with her index finger. "We observed her interactions with each candidate, and every time, she remained friendly but professional. I adore Lacey. There isn't a kinder, more considerate person on this ship, but when it comes to romance, the girl is an ice princess. The only reason we settled on the pastry chef is because she loves his cherry tarts."

"I could go for one of those tarts." Althea moaned and rubbed her extended belly. "When do we eat?"

"It's a cruise ship," Gerry said. "You can eat whenever the urge hits."

"But I can't go alone." Althea's eyebrows flew high as the Gateway Arch while her lower lip jutted out.

"Althea. Gerry. Please focus." Emily tapped the list one more time. "As I was saying, Lacey showed zero interest in the other men, but you should've been in that hallway an hour ago. They needed a fire extinguisher for the sparks those two were throwing around. They definitely seemed familiar with each other, already on a first-name basis. And Jon made a telling comment about knowing Lacey's softer side. I'd give all my cruiser reward points to know what he meant!"

"It appears they have a history." Daisy took a packet of peanuts from her purse and passed them to Althea. "How do you think they became acquainted?"

"I overheard Lacey mention he was good at his job." Emily walked to the end of the long paper and picked at the tape holding it on the wall. "She's worked for Monarch for over four years. The logical assumption is they sailed together on a different ship in the past."

The scent of peanuts wafted through the air as Althea crunched. "You know how workers on a cruise ship can be. It's like a dating reality show from the moment we leave port."

"Small wonder," said Gerry. "They spend day and night in close quarters for a six-month stretch. It would be difficult not to grow attached to someone with that much togetherness."

"Or get sick of someone." Althea twisted her lips, and Gerry stuck out her tongue in response. Althea ignored her and turned her attention back to their fearless leader. "What type is this new man? How does he look?"

Emily sighed dreamily. "He reminds me of the classic Hollywood movies when men wore suits and stood up as a lady came to the table. Tall, dark, and every other cliché you can imagine. Jonathan King's shoulders stretch for miles, and his easy way of talking exudes confidence."

"Yes, please." Althea clapped.

"But more importantly, the man is smitten. He kept his eyes glued to Lacey no matter how fast she marched without sparing him a glance. He's the one." Emily's chin bobbed as she pulled the last bit of tape off the old candidate list and crumpled it. She tossed the wad into the waste can by the desk and motioned to the woman beside it. "Daisy, get me that roll of butcher paper in the closet. Time to make a new battle plan. This match will be our crowning achievement. I feel it deep down in my bones."

Gerry took out her laptop, and the Shippers settled in to chart a new course for Lacey's love life, whether she wanted it or not.

Their little club name came about a few weeks into their friendship. Althea had said every team required a proper moniker. Her first husband played hockey, and she suggested the Wedding Ringers—referring to players who can turn the tide of a game with their skills. A casual observer might dismiss Emily and her friends as the sweet little old ladies on the boat, but they were the ones making things happen.

Daisy had protested that the term *ringer* was a little crass. They were in the romance business, not a sports franchise. It was Gerry who brainstormed the name that stuck: the Shippers, because they were all about relation*ship*s. It sounded nautical and didn't give their true purpose away.

Emily didn't care what they were called so long as they got the job done. And intuition told her she'd found the right match for Lacey Anderson.

Handsome, mannerly, and charismatic, with an honest smile. A man with nothing to hide.

He was perfect.

CHAPTER 3

"CRUISE DIRECTOR IS THE PERFECT cover." The man lounging across from Jon tugged on the front of his wrinkled Hawaiian shirt as its buttons made a valiant attempt to join the overextended fabric. He threaded a hand through his graying hair and leaned back in the office chair. Reid Collins looked more like a retired accountant from Baltimore than a now-private detective who'd spent thirty years in the FBI.

Jon forced his attention away from the white T-shirt peekabooing from the gaping holes in the man's outfit—though he was grateful for the barrier it offered from the skin beneath—and adjusted the stapler on his desk. "Not that I object to the job, but why is it perfect?"

"You have the run of the ship, and no one will question you for being up in people's business. Watch for the warning signs. People traveling alone. Passengers arriving from a day in port with large amounts of luggage. Jumpy crew members."

Jon typed into his computer. "Have you noticed anyone suspicious?"

"Lots." Collins popped a piece of gum in his mouth. "You can't dismiss anyone. I remember one drug ring I busted on a cruise ship in '99 was headed by a seventy-year-old grandma. She tried to plead senility."

Jon made another note. "I met a woman like that today. She lives on board the ship."

"Did you catch her name?"

"Emily Windsor. A very friendly lady. But I doubt she has anything to do with this. Too nice."

Collins smirked. "You'd be amazed how many nice people I've slapped the cuffs on through the years. Have any of the crew appeared overly interested in the missing cruise director?"

"No. More like relieved he's gone. I don't think they cared for Newberg much. Apparently, he was great at schmoozing the passengers but was a stuck-up snob to the employees."

"I understand he died while everyone was off ship for repairs." Collins yanked a small notebook from his pocket and flipped the pages. "Dexter Newberg. Age thirty-two. Found floating in the ocean with enough cocaine in his system to choke a horse. The police wrote it off as an accidental drowning due to overdose." He snapped his gum. "Good thing Monarch's general manager still had my number and gave me a call. How 'bout you give me some background on this case in your own words?"

"It's not uncommon for people to sneak recreational drugs on a cruise for party purposes." Jon closed the lid of his laptop. "But large amounts of narcotics are showing up on Monarch ships with alarming frequency. Two months ago, a drug-sniffing dog unearthed five kilos of cocaine on the MS *Versailles* in the wall behind a crew member's toilet, and last week, the FBI busted a couple of passengers on the MS *Alhambra* smuggling more cocaine in hollowed-out Virgin Mary statues. Tabloids got ahold of the story and slapped us with the label Ship of Sin. My deacon father strongly objected to that term. After all, we bill ourselves as family friendly and don't even offer casinos, unlike a lot of the other cruise lines. This situation puts a major dent in our squeaky-clean image. The PR department isn't happy."

"Too many scandals, too close together." Collins nodded. "Be glad you brought in an expert from the outside. Can't trust anyone on board."

No. There was one person he could trust. Jon's thoughts drifted to Lacey. Intelligent and loyal to a fault, she'd be a valuable asset in the search for a culprit. *Maybe I could—*

The memory of Dexter Newberg's swollen, waterlogged body stopped that thought cold. He'd seen pictures of the corpse, and they weren't pretty. The idea of putting Lacey in harm's way was unthinkable. Better keep her as far from this as possible.

Collins spit his gum in the trash can by the desk. "What's our first move?"

"My first move is to give the welcome orientation." Jon stood from behind the desk. "Time to distribute door prizes."

"Hey, babe, can you get me one of those drinks with the little umbrellas?" A middle-aged man with a too-tight T-shirt, a diamond stud earring, and jet-black hair that didn't match his thinning eyebrows stopped in front of Lacey.

"I'm so glad you asked me." She'd perfected the art of answering stupid questions with a believable smile. "But we don't offer beverage service during our welcome orientation. I'm sorry to disappoint you."

"What!" His voice rose, and the female companion holding his arm cringed. "That lifeboat practice took forever, and I still can't get a drink?"

"The muster drill can be a bit overwhelming, can't it?" Lacey made sure her tone was appropriately consoling. "We have bottled water on a table in the hall if you're thirsty, but if you're willing to wait, I promise our cruise director will make this orientation worth your time."

He sucked a giant breath through his nose and tilted his head forward, but his girlfriend tugged on his sleeve. "I'll mention this in my online review." He glared at Lacey as he emphasized the words.

"There's also a phone number for customer service on the card in your cabin." Her smile remained at full capacity. "Have a wonderful cruise, sir."

She left the man with the midlife crisis and found the whole Shipper posse waiting with sympathetic expressions.

"Don't listen to him, sugar." Daisy laid a hand on her arm. "That kind is never satisfied."

Althea wrapped her soft arms around Lacey. "You give me a squeeze and forget all about him."

"I'm surprised to see you here." Lacey patted Althea's back before she let go. "Don't you usually skip the embarkation meeting? You must have the speech memorized by now."

Gerry waved her novel. "Never fear. I came prepared."

Emily stood clasping a pen and a black three-ring binder. "Besides, this embarkation features the new director's welcome speech. We want to check him out."

As if on cue, Jon poked his head into the group. "I love it when beautiful women check me out. Be sure to let me know how I rate." He pointed a cheesy finger gun at her. "You too, Lace."

Lacey's eyes started to roll upward, but she stopped them in time.

Jon held two elbows out to the women at his sides. "May I escort you ladies to your seats?"

"Yes indeedy." Althea grabbed an arm before he even finished making the offer, and signaled for Daisy to take the other.

"How kind of you." Daisy placed her hand in the crook of his arm. She received his attention as if it were owed her. Jon accompanied them down the aisle, bending his head toward Althea as she chattered. Gerry and Emily followed in their wake, part of the honored procession.

Lacey watched as the group passed rows of sturdy navy-blue couches and chairs until they reached the front. Jon waited while they settled, then walked up the center stairs and onto the stage. He studied the room and rested his gaze on her for a brief instant before he raised his microphone.

"Ahoy, everyone. Welcome to the MS *Buckingham*. Are you ready for the best vacation of your life?"

Hoots and hollers answered.

"You came to the right place. Let me ask another question. Is this the first cruise for anyone?"

Hands rose around the room.

"Whether this is your first time or you're an old sea dog like my friend Emily"—he motioned to her on the row below him and winked—"I'll try to keep this short and sweet so you can get out of here and hit the buffet."

"I'm in no hurry." On Lacey's left, a ruby redhead wearing cutoff jeans and a neon pink tank top snickered with her friend. She flipped open the bejeweled case on her cell phone and recorded Jon as he made his speech. "Keep talking, hot stuff." She perched on the edge of a row, leaned out at a precarious angle with her device pointed at the stage, and pinched at the screen to enlarge the picture. "Whoo, check out the muscles."

Lacey paused for all of five seconds before she wandered into the aisle and stood a few feet in front of the redhead. After years of being asked to "take a quick picture" for social media junkies, she knew camera angles cold. If she calculated correctly, this should be the spot.

"Hey," the woman behind her whispered. "You're in my shot."

Lacey pretended not to hear.

"Cruise ship lady. Hey!" The woman's voice got louder.

People shushed her, and she sat on her seat with an offended huff.

Lacey enjoyed the silent victory—until she surveyed the auditorium and saw at least seven other females with their phones out. Call her cynical, but she didn't think they were recording Jonathan King for informational purposes.

Fine. Let them drool. What did it matter to her? It wasn't like she'd never been leered at by a passenger. It was part and parcel of working on a cruise ship. Inappropriate people did inappropriate things. Jon was getting ogled. So what?

"Lacey."

Her attention jerked to the stage, where Jon was motioning for her. "Can you join me please?"

Lacey smiled bigger and shook her head.

"Oh, come on." Jon waved his arm a little more.

Lacey shook her head a lot more.

"Looks like she's shy." Jon grinned at the crowd. "How about a round of applause for encouragement?"

The crowd cheered and clapped.

"La-cey. La-cey. La-cey." Jon chanted into the mic, and the audience chimed in.

Her name echoed through the room, and Lacey hurried forward to make it stop. She climbed up the stairs to center stage. The last step was wider, and Jon held out a hand to assist her. She grabbed it and dug her nails into his fingers. His bottom teeth showed as he smile-grimaced and pulled away.

"Can we get another microphone for our fabulous hostess?" Jon called to a worker backstage.

Lacey faced the audience. The house lights were up, and she had a clear view of the entire room. Tiny-Umbrella Man slouched in the sixth row with his arms crossed, still pouting. Leering Lady in the back curled her lips and eyed her with disdain. And the Shippers were front and center, observing everything. Daisy sat with perfect posture, while Althea whispered in her ear. Emily took Gerry's book, handed her the binder and pen, then raised her phone and pointed it at the stage. A crew member appeared with the extra microphone and passed it to Lacey.

"Don't worry," Jon said. "I won't make you sing."

"If you value your life." Her smile dripped honey and her voice retribution.

The passengers laughed and applauded.

"I'm going to let you in on a secret." Jon leaned out to the crowd and whispered. "This is my first cruise too, at least on this ship, so I wanted to introduce the woman with the answers. Anything I don't know, she does. Take note of her uniform. She, or any other person wearing this white jacket with gold buttons, is your sailing sage. If you have any questions, please ask."

"How about a date tonight?" A college-aged guy stood from the front row on the left side and leaned his arms on the stage.

Jon bristled, but Lacey spoke into her mic.

"You'd have to get permission from the captain first."

The young man stuck his bottom lip out, and his friends jeered as they dragged him to his seat.

Jon maneuvered to stand between the frat boys and her. "Trust me, you'll have to take a number and get in line for a date with Lacey."

"What number do you have?" Another voice from the audience called out.

Jon flinched. "Not high enough."

The listeners moaned.

He shrugged and looked at her. Their eyes connected.

Suddenly, Lacey's feet didn't feel so steady. Had the ship hit a rough patch? It must be motion sickness. *Breathe, girl.*

In and out.

In and out.

She was going to need a Lamaze coach before this cruise finished. For breathing. Not for anything— Whatever.

Lacey tore her gaze away and found the Shippers. They sat in a row like four satisfied cats eyeing a bowl of cream. Gerry scribbled in the binder. Althea fanned herself with splayed fingers. Daisy hid her mouth behind a handkerchief. And Emily popped a piece of butterscotch candy past a pair of smiling lips.

Lacey's neck tingled like Marie Antoinette's as she was led to the guillotine. Was it too late to swim back to shore?

CHAPTER 4

Jon wove through the gauntlet of sunbathers as he made his rounds on the upper deck. He passed a young man stretched out on a lounge chair. His pasty complexion and bushy beard would put any caveman to shame. Beside him slept a teenage girl with a smiley face drawn on her stomach in sunscreen.

She'll regret that in the morning.

But he didn't have time to offer unsolicited advice. How was he supposed to catch a band of smugglers when people kept asking so many questions? Passengers stopped him every few feet, and he gave the same responses over and over.

"The earlier dinner time has seats available."

"There's a shop on the promenade deck that sells Dramamine."

"No, I can't set you up with a cruise hostess, but I highly recommend the Single Mingle at midnight."

At least three men asked the hostess question. Did they all mean Lacey? Not that he blamed them. He scanned the deck for the lady in question and noticed four aged heads bent together around a table. Collins's suspicions replayed in his memory. A grandma drug syndicate? Sounded ridiculous even in his brain. But he had to check every angle.

Jon skirted the pool and found the Shippers sitting with a large purple-and-gold umbrella shielding them from the sun. A thick novel with a racy cover hid the thin one's face, while Emily wrote in a binder, and the other two watched him approach, whispering behind raised hands.

"Good afternoon, ladies. How would you rate my opening speech yesterday?" Jon noted a spreadsheet Emily was working on and craned his neck for a closer look. "Did I pass muster?"

Emily shut the binder and nodded her head. "I think you'll do, Jon."

"That's a relief. I really didn't want to go back to washing dishes."

"Did you work in the kitchen?"

"There's hardly a place on board I haven't worked. Busboy, steward, art auctioneer, photographer, waiter, disc jockey—"

"Your résumé must be an inch thick." The large woman with the rhinestone-studded baseball cap and matching fanny pack who was sitting beside Emily interrupted him. "Couldn't find a position you favored?"

"I don't believe we've met, at least officially." Jon held out a hand. "Allow me to introduce myself. Jonathan King, cruise director extraordinaire, at your service."

"Mrs. Althea Jones." She gave his hand a hearty shake. "Bingo player extraordinaire."

"That's a lovely name, Mrs. Althea Jones."

"My father was an English teacher. He named me after his favorite poem."

"Ah, Richard Lovelace. I remember from my college lit class: 'When Love with unconfinèd wings hovers within my Gates, and my divine Althea brings to whisper at the Grates.'"

"Mmm-mmm." Her eyes sparkled as she rested her elbows on the table and propped her chin on her laced fingers. "Baby, you must have to beat the ladies off with a stick."

"Were you an English major?" The woman with the cat-eye spectacles spoke with her gaze still fastened on her novel.

"No, ma'am."

"Call me Gerry. It's short for Geraldine."

"Thank you, Gerry. I wasn't an English major. I just had a penchant for reading." He reached out to the remaining unnamed woman at the table. "Jonathan King, ma'am."

"Daisy Randolph Masterson. How do you do?"

She rested her manicured fingers against his, and he gently pressed them instead of shaking. Nobility encompassed her like an invisible mantle. He wouldn't be surprised to learn she descended from a queen of England. She retrieved her hand and reclined on her chair, pulling the brim of her large black sun hat over one eye.

Emily clicked the top of her pen. "Where did you go to school?"

"Someplace I couldn't find a decent taco." Jon gave an exaggerated shudder.

"You're a fan of tacos, then?"

"I'm Florida-grown. We've got some of the best food trucks in the country. You haven't lived until you've tasted the sweet fusion of juicy Korean bulgogi and spicy coleslaw wrapped in a fresh corn tortilla." He pulled an empty chair out and sat next to Althea. "Did you ladies know each other before you came aboard?"

"Only Althea and Daisy." Emily motioned to the women on her right. "They share the same hometown."

"Where would that be?"

"The Big Easy," Althea said.

"Ah, New Orleans natives. Were you friends for a long time?"

The two shook their heads, Daisy with her hat still covering half her face.

"Hardly," she said. "We met a week before sailing."

"It was my idea to share a cabin." Althea leaned over and swallowed petite Daisy in an affectionate hug. "I was going to have to pay a single supplement without her. This way, it's cheaper for both of us. She's got me to thank for all this luxury."

Daisy tilted her head and granted a soft smile to her roommate. "I couldn't have done it without you."

"But why a cruise ship?" Jon asked. "Doesn't it get tedious? Visiting the same ports? Attending the same shows?"

Gerry poked her head out of her literary foxhole. "More tedious than an overpriced retirement community where the highlight of the year is a pack of screeching first graders singing Christmas carols?"

"Gerry." Daisy stuck her hand up, her pinky tipping a little farther back than the rest of her fingers. "Mr. King doesn't know you very well. He won't understand you're joking."

"Who said I was joking?" Gerry mumbled as she descended into her book.

"Consider the facts, Jon." Emily raised a finger and pointed at it with her ballpoint pen. "It costs approximately the same amount of money to live on board as a retirement community these days. But you make our beds, do our laundry, offer nightly shows, and provide a wide variety of food options." She ticked off the amenities on her fingers. "We eat what we want, when we want, and have it delivered to our room if we don't feel like going out—and it's a lot better than cafeteria food."

Jon admired their ingenuity. "I concede to your point."

"Excuse me." A pudgy man in a Speedo approached Jon. A bloated green snake tattoo with a rose in its mouth curled around his milky-white belly button. "My wife wants me to ask when the ballroom lessons start."

"Day after tomorrow." Jon stood. "I can help you register, if you're interested."

"Are you crazy?" The snake charmer lowered his voice. "Why don't you schedule me a root canal while you're at it? Day after tomorrow, you said? I'll make sure I'm sick in bed." He stalked away and caused a minor tidal wave when he jumped in the pool.

"Did you notice the artwork?" Daisy said. "Bless his heart."

"I bet that python was a grass snake twenty years ago." Gerry quipped from behind her novel.

Althea laughed and slapped her on the back.

Jon clocked a familiar shabby Hawaiian shirt and Collins's face frowning above it in the distance. The detective made eye contact. His head jerked to the right before he headed for the stairs, and Jon pushed in his chair. "I'd love to stay longer, but I should continue my rounds. We're docking in Cozumel tomorrow. A port call generates lots of questions. Are any of you getting off the boat?"

"Why yes," said Daisy. "The ship's manicurist recommended a little salon we plan to visit."

"Be sure to tell me if you need anything." He tapped the table with his knuckles.

"Good talking to you, Jon." Emily rested her pen against her chin. "I'm glad the Lord brought you to our ship. I'm sure he had a good reason."

"He always does," Jon agreed.

"So you're on speaking terms with the Almighty?"

"Every single day."

Emily's smile broadened. "That's good to hear. I hope you and I can get better acquainted soon."

"My pleasure." Jon bowed his head in a courtly fashion and left the ladies on the upper half of the lido deck. He headed in the direction Collins had gone. As Jon descended the stairs, he spotted Lacey a few feet away, observing him. He jumped down the last two steps and approached her. "Good morning!"

"What were you talking about?" She manufactured a counterfeit smile with both rows of teeth showing, then pointed above his head.

Jon looked up. Three of the four women peered over the rail like a row of expectant children watching for Santa Claus. He waved with a big grin. "This and that. They're quite the characters."

"Keep on your guard." Lacey turned her back to them, and her smile disappeared. "The Shippers will have you tied down before you can blink."

"Tied down?" Jon's muscles tensed.

"Married. They imagine themselves the ship's unofficial marriage brokers. They already matched two couples in the crew and reconciled one set of passengers who were on the brink of divorce."

"Isn't that a good thing?" The left side of Jon's mouth quirked upward.

"Absolutely. If you want to be married. But if you don't, no amount of argument will dissuade them. Once they have you in their cross-hairs, you might as well start shopping for a tuxedo."

Jon pictured himself in formal wear. His vision of the future quickly shifted to the woman beside him at the altar—Lacey in a flowing white dress. Beautiful. He tried to pull his attention back to the conversation, but a breeze playing with her hair distracted him. A shiny strand dipped and swayed above her long eyelashes in a flirtatious, silken dance. Should he fix it?

"Jon?"

"Hmm?" He ignored the blond temptation and focused on Lacey. Time to pull it together before he found himself dumped by the same woman again. The first experience hurt enough. Besides, he had bigger issues to worry about than dating. His family's reputation was on the line, he had responsibilities, and Collins was waiting for him.

Emily and her friends didn't miss a second of the drama playing out below. The Shippers observed everything from their chairs on the deck, except for Daisy, who lounged with eyes closed under her sun hat.

"This new candidate is a good choice." Gerry nodded her head, settled back on her seat, and pulled her laptop from the canvas bag at her side.

"Isn't he perfect?" Emily clasped her small hands and squeezed her shoulders so tight they formed tiny, euphoric points. "I'm sure we're on the right track this time."

"I see why you switched horses." Althea patted Emily's leg and gave her a thumbs-up. "If I were ten years younger!"

"If you were twenty years younger, you'd still be old enough to be his mother." Gerry typed on her computer without looking at the keyboard.

"Age is just a number, baby." Althea rose from her chair, took off her fanny pack, and smoothed the fabric of her bright-red swimsuit with sparkly pink strawberries on it. "Seventeen years separated me and my third husband, and he had zero complaints. I must admit, I enjoyed being the older woman. We never needed an electric blanket in our marriage." She sashayed to the nearby hot tub, climbed in, and sat between two men.

"I've created a new file on Jonathan King." Gerry paused with her fingers poised over the keyboard. "What did we gather from our conversation?"

Emily studied her binder. "He talks to God. A major point in his favor. Born and raised in Florida. Attended college somewhere else. Didn't major in English literature. Likes poetry and tacos." She threw her pen on the table. "Not much to go on. Are we losing our touch?"

Gerry entered what little they had gleaned. "Was it my imagination, or was he being evasive?"

"You aren't imagining things," Daisy drawled from under her hat. "My late husband used to answer questions the exact same way. He would change the subject and have you off on a rabbit trail before you knew it."

Emily's gaze followed Jon as he walked away from Lacey on the lower deck. "My bones tell me he's one of the good ones, but we have to be careful. Gerry, you're the research queen. Fire up the internet engines. Let's find out a little more about Mr. King before we give him the official Shipper stamp of approval."

"Is that the old lady you told me about?" Collins smacked his gum as he rested his girth against the metal railing.

Jon surveyed the flocks of sun-drenched tourists. No one was close enough to hear them. "Emily Windsor. And she's got three friends who are equally curious. I'm not sure who was grilling whom back there. Lace . . . someone I know, called them the Shippers. She said they live on board year-round and amuse themselves by matchmaking. Which might explain why they asked so many questions. I'll keep an eye on them, but I'm pretty sure it's a dead end."

"Do we dock in Cozumel tomorrow?"

"Yes. Because it's festival time, we bypassed our usual stop in Progreso and are spending two days in the Cozumel port as opposed to the normal one and done."

Collins spit his gum over the side of the ship and drew a fresh piece from his pocket. "Prime time to sneak a stash aboard." He unwrapped the stick and shoved it in his mouth. "Are the grandmas planning to get off?"

"They said something about visiting a salon. But I don't—"

"Got it." Collins raised both hands. "You don't think it's them. But go with me on this. I'll trail the old biddies a while, mark their names off the suspect list, and then we have fewer people to track. Make sense?"

Jon shrugged. It was corporate's idea to bring the retired FBI agent on the case, and he'd come highly recommended by their general manager, who'd worked with Collins on another cruise line. The idea sounded good at the time, but now he was beginning to wonder. Was the man on the job or enjoying a free vacation? Either way, while Collins was wasting his time on the wrong people, Jon would monitor the crew members. Port time provided a golden opportunity for an off-duty worker to make a pickup.

His phone buzzed, and he checked his text messages. Being the cruise director, he got plenty. Jon's eyebrows scrunched as he read.

"Bad news?" Collins asked.

"It's a message from Emily Windsor."

"You gave her your number?"

"No."

The detective chuckled. "Resourceful woman. What does she want?"

Jon rubbed his neck. "She says Lacey's at the front desk, and she's thirsty."

"Lacey? Ah, that *someone you know* you started to mention earlier. Why is the old lady telling you this?"

"Guess I should've paid more attention when Lacey warned me the Shippers' hobby is matchmaking."

"Or they're onto you and trying to divert your attention elsewhere," Collins said.

Jon tapped his phone against his hip. This was going to be a problem. Balancing the investigation with regular cruise director duties was difficult enough without a bunch of well-meaning but insistent busybodies pushing him toward romance. Even if the woman they had in mind was the one that got away.

CHAPTER 5

LACEY DRAGGED THE CURTAIN BACK from her tiny lower bunk, dived on the narrow mattress, and moaned into the pillow. Only a day and a half since Jon's reappearance, and her emotions felt like an empty ketchup bottle that had been whacked too many times. How could she survive this for three more months? A soul-deep groan escaped her throat.

"That doesn't sound good." Lacey's roommate, Abigail O'Brien, entered their compact cabin and swerved around a pile of dirty clothes. A fruit punch–colored stain covered the bottom half of her white Monarch polo. The five-foot-two fireball with flaming red hair to match was the sole person aboard who knew her secrets. "Is it your ex-fiancé again?"

"We were never engaged!" Lacey's smothered voice rose from the pillow. She turned on her side to look at Abby.

"Fine. Is it your ex-boyfriend again?"

"Technically, we never officially dated." She picked at a loose thread on the blanket. "We just hung out during our free time and port calls and meals and—"

"Did you ever kiss?"

Lacey averted her eyes. "Maybe."

Abby snorted. "Sounds like dating to me. Who cares if you never announced you were going out? But let's get back to where we started.

39

Was it your ex-not-quite-official-boyfriend who put that frown on your face?"

"Who else? He crashed my art gallery tour this morning and charmed the passengers. Then he stood in the back of the room while I gave another group a presentation on Cozumel. Oh, and he brought me a glass of lemonade while I was covering the front desk, because the Shippers told him I was thirsty."

"He brought you lemonade?" Abby leaned against the wall as she tugged her sneakers off and threw them across the messy room. "What a jerk."

"Every time I turn around—there he is, bothering me."

"I wish someone would bother me that way." Abby ducked her head and plopped on the foot of the bed. Lacey scooted to make more room, banging her elbow against the ladder leading to Abby's bunk. She rubbed her arm and leaned against the wall. Abby propped one leg up and massaged her toes. "Forget fancy presents. All I want is a man who will rub my feet without complaining." She pointed her best puppy-dog face at her roommate. "Of course, if a friend offered . . ."

Lacey shimmied forward and held out a hand. "Give it."

Abby stretched her leg and dropped it on Lacey's lap. "Did I ever tell you you're the best roomie I ever had? Including all three of my sisters."

"You're just saying that so I'll do your other foot."

"That's one of the reasons, but the sentiment's still true." Abby put both hands behind her waist and arched her spine. "I don't get it. The guy is sweet and thoughtful, and you won't go blind looking at him, unless it's from an overload of gorgeousness. Did he cheat on you or something?"

Lacey really didn't want to talk about this. "He's not the type."

"Okay. Did he kick a puppy? Put pineapple on his pizza?"

"Very funny. We weren't meant for each other. Let's drop it."

Abby shook her head.

Lacey squinted and pointed at the doorjamb. "Is that a spider?"

"If it were, you'd be the first one screaming. Don't even try to distract me."

Lacey dug her fingers into the ball of Abby's foot.

"Ow." The redhead winced. "Easy there. Was he a bad kisser?"

Lacey threw the Cinderella-sized foot off her lap. "I don't have to finish this favor."

"I'm sorry. I'm sorry!" Abby held out her other foot and waggled her toes with a pathetic whimper.

Lacey grabbed it and kneaded the bottom with her thumbs.

"Was he a *good* kisser?" Abby was part bulldog. That was how she'd discovered Lacey's secrets. Wearing her down. Little by little.

"Abb-yyyy," Lacey warned as she rubbed tiny circles in the arch of her roomie's foot.

Abby leaned forward with a glint in her eye. "Fireworks?"

"Like New Year's Eve in Times Square." Lacey's fingers stilled as her mind strayed to the memories of those heart-stuttering kisses. Unforgettable. No matter how hard she'd tried to erase them.

"I'm drawing a blank. It must have been something serious to reject a guy who looks like that *and* brings you lemonade. Was it a spiritual problem?"

"I'd hardly be in a position to judge someone else's faith. You know I don't read my Bible nearly as much as you do. Besides, Jon was a very moral, God-fearing person."

"Come here and let me pray for you." Abby hollered at the ceiling. "Lord! We've got another pair of blind eyes that needs opening." She studied Lacey. "The man is faithful, handsome, and kissable. What's not to love?"

"It's complicated."

"Is that what you told him?"

"Not exactly." Lacey examined the foot she was holding. The toenails were cropped short, no polish. "You could use a pedicure."

"What exactly *did* you tell him?" Abby ignored her redirection.

Lacey ignored Abby ignoring her and kept massaging. Someone bumped along the passageway and entered the laundry room on the other side of the wall. She pointed in the direction of the noise. "It's such a pain sleeping right next to the dryers."

"Please tell me you explained why you left him." Abby pulled her foot away. "You told him why it wouldn't work, right?"

Lacey said nothing. She grabbed a wet wipe from the dispenser on the dresser and scrubbed at her fingers.

"You left him cold? Changed ships and didn't even leave a forwarding?" Abby stuck a short, unpainted fingernail between her teeth and stared at her. "That's hard-core harsh. The poor guy deserved a breakup text at the very least."

"I told you. We weren't—"

"I know. I know. You weren't officially together. Except . . ." Abby's lips pinched, and her eyebrows rose. "You totally were. Don't you owe him an explanation?"

Lacey's stomach churned, and she pushed the guilt behind a barrier of every excuse her brain could generate. Better she left the past dead and buried. It didn't matter how many shovels the Shippers brought. Her relationship with Jon belonged in the graveyard.

CHAPTER 6

THE LONG CONCRETE PIER STRETCHED in front of the Shippers like an airplane runway. Women in colorful voluminous Mexican dresses and flowered hairdos posed with the picture-hungry passengers after they disembarked. A line of faux-grass roofs sat in the distance, where the first hurrah of overpriced souvenir shops waited.

"Hello, Cozumel." Emily stood on the pier and counted in her head how many voyages she had docked there. "For the twenty-third time."

Behind her, Althea groused at the gangplank, scooting her feet along as she grasped the rail. "Why do they put everything so stinkin' far away? The boat should pull up to Main Street and drop us off."

"The Caribbean Sea doesn't flow through Main Street." Gerry stomped down the metal walkway. "But I'm with you. I'd rather stay on board and work on the novel I'm writing. Why are we doing this again, Daisy?"

"Magda recommended an exceptional pedicure place." The genteel woman adjusted her designer sunglasses and brushed a stray hair from her forehead. "They offer ichthyotherapy."

"Icky-what?" Althea asked.

"Trust me. It will be worth it."

"It better be." Althea scowled at the sizable walk awaiting them and groaned.

The foursome started toward the shops when two bright-red bicycle taxis with yellow sunshades arrived.

"We will give you ride," one of the drivers said with an appealing accent.

"Praise the Lawd!" Althea lifted her hands to the sky and headed for the nearest padded seat.

"Hold it, Althea." Emily grabbed the eager woman's arm. "We don't want to spend our life savings." She eyed the taxis and their operators. "How much will this cost?"

"It is free."

Gerry snorted. "Do we look stupid?"

"No, no." The man waved. "For you, it is free. You are sheepers, no?"

"Sheepers?" Gerry wrinkled her nose at Emily. "Baaaa?"

"Oh, *Shippers*." Emily nodded. "We are Shippers. Yes."

"*Mucho gusto*. I am Rafael. A man named Jonathan call me to pick you up. He already pay."

"That's good enough for me." Althea clambered into the taxi and plopped onto the bench. "Come on, Daisy. Jonny hired these nice gentlemen to carry us to the salon." She patted the empty spot beside her.

"What an obliging gesture." Daisy joined her without argument. "We must write him a thank-you note."

The more suspicious Emily and Gerry paused a few seconds before boarding the other taxi. The drivers climbed on their bicycles and transported the ladies down the long pier and through the fake village in just a few minutes. Daisy directed them to the nail place, and they zipped through the city, eventually dropping them off at the entrance.

Rafael grinned. "We will wait until you finish."

"We may be a while," said Emily.

"It is fine. Jonathan paid me for all day."

Daisy put a delicate hand to her chest. "I think we owe him more than a thank-you note, ladies."

Gerry shooed her into the building. "We're helping him win the love of his life. That's worth much more than a greeting card."

A bell rang as the four entered not a salon but a convenience store.

Althea looked around. "Baby, are you sure you got the address right?"

"Don't be put off by the surroundings." Daisy waved to four cushy chairs shoved against the side wall. "This is where we want."

In front of each chair sat a large glass box with water. Tiny gray fish about the size of pinto beans swam inside.

"Hello." A woman appeared from the recesses of the store. "You want a treatment?"

"Yes, one for each of us." Daisy motioned to her friends.

"Good. Sit here, please." The attendant grabbed a pile of towels from a side table.

Gerry's skinny fingers shot in the air as she held up her palm. "Hold on a minute. I'm not sitting anywhere until I know what this is."

"It's perfectly safe, Gerry." Daisy took the chair on the far right and unbuckled her low-heeled leather sandals. "Ichthyotherapy is an all-natural pedicure. You place your feet in the water, and the fish eat the dead skin off your soles."

"My cracked heels are their lunch?" Althea made a face but sat on the chair next to her. "Doesn't sound very appetizing."

The proprietor passed Gerry a laminated flyer, and Emily examined a bowl of Mexican candy as Gerry read aloud. "'Ichthyotherapy is an organic treatment where *Garra rufa* fish micromassage your feet as they eat the outer layer of your skin. A relaxing, chemical-free experience.'"

Daisy rolled her pants legs to her knees and lowered her slender feet into the tank. "Ahhh." She wilted on the chair. "The cool water refreshes my tired arches. Indulge yourself, Gerry."

"They spelled *chemical* k-e-m-i-c-a-l." Gerry waved the sheet under Daisy's nose.

She ignored the typo and rested her head against the wall.

"Ooooh." Althea giggled as the fish in her own tank swarmed around her toes. "It tickles."

"Oh well." Emily walked to the chair beside her. "If you can't beat them, et cetera."

"There will be no 'et cetera' for me." Gerry crossed her arms.

"Don't be so stuffy, baby." Althea flapped her hand at the empty seat. "It feels good."

"I'll stay over here, thank you. One of us should keep her shoes on to run for help."

"Do whatever makes you comfortable, Gerry." Emily learned a long time ago the woman had a stubborn streak the length of the Chesapeake Bay Bridge-Tunnel. Arguing was pointless.

The holdout Shipper eyed the process with skepticism as enthusiastic fish nibbled at her friends' toes, but Emily chuckled when she saw her pull a small notebook from her pocket. Gerry might not get a pedicure out of the trip, but she must have gotten inspiration for her book.

Emily leaned farther back on her seat.

The sounds and smells of Cozumel drifted through the open doorway. Meat sizzled on the griddle of the taco cart at the curb, and the spicy scent of carne asada with grilled onions wafted on the breeze. A store owner across the street beckoned at a man in a loud, ill-fitting Hawaiian shirt lingering outside. "Let me give you a tequila shot. Come on." It was a common sales tactic in the port town for getting customers into one's shop.

Emily's gaze met the tourist's through the glass window, and she shook her head at him. He tugged his panama hat lower on his forehead, hunched his shoulders, and followed the owner inside.

She tsk-tsked. "I hope he doesn't visit every establishment on the strip."

A swayback horse pulling a silk-flower-bedecked carriage clomped to a stop nearby. Dirty tan netting covered the animal's hide to protect it from the sun, and a bag stretched behind its tail to protect the street from the remains of the horse's breakfast.

"Wasn't it sweet of Jonathan to provide a ride for us?" Daisy said from the end of the row.

"That one's a keeper." Althea rubbed her stomach. "Have you got anything to eat?"

Daisy dug around in her pink suede purse and passed her a mini candy bar.

"I wonder how much he spent," Emily said. "Hiring two taxis for the whole day? Couldn't have been cheap."

Gerry scrawled in her notebook. "They pay cruise directors well."

"Still." Emily quirked her head. "We should delve deeper into Mr. Jonathan King's background. And for that, we'll need more basic details."

She raised her legs and swung her feet out of the water. A tiny fish clung to her heel, and she shook it off. "Come on, Shippers. Time to get to work."

The women dried their feet and paid the store owner. They exited to find Rafael and his buddy waiting as they'd promised.

"*Swing low, sweeeeeeet chariot,*" Althea sang as she climbed into the bicycle taxi. "*Comin' for to carry me home.*"

The other three took their seats on the open-air benches.

"No beach *hoy*?" Rafael asked.

"Not today," said Emily. "To the ship, please. *Ándale!*"

She tapped her chin with an index finger. *Jonathan King. Good-looking. Considerate. Generous.* But her bones whispered there was more to the story, and she meant to find out what.

CHAPTER 7

"Slow. Slow. Quick-quick, slow."

Wooden floorboards rattled as the lead-footed passengers stomped across the stage of the main auditorium. The Argentine tango sounded more like a military march. Jon's left temple pounded to the beat of the live accordion music. Why would anyone schedule a ballroom dance class for nine o'clock in the morning? The high-pitched voice of the instructor, Marcel, grated on Jon's nerves as his middle-aged partner tromped on his big toe for the second time.

The woman in the fluorescent-yellow beach cover-up hopped back. "I'm sorry."

"Don't worry." Jon smiled. "I'm sure Fred Astaire would have put up with much worse for the beautiful Ginger."

"Who are they?"

"A famous dance pair in classic movies."

"Oh."

She tittered like a canary, and he wondered why he was wasting his day here when he should be vetting the crew for possible suspects. Marcel had roped him into the class when the assistant dance instructor caught the flu. Jon's job was to partner the single ladies. Chances were they weren't really single. Their husbands and boyfriends likely possessed a strong preservation instinct that kept them away.

He felt pressure on his left pinky toe, but his partner didn't even notice she was trampling his foot.

"Pardon me." He tapped her, and she beamed at him. "You're standing on my toe."

"Oh." She wobbled backward. "I'm sorry, Fred." Her shrill bird laugh hit him again.

"It's okay, Ginger."

"Excuse me, baby." Althea's voice sounded from the theater floor below them. She hauled herself onto the stage, pranced over, and sidled up to his partner. "Mind if I cut in? It would be such a shame if I got all gussied up for nothing." She wore a black leotard with a ruffled skirt in a scandalous shade of red. Her silver hair was slicked flat and confined in a low bun with curls surrounding it. A silk rose rested behind her ear.

"I . . . I guess not." The woman moved aside, and Althea took her place.

"My divine Althea comes." Jon held out his left hand, and she placed her right one on it.

They moved to the sultry music without speaking. The woman's light motions belied her size as she nimbly followed him in the dance. His former partner stuck her tongue out at Althea's back before slouching away.

"You do realize you saved eight of my toes," Jon said when they were out of earshot.

"Sorry I was too late to save the other two." The hand resting on his shoulder patted him. "Consider it repaying the favor for the taxis yesterday. Years ago, I was in a city bus accident, and walking long distances is difficult."

"Glad to be of service." He observed the other people on the stage. Daisy danced an elegant pattern off to their right, partnered by one of the waiters, but the other two Shippers were nowhere to be seen. "Don't Emily and Gerry enjoy ballroom?"

"I imagine they do, but they're making arrangements for a quick trip later this morning. We don't often stay two days in Cozumel, and they wanted to do some adventuring."

"I hear the higher-ups made an exception because it's carnival season. They figured the passengers might relish the festivities. Where are Emily and Gerry headed?"

"A park on the other side of the island. Pointa Verdad?"

"Punta Verdad?" Jon's brow furrowed. "That's a fair distance from the ship. The tour takes six to eight hours on a dune buggy."

Althea flinched. "Glad I'm not going, then."

"It's a demanding ride. Are you sure they're planning to—"

The tango music swelled around them and built to a frantic crescendo.

She thrust her hand into the air. "Dip me, darling," she cried.

Althea jerked herself back before he could respond. Jon wrapped both arms around her waist and held on for dear life. She reclined her head and shouted. "Olé!"

"Ooooooooo-lé," Jon ground out from between his clenched teeth. He tried to hoist her, but she leaned horizontal again, and he spread his legs farther to support the weight. "Mrs. Jones, can we please stop dipping? Althea?"

"Not yet. Daisy, take a picture." She waved at her friend, who glided to the couple and pulled a disposable camera from the pocket of her wide-legged black trousers. "Say cheese, handsome."

With effort, Jon lifted the corners of his lips. Were his arms shaking? It wouldn't look good if the cruise director dropped a senior passenger on the floor. His eyes swept the crowded stage for any source of relief.

"I'm missing the fun," said a familiar voice. "Can anyone participate?"

Jon craned his neck and beheld Lacey. The blinding stage lights behind her head hid her expression. To him, the glow resembled a halo, and she was his angel of mercy.

"Yes." He gasped. "Please."

Lacey propped a supportive hand behind Althea. "May I cut in, Mrs. Jones?"

"Why, yes, of course, baby." Althea popped up like a piece of toast and slipped out of his arms.

Jon resisted the urge to grab his spine. Lacey was way smaller, but could his vertebrae handle another round of dipping? She smirked at him as if she read his thoughts. Placing her right hand in his left, she rested the other one on his biceps. It tightened under her touch. Her body moved forward until it was perfectly aligned with his own.

Lacey's mouth twitched. "Dip me, darling."

She repeated Althea's words, but they sounded different coming from Lacey's soft pink lips.

He twisted her to the side, and she bent over his arm. Her right leg stayed steady underneath to help brace her weight as her left leg stretched out in front at a graceful angle. Jon regarded her upturned face. Heaven help him, she was beautiful.

This was a bad idea. This was a bad idea.

The words repeated on a loop in Lacey's head. She'd tried hard to keep her distance from Jon the past few days. But when she'd seen him struggling with Althea, the veins popping out on his neck, she'd weakened. He had plenty of muscles, but Mrs. Jones indulged in second and third trips to the dessert bar.

Now Lacey didn't have to rely on faulty memory for what it felt like to be in his arms. Her whole body downloaded the feeling and saved it to her brain so she'd never forget the sensation. Or the look in his eyes. She recognized that expression but preferred not to put a name to it.

The sound of applause saved her from studying it further.

"*Magnifique*," the dance instructor exclaimed. He ran to them as they stood upright. "I know who to call if one of our dancers ever falls under the weather, no?"

"No," Jon said as Lacey moved out of his arms.

Althea rushed to them. "You two were amazing. Can't you show us one more time?"

Lacey jumped in before Jon had the chance to comply. "I'm sorry, Mrs. Jones. No double-dipping. Besides, isn't it time for bingo in the main lounge?"

"Bingo?"

The woman's gaze shifted, and Lacey delivered the final blow. "I hear they're tripling the prize money today."

Althea's head snapped in the direction of the exit. She plucked the curly hair extensions from her bun and shoved them in her pocket. "Sorry, Jonny. We can finish another time. I got a pressing engagement."

She scuttled off the stage as the instructor clapped.

"Everyone take your starting positions. Slow. Slow. Quick-quick. Slow."

The tango music swirled around them as they stood to the side. A brash accordion whined, and the melody rose in a passionate, tremulous fervor.

Lacey quirked a suspicious eyebrow at Jon. "Don't tell me you've switched jobs already."

"What do you mean?"

"You never did stay in one position long—always on the hunt for greener grass."

Jon shook his head. "Cruise director is about as green as it gets unless you're the captain. I'm just filling in for a sick dance instructor who's sleeping off his cough medicine. But I didn't understand I'd be taking my life in my hands. I owe you big-time."

"Forget it." Lacey turned to leave, but he caught her.

"Not a chance." He dragged her back until she was right under his nose. "Please know we all thank you."

"We?" Lacey looked around.

"Me and every disc in my spinal column."

Lacey laughed and pulled away to swat him. "You're right. You do owe me."

"I wait with bated breath to see how you'll collect."

He amped the wattage in his smile, and Lacey experienced the same old equilibrium problem. She should get some motion-sickness pills.

If only the malady was that easy to fix.

"Punta Verdad?" Collins tapped his notepad against his chin. "Where have I heard that name?"

He flipped through the pages as Jon updated the duty rosters in his computer. His toes still ached from dance practice, and there was a strange sensation in his chest. He rubbed the spot. Not exactly pain. A ghostlike hollowness mixed with anticipation had started the moment he held Lacey in his arms. He shook his head. *Concentrate.*

"Here it is." Collins thumped a fist on the desk. "Last year, another cruise line caught three busboys transporting narcotics by taping them to their bodies underneath their clothes. When the Mexican authorities questioned them, they confessed they bought the drugs in an isolated location near Punta Verdad, where there weren't any witnesses. Quite a coincidence the grandmas chose the same place."

Jon refrained from arguing. He was 99 percent sure the Shippers had nothing to do with the smuggling. But on the 1 percent chance he was mistaken, he'd let Collins have his way. "Are you going to follow them?"

"Can't. One got a good look at me in Cozumel while I was tailing them. Suspicious old gal. And curious as a cat. In an out-of-the-way site like Punta Verdad, she'd recognize me right away. You'd better go. I'll set up surveillance on the ship and keep an eye on any possible suspects from the crew."

"The Shippers are harmless. I'm sure they're not—"

"Indulge me." Collins tossed his notepad on the desk. "I'm the one with thirty years of experience. Remember?"

Jon twisted on his chair. How could he forget? Even if the aging detective didn't seem to excel at his job, thirty years had to mean something, right?

The gentle buzz from his laptop filled the silence as he considered. He had fewer activities to supervise on port days with most of the passengers off the boat. He could get the dance instructor to cover for him. But what excuse could he give the Shippers for his tagging along?

CHAPTER 8

"HI, MOM." LACEY LEANED ON the railing and watched the passengers disembark as she talked on her phone. "How are you?"

"Not too bad. My new medication is better than the old one. I haven't had nearly the pain."

"That's good." Lacey untied the purple scarf around her neck with one hand and stuffed it in the pocket of her uniform. "Are you still working two jobs?"

"Yes, but it's part-time. My schedule's a lot easier these days, thanks to the money you keep sending. You're sure you still have enough to live on? I hope you're not working too hard."

"No more than usual. I even have a few hours off. The ship's docked in Cozumel an extra day, so I'm going shopping."

"Good for you. Buy yourself a pretty outfit."

"Who would I wear it for?" Her sarcastic response was automatic, but a familiar face popped in her mind. Brown hair. Square jaw. Rock-solid arms that dipped a girl like she weighed less than a life preserver.

Lacey realized her mother was talking and tried to refocus.

"I hear your father coming in from his softball game."

"Softball? He must be feeling better."

"Not much. He still suffers from the chronic fatigue. But the doctor says it's good for him to exercise. He forces himself to get out. Wait a minute. I'll put him on the phone."

"Don't bother." Lacey walked down the empty side deck. "I have to go. Love you. Bye." She hung up and entered the glass doors into one of the small lobbies.

Static crackled.

Lacey tensed, and her head whipped around. Daisy and Althea sat at a small table by the window playing cards. Not a walkie-talkie in sight.

Did she imagine it?

She strolled over and eyed the setup. "What game is this?"

"Gin rummy." Althea placed an eight of hearts on the discard pile. "Care to join us?"

"Thanks, but I have to change my clothes." Lacey scanned the room. "Where are the other Shippers?"

Daisy drew a card from the stockpile. "Emily and Gerry reserved a special trip to a lighthouse. They're getting ready and meeting us here before departure."

"A lighthouse? Where?"

"I'm not sure," Althea said.

"I've told you three times," Gerry grumbled as she and Emily walked in together. "We're visiting the El Grande Lighthouse at Punta Verdad."

"Like I'm really going to remember that." Althea waggled her head.

Lacey observed the approaching pair. "Punta Verdad is thirty kilometers away. Don't tell me you're taking one of those all-terrain vehicle tours."

"Oh no." Emily flapped a hand at her. "Can you picture a body my age bouncing through the Mexican jungle for hours?"

"Exactly. It's a crazy idea."

She nodded. "That's why we're riding a motorboat."

"What?" Lacey leaned forward. "You're riding what?"

"I found the sweetest young man online. His name is Fernando. He takes you out to the lighthouse on his boat and even provides lunch. He makes the sandwiches with his grandmother's fresh homemade salsa."

Lacey pressed her fingers against her temples. "You can't be serious.

The four of you are going to climb into a motorboat with a total stranger and go careening across the water to Punta Verdad?"

"Mercy, no." Althea raised her head from her cards. "You couldn't pay me to get on that thing. The website said you had to get out of the boat on your own and wade ashore. I might be able to manage the exodus, but imagine me trying to climb back in." She laughed. "He'd have to haul me up with a fishing net. The locals would think he caught a two-hundred-pound tuna."

Daisy laid her cards on the table. "The trip doesn't appeal to me either. Althea and I decided to stay here."

Lacey turned to Gerry. An ex-librarian might be an easier sell than the career-military-wife Emily.

"Ms. Paroo, this sounds kind of dangerous."

Emily slid in front of her friend. "It was Gerry's idea. She needs material for her book."

Gerry peered over the frizzy gray mop of hair. "I *need* material for my book."

"She believes the lighthouse will be a great location for the feuding couple to reconcile."

"It's a *great* location," said Gerry.

Lacey glanced from one to the other. Their placid expressions told her she wasn't reaching them. "What if someone gets sick? Or you have trouble reentering the boat? There will only be the guide to take care of you."

"I'm sorry, Lacey." Emily's smile didn't look sorry. "You can't talk us out of this."

"I don't . . . this isn't—"

"Of course, you're welcome to tag along." Emily focused on her khaki slacks and picked at a stain.

"What?"

"Come with us." Gerry propped her bony arms on Emily's shoulders and leaned forward. "Do you have some time off?"

"Yeeees . . ."

"It requires one hour to get there, one hour back, and I can take the pictures and notes for my book in an hour. That's three hours, tops."

Lacey studied both ladies. Gerry's stoic face waited, and Emily scrubbed her pants leg. "You're sure I can't talk you out of this?"

"We're sure," Gerry said.

Lacey sighed. "I'll have to do my shopping later."

"That's wonderful, dear." A gleam entered Emily's eye. "I'm sure you'll enjoy yourself." She hummed a little tune as she walked away.

Lacey's insides tugged like a fish with a hook in its jaw. It was too late now. She'd taken the bait and wanted to make sure the women returned safely. Her gut told her there was more to this lighthouse excursion, but what could it be?

CHAPTER 9

"WHAT ARE *YOU* DOING HERE?"

Jon wished Lacey's tone sounded less like a kindergartner staring at a piece of broccoli. He stood at the marina, eyeing the trio before him. Emily wore a blue-and-white-striped shirt with khaki pants. Gerry had gone bohemian with a gauzy tie-dyed skirt and matching top. Lacey had traded her crisp white uniform for a pair of capris and a loose cotton blouse with colorful flowers embroidered on the lapel. Her silky hair was pulled into a ponytail. A trickle of sweat dripped down the side of her slender, exposed neck and cascaded to the hollow of her throat, drawing his eyes along the same path.

"Jon." She waved a hand in front of him.

He snapped out of it. "Yes?"

"What are you doing here?"

"I came for the fun." Jon gestured at his T-shirt and cargo shorts. "Althea told me Emily and Gerry planned to take on the south side of the island alone. I wondered if it was such a good idea, so I offered to escort them."

"When exactly was this conversation?" Lacey frowned at the silver-topped instigators.

The two found interest in anything but her. Their faces moved this way and that, as if they hadn't heard the question. Emily picked at a fishnet drying on top of a blue plastic barrel.

Jon's lips twitched. That explained why they'd jumped at his offer to come with them. The Shippers were up to their old matchmaking tricks.

"Buenos días. Hello." A young man in his twenties approached them. He wore ragged jean shorts, a sleeveless shirt, and a dirty white captain's hat. "Are you Mrs. Emily?"

"Yes, I'm Emily." She navigated around Lacey and shook his hand.

Lacey switched her attention to Jon. "I'm here to watch over them. You can return to the ship. I'm sure you're wanted there."

"Marcel is covering for me. He owed me a favor."

"But . . . you're the cruise director. You work fifteen-hour days. You can't take off."

"Even cruise directors get a little time away. You know that." Truth be told, he had lots to do. But her veiled insistence that he wasn't welcome irked him.

Lacey turned her back to him. She walked closer to the waiting motorboat and muttered, "Flaking out again."

"What did you say?" Jon came around in front of her.

"The paint is flaking, and it seems awfully small." Lacey motioned to the compact craft. It was a faded lime green, about the length of a minivan, with a blue tarp stretched across the metal-frame canopy to block the sun. An outboard motor hung off the rear. "I don't think we'll all fit."

"No. No." Fernando bounced around and waved his hands. "Mrs. Emily said four people. It is good."

He fanned his arm toward the boat, and everyone climbed aboard. Jon sat in front to take the brunt of the sea spray, while the women lined the side. Fernando fired up the engine. They pulled away from the wooden pier and were soon jetting through the crystal-blue water.

Jon's eyes traveled to Lacey like a homing pigeon, but her leave-me-alone expression was less than encouraging. Next to her, Gerry lost inches to her stature with each bounce of the boat.

"Are you okay, Gerry?" Jon shouted above the motor. "You look a little green around the gills."

Her lips twisted into what might have been a smile on dry land. At sea, it was more likely the precursor to losing her breakfast.

"Serves her right," Lacey muttered as Fernando killed the motor.

"What did you say, dear?" Emily leaned in from her right side.

"Nothing."

Jon pressed his lips together to keep from chuckling. Did the lady not hear Lacey, or was she calling her out? He guessed the latter.

Their guide slowed to point out a famous landmark, then tugged on the engine cord, and they were off again. After fifty-five minutes of bounding through the choppy waves like a clown on a pogo stick, even Jon prayed for a reprieve. They cheered when the red-and-white El Grande Lighthouse appeared in the distance.

Fernando dropped the anchor when the boat was a few yards from the beach. He jumped into the shallow water and beckoned to his customers. "You come and wade ashore." He waved his arm toward the sandy stretch.

"Gerry, are you sure you can make it?" Jon rested a hand on her shoulder. "Let's ask him to take us home."

"No." She stood and swayed. "I'm fit as a fiddle. Truly." She put her hand on his. "I must observe the lighthouse. It's important to me."

Lacey grimaced and shook her head at him. He ran the different scenarios in his mind, but Gerry's pleading trumped everything else. Jon grabbed the rim of the boat and vaulted over. He landed knee-deep in water. The bottom of his shorts soaked up the surf, and the breeze blew his hair in all directions. He turned and faced away from the waiting women.

"You're already woozy." He stretched his arms behind him in Gerry's direction. "How about I give you a piggyback to shore?"

"Oh, I couldn't do that. It's been sixty years since my last piggyback ride."

"Then I say you're about due." Jon peeked back at her and grinned. "Climb on."

"Yes, do what he says, Ms. Paroo." Lacey led her toward Jon. "It will be safer."

Gerry held on to Lacey's arm as Jon maneuvered closer to the boat. The retired librarian squatted and sat on the edge, swung her legs, and wrapped her thin arms around his neck. He took hold under her knees and pulled the rest of her down.

Fernando eyed the remaining ladies, and his mouth scrunched. "Do I have to carry someone too?"

"Don't be ridiculous." Emily sniffed.

Lacey laughed. "If you help us into the water, we can manage on our own."

With Fernando's assistance, the two exited the boat without incident and headed for the beach.

The waterlogged sand shifted, and Jon's feet sank. He listed to the side. Gerry squealed. She wrapped her arms tighter around his throat.

"Have no fear," Jon choked out. "They train us for this in school."

"Cruise directors have a school?"

"I was talking about elementary school." He lifted his foot in the unstable sand and carefully took another step. He arrived on dry land at the same time as the other women and lowered his knees to deposit Gerry on the soft white beach. Scanning the vicinity, Jon made note of the sparse buildings and deserted landscape—not a person or drug runner in sight. He'd tried to tell Collins. This trip was a waste of time.

"Look." He pointed in the distance. "There's the lighthouse."

"Uh-huh." Gerry curled over her knees and rested her head on top.

"Gerry?" Jon knelt beside her, but she waved him away.

"I'm fine. I just need to sit very still for a very long time."

He saw a white stucco store next to the lighthouse. The dinky establishment boasted a plastic picnic table and mismatched chairs under an awning. "They have a place where you could get out of the sun and rest. Can I help you?"

She nodded without raising her head, and Jon took her by the arm. Lacey looped her hand under Gerry's other elbow, and they lifted her up.

"Oh, Gerry." Emily bit her lip as she hovered. "I'm so sorry."

"It's nothing." She took a deep breath. "All that rocking and rolling through the waves got to me. I'm doing better on terra firma."

The group walked to the small store, and Gerry sank onto one of the battered chairs by the warped table. Jon sat beside her and patted her back.

"Don't let me worry you." She slipped the strap of her bag off her shoulder and took out a notebook and pen. "I'll sit here and absorb the ambiance. I'm already getting a flood of ideas."

"I'll buy you a drink, dear." Emily disappeared inside and exited a few minutes later with a glass bottle of mineral water. She handed it to her friend and motioned to the others. "Why don't you two check out the lighthouse while I discuss lunch with Fernando?" Emily pointed at the tower beside them.

"Good idea." Jon rose. "Come on, Lace."

She looked at Emily. "Don't you want to come?"

"The steep climb would be too much for these old legs of mine. You two go and enjoy yourselves."

"Are you sure you'll be all right—"

Jon took her elbow and steered her away from the table. "Humor them," he whispered. "If they went to this trouble to set us up, might as well play along."

"Don't encourage their schemes." Lacey knocked his hand away from her elbow as they walked. "An inch is a mile with that group."

Jon laughed as they entered the lighthouse. A narrow stone staircase lay before them.

"Ladies first." He motioned for her to lead the way.

The humidity hung on Lacey like a heavy, wet blanket. She climbed the cramped staircase—too aware of the man following behind. She had successfully limited their interactions to group settings on the giant MS *Buckingham*. How had they wound up in this tiny building? Alone?

Those Shippers.

They reached the top and exited onto the circular walkway surrounding the lantern room. Red columns supported the balustrade, and Lacey leaned on the stones. The Caribbean Sea grew darker by degrees. The shallows washed around in a friendly teal blue, but dusky indigo sat waiting a few hundred yards beyond.

"Beautiful, isn't it?" Jon bent forward and crossed his arms on the stone guard. "I'd love to do some diving out there."

"Too deep for me. I prefer to stay close to shore."

Jon tilted his head her way. "You were always cautious by nature. In everything."

Lacey eased away and tucked her shirt in her waistband. The wind blew a stray hair from her ponytail, and she pushed it behind her ear. She walked to the other side and observed a signpost on the beach below. Large, colorful arrows were nailed to a weathered piece of wood with various city names and their distances in kilometers.

"It appears you can get anywhere from here." She pointed, and Jon joined her. "Filipinas, Cuba, Halifax, Jamaica."

"Key West."

Lacey winced. That was the spot of their last date . . . nondate . . . whatever it was they'd had two and a half years ago. The ship they were working docked in Key West, and they'd spent their free time eating dinner in a romantic restaurant in town. Their six-month contracts concluded when they reached Orlando the next morning, and mandatory vacation time commenced.

"Do you remember what I said that night?" Jon asked.

"What?" Lacey's mind returned to the present. He stood a safe two feet away, studying her. She cleared her throat and leaned on the guardrail, crossing her arms. "What night?"

"Key West." Jon mirrored her pose. "I said I had something important to tell you when we got home to Orlando."

The sound of the waves crashing below them answered. Lacey said nothing. She was too busy keeping a neutral expression.

"You asked me to wait to say anything until after you'd visited your family . . . and then you never came back."

"I heard they were giving out promotions on a different ship, so I transferred." Lacey trailed her hand along the railing as she walked to the other side of the tower, aiming for nonchalance. "I guess we didn't get a chance to say goodbye."

"*Goodbye* wasn't what I planned to say." Jon matched her stride and stood closer this time. "As you're well aware."

"Hmm?" His intensity surrounded her like a thick fog. Lacey pretended interest in the view below, but he took hold of her arm and spun her around.

"Why did you do it?" His eyes stared into hers, searching.

"What do you mean?" She avoided his gaze.

"I've spent the past few days trying to make amends for whatever I did wrong back then."

Lacey's head jerked his direction. "Who said you did anything wrong?"

"You did. With your disappearing act."

"I had a great opportunity for a promotion, and I took it."

"Did you also have a great opportunity to change your phone number, and you took it?"

"I'm no good at goodbyes." Lacey stood still, meeting his scrutiny without wavering. "Sometimes it's easier to pack and go. Parting from friends is painful."

"Friends?" Jon released her and retreated. "Is that what you would have called our relationship?"

"Absolutely." Lacey's wide smile raised her cheeks until they ached. "We ate together, hung out together, laughed together. That's what *friends* do." No need to mention the rest. The staring into each other's eyes without speaking. The butterflies in her stomach. The tingly embraces.

Jon opened his mouth and closed it. He opened it again. And closed it again. The air left his nostrils in a violent snort. He turned around and walked through the door by the lantern room. His heavy footsteps echoed off the stone as he descended the stairs, leaving Lacey alone at the top.

Her smile and shoulders drooped in tandem. She sank to the floor, pressed her fingertips to her temples, and took a deep breath. Then another. A seagull mocked her with a raucous cry.

She glared at the bird. "What are you laughing at?"

Fluffy white clouds stretched overhead. They reminded her there'd been another witness to the whole conversation. Someone who knew what a pack of lies she'd spouted.

"Sorry, God." She dropped her gaze. "I know I'm a coward. But . . . it's safer this way."

The sunlight shone through the stone columns of the walkway—casting thick, rigid shadows on the floor at her feet. She'd realized the inevitability of "the talk." But it was finished, and it hadn't been the disaster she'd expected. They'd rehashed the past, and Jon would leave her alone. This trip was a good idea after all. So good she wanted to cry with relief. Yes, that's why tears were stuck in her throat. *Relief.* Everything would be fine from here on out. She was sure of it.

Until she looked at the beach.

Lacey jumped up and hollered over the railing at the woman sitting below. "Emily, where's the boat?"

CHAPTER 10

LACEY CAREENED DOWN THE STAIRS. She descended round and round the narrow lighthouse. Her speed increased until she reached the bottom and slammed to a stop. Right into Jon's back. He stood in the open doorway and lurched forward as she crashed into him.

"Sorry." She ducked under his arm and ran to the beach. Her feet sank in the powder-soft sand, slowing her gait. Lacey pushed harder, not that it did any good. The lazy teal waves rolled in front of her without a single boat to mar their postcard perfection. She doubled over, bracing her hands against her knees, and gasped for air.

Jon caught up at the water's edge. "What's wrong?"

Chest heaving, Lacey waved at the spot where Fernando's boat used to be.

Jon groaned. He scanned the water and pointed to a speck on the horizon. "There."

Lacey straightened, and her neck swiveled to Emily and Gerry at the table. She marched across the beach, Jon at her heels.

"Where's Fernando?" Lacey stopped in front of them and twirled around as if she expected him to appear.

"He had an emergency." Emily held a plastic bag. "Don't worry. He said he'd be back in a bit. And he left the sandwiches for us, so we won't starve."

"A bit?" Lacey swung her head from side to side. "What does that

67

even mean? It took us an hour to get here. If he's going home, that's two hours round trip. Did you even bring your medicine with you?"

"Relax, dear." Emily unzipped her purse and riffled through it. "I took a dose before we left. And there are lots of things to see here in the meantime. Fernando said that path over there leads to a crop of ancient Mayan ruins." She withdrew a pair of aviator sunglasses from a leather pouch, put them on, and motioned to a trail at the far end of the beach. "You and Jon go explore them while we wait."

"I'm supposed to return to the ship in time for the first dinner seating." Lacey's hands rose to her waist, palms up as if asking for a benediction from above and waiting for the right answer to drop into them.

"This won't do." Jon moved around Lacey and crouched in front of Emily. "You must have his phone number. Call him. Even if he's already left, it won't add too much time to his trip to come and get us now."

"Out of the question." Emily stared him down, his face reflected in her mirrored lenses. "It was urgent."

"Don't worry." Gerry pulled a novel from her woven purse. "He'll be back soon. I brought an extra book if someone wants to borrow it."

Gerry passed the novel to Lacey, who cringed at the amorous couple embracing on its cover. She tossed the book on the table.

Emily shook her head as she retrieved the novel. "Young people are always in such a hurry." She hummed as she opened the story to the first chapter.

Jon was no help. He said nothing.

Lacey's mouth formed words, but no sound came out. This must be illegal. They were being held hostage by two granny gangsters. She clenched her fists, gave a tiny squeal, and stomped away.

Jon eyed the placid little ladies as they read, then suppressed a chuckle. The whole crazy situation would be funny if Lacey weren't so peeved.

In the distance, she stormed along the beach, kicking sand right and left. A perfectly understandable reaction.

The setup was too blatant. An obvious bid to force them into close proximity. This remote south side of the island took hours to reach by dune buggy. Calling a Monarch employee to come and get them was an option. But by the time they reached the ship, it would be the same difference as waiting for Fernando. Plus, the journey might be hard on the senior citizens, and he wouldn't abandon them to wait for the motorboat alone.

They were stuck.

Fifteen minutes ago, he'd have welcomed the chance to spend quality time with Lacey—before she played the just-friends card, consigning every tender memory they'd ever shared to the garbage pile. He wasn't feeling friendly right now.

Had the good old days only been good for him? Granted, they never officially defined their relationship back when they were together. But they *were* together. Any spare moment was spent in each other's company.

Jon wandered around, digging in the dirt and collecting seashells, but somehow his feet kept pointing Lacey's direction. He gave up and walked toward the beach. She sat in stony silence next to the water's edge, staring at the last place they'd seen Fernando's boat. She spoke as soon as he stopped beside her.

"I can't believe they went this far." She hunched, hiding her face in her hands.

"Who?" He sat on her right, careful to leave a few inches of empty space between them.

"The Shippers." She pounded a fist into the sand. "This has their fingerprints all over it."

He knew she was right but didn't want to admit it out loud. He was enjoying the rare sight of her normally battened-down self so out of control.

"The man had an emergency, Lacey." Jon shifted to find a comfortable position. "Let it go."

"So why didn't he load everybody on the boat before he left?"

"I concede your point. That would have made more sense."

She snatched a pebble and chucked it at the waves. "They wanted to give us plenty of time alone to reminisce."

"About our *friendship*, you mean?" Jon grabbed a jagged rock and hurled it in the same direction.

"About whatever." Lacey leaned on her arm, away from him.

"Let's reminisce, then. Do you remember the first words you ever said to me?"

She glanced at him from the corner of her eye. "Were they 'nice to meet you'?"

"No. You skipped the formalities." Jon's mouth twitched as he studied his fingers. "You said, 'Are you going to pick up that trash?'"

"Trash?"

If Jon had asked her *where* she first saw him, she could've named the exact location. Lacey was a maid then. She remembered standing in the housekeeping line as the chief steward belabored their duties. The bellboys stood opposite, and long-legged Jon with the quarterback shoulders and toothpaste-commercial smile had caught the eye of more than one lady. But there was no trash involved.

"It must have been commonplace to you." He laughed. "You always had a bossy streak with everyone."

"I'm not bossy." Lacey dug her toes in the sand. "I'm assertive."

"That you are." Jon stretched out his legs and leaned back on his elbows. "You're assertive a lot." She opened her mouth to defend herself, but he interrupted. "I admire that about you."

She closed her lips and slowly reclined on the sand—keeping a Bible's length between them, the safe distance all the youth pastors in her adolescence had prescribed. And she definitely needed safety at the moment. "Were you littering?"

"No. I was walking down a stateroom corridor and passed a crumpled coffee cup on the floor. You didn't like that I left it there."

"I still don't." She squinted his way. "Why didn't you pick it up?"

"Can't remember. Maybe I didn't notice it. Maybe because it wasn't mine."

"If you work on a ship, then it belongs to you. Every part. Even the trash."

Jon rolled on his side to look at her. "I agree. Now. But I was still learning the ropes then. Many of which I learned from you."

It was hard to keep her distance from such an insightful, gorgeous man.

But she would persevere. Stay safe.

Charming people let you down.

The reminder sounded hollow, even in her head. Lacey wiggled a little to the left, widening the space between them by another Bible's length. She lounged on the toasty sand and propped her hands behind her head.

"No charge for the lessons." She lowered her lids.

The Mexican sunlight warmed her skin, and a salty-sea aroma tickled her nostrils.

Lacey felt rather than saw Jon relax beside her. They were on an open beach with two nosy chaperones a few yards away, but the intimacy rocked her insides. The Shippers were good. She'd give them that. Throwing her together with this sweet, sincere, and good-looking-enough-to-make-your-earlobes-tingle guy was a savvy plan. She moved her hands in front of her, folded them on her torso, and stayed still as a mummy. The ancient Egyptians embalmed people after removing the heart and other organs from the body to preserve a beautiful, empty corpse.

A morbid thought for a sunny day at the beach.

And completely irrelevant.

Her heart was alive and well and pulsing away like a noisy, unwelcome alarm clock.

The cool breeze swirled, and a spicy scent wafted from the chili peppers hanging from the store's doorjamb. Emily and Gerry stared out at the beach, watching Jon and Lacey from behind their open books. The couple scooted back and forth on the sand like a pair of lobsters doing a mating dance.

Emily slammed her novel on the table. "What do you suppose they're saying?"

"Probably not much with words." Gerry scribbled in her notebook. "But their body language is fascinating."

"Are you plotting another book?" Emily propped her elbow on the table and rested her cheek against her palm. "You should finish the first one before you start something new."

Gerry ignored her. The pen tip flew across the page. She scratched her nose, and a speck of ink smeared on her upper lip.

"Go ahead." Emily flopped back on her chair and crossed her arms. "Keep writing. At least some kind of romance—albeit imaginary—will result from this failure." The fingers of her right hand drummed against the tabletop. "What are we missing? Lacey likes him. I'm sure of it. Why is she fighting this so hard? I worry Jon will take no for an answer and stop trying." She raised her gaze to the blue sky. "Lord, I'm stumped. I believe you brought Jon here for Lacey, and I'd like to help. But I don't know how."

Her eyes narrowed as she studied the uncooperative couple on the beach. This called for an Alpha strike. She pulled out her phone and typed a list of things she wanted to tell the other two Shippers. The next operation required all hands on deck.

The sun dipped low in the sky as Fernando's boat approached the shore. The water shimmered a pearly white in the early evening glow.

He killed the motor, leaped over the side, and waded through the gentle waves toward the four waiting passengers.

Jon headed for the plastic table and squatted in front of Gerry. "Are you ready for another piggyback, Ms. Paroo?"

She pushed his shoulder. "I'm fully recovered. No sense in throwing your back out for an old woman. I can walk to the boat."

Gerry gathered the gauzy fabric of her skirt and tied it in a knot above her knees. Emily rolled up her khaki pants legs. The two locked arms, and Lacey hovered behind them as they headed to the craft, her hands outstretched—prepared to catch anyone who stumbled.

She'd probably let me take a nosedive and not lift a finger.

Jon's feet sank lower in the wet sand as the crystal-clear water lapped around his toes. Fernando splashed to his side. He bent forward and swept his arm at the boat like a doorman at a fancy hotel.

"Was everything okay?" Jon asked.

"What?"

"Didn't you have an emergency?"

"No." The young man tilted his head. "Mrs. Emily asked me to leave and not come back for a few hours."

Jon's gaze swung to the older woman. She stood at the side of the boat, whispering with Gerry. It was a setup from the beginning, but with what intent? Even now, he didn't buy Collins's cockeyed theory they were involved in the drug smuggling. The matchmaking strings were so obvious. He hoped that's all there was to it.

Better not tell Lacey about Fernando's confession. No need to add more fuel to her paranoia fire. Of course, was it truly paranoia when she was 100 percent right? The Shippers were out to get them.

He should be upset. Their little scheme cost him valuable time away from the investigation. But the matchmakers' interference got him something he'd lacked for two and a half years—answers. They weren't the ones he wanted, but at least he knew where he stood.

Firmly in the friend zone.

That was fine. All the better. His brain listed the reasons this wasn't the time for romance, but his eyes cut to the alluring blonde who stood facing away from him—a common sight these days. Jon kicked at the water surging around his feet.

He was tired of playing puppy. How many times did he have to taste rejection before he got the message? Still, every time he thought his feelings had ebbed, his heart washed right back to Lacey.

CHAPTER 11

FISH SKELETONS WITH PREHISTORIC-SIZED teeth decorated the chalkboard ceiling of Hibachi Coast, the MS *Buckingham*'s Japanese restaurant. Multicolored glass ocean creatures hung on the walls. Their comedic pupils bulged at anyone who dared to look at them. Emily ignored the fanciful decorations as she and her fellow Shippers settled in at a booth for their once-a-week treat of the ship's private dining options. She opened her binder and spread her notes on the table.

"Aw, baby." Althea stared at the stacks of paper. "Can't it wait till after dinner? I'm starving."

"Just a short strategy meeting. Then we can order the food."

"But the sushi's calling my name." Althea cast a longing glance at the bar, where a chef wrapped the fresh seaweed rolls in front of waiting diners.

"It won't take long." Emily passed a one-sheet summary to each woman. "They always bring miso soup."

"But me so hungry." Althea nudged Daisy with an elbow, and her roommate chuckled obediently.

Gerry took out her spectacles and studied the handout on Jon. The short list of details regarding their cruise director didn't even fill half the page. "Not much to go on, is it?"

"What new information have you found?" Emily held her pen above the paper, ready to write.

"I combed the social media sites," Gerry said. "He's not listed on any of them. I even tried the Florida government page. I found thirteen men with the name Jonathan King in Fort Lauderdale alone. Who knew it was such a common name? In the end, I got zilch."

Emily dropped her pen. "Nothing?"

Gerry leaned back on the bench seat, crossed her arms, and wrapped her long fingers around her elbows. "I employed all the usual methods. When using his name didn't work, I ran an image search on Google. I even checked the sex offender registry, but still nothing."

"Thank heaven for that," Daisy said, shivering.

Althea grabbed a cloth napkin from the table and spread it across her lap. "What do we do now?"

Gerry rubbed the nape of her neck. "Without a hometown or the name of his school to narrow the results, there are way too many Jonathan Kings in the public records. It would take forever to sift through the agglomeration. Details. We have to find them."

Emily reached over and patted Gerry's arm. "You've done your best, dear. But the fact that we can't easily locate any information is highly suspicious. Let's consider other options."

Daisy's drawl was tinged with a hint of trepidation. "Such as?"

"Tell me, Gerry." Emily picked up her pen and slid it in her pocket. "Don't you have a cousin who's a retired detective?"

"Yes, I do." Her sudden catlike smile matched her spectacles. "And as a matter of fact, he owes me a favor."

"Wonderful." Emily closed her binder. "Give him Jonathan King's name and profession and see what he can uncover. We'll continue this discussion after your cousin does some research. Meeting adjourned."

Althea's arm shot in the air. "Waiter."

One round of miso and two appetizers later, the Shippers dug into the main course.

"They hired a new magician for the after-dinner show," Althea said around a mouthful of chicken katsu. "We should go."

"I lost my interest in magic shows at the age of twelve," Emily said.

"Think of it as matchmaker research. A new man means a new

workup for our employee files. You're the one who insists we keep them updated."

"She's right." Gerry squeezed her chopsticks to grab a lone fried dumpling on the appetizer plate. "He might be a prospective client."

Daisy set her fork down and fingered the high neckline of her dark cotton blouse. "I'm not dressed for a show. I'll have to change first."

Althea waved her fork. "You're wearing black from top to toe. That's dressy enough. I bet some people will come in flip-flops."

Daisy smoothed her shirt and buttoned it at the collar. After reaching in her purse, she withdrew a rose-tinted cameo brooch and pinned it at her neck. "I suppose you're right. Young people these days lack proper fashion sense."

"Or common sense." Gerry pushed her plate away. "It's settled, then. Let's head to the show."

They left the restaurant, maneuvered through the crowded lobby, and entered the main auditorium. Emily led them to their usual couch in front of the stage, and the Shippers made themselves comfortable. The opening numbers remained the same. An overblown master of ceremonies in a flashy blue-sequined jacket introduced the next performers, and an energetic samba group spilled onto the stage. The dancers jiggled and shimmied to the syncopated music.

Emily's attention wandered to her friends. Althea clapped along even though she'd watched the show many times. Gerry's eyes held the faraway look she got when she was plotting a new story, and Daisy had shut her eyes altogether. The Southern matron wore a pained expression.

Daisy whispered, "Those women haven't got enough clothes between them for one decent outfit."

"Bless their hearts." Althea squinted. "Not a panty line to be seen on any of them. I wonder if the men are wearing thongs."

Emily couldn't care less about the performers' underwear. She scrutinized the room, but Lacey wasn't there. She'd been out of sight since Punta Verdad. The hardworking hostess was usually easy to spot. Was she angry enough to cut them out completely? Emily sucked the inside of her cheek between her teeth and chewed. Perhaps they *had* gone a bit far . . . Emily straightened at the thought, rejecting it. They would go further still if it meant helping Lacey find love.

A deafening crescendo jolted Emily from her musings. The MC dashed from behind the curtain and bellowed into his microphone.

"We hope you're enjoying the entertainment, ladies and gentlemen. You're going to love this next guy, a new addition to our Monarch family. We imported him straight from Ireland for your entertainment pleasure. Please put your hands together for Seamus O'Riley."

A man in his late sixties dressed in an old-fashioned tuxedo with pointy tails, white silk vest, and matching bow tie strutted onstage carrying a small magician's table with a black velvet cloth covering the top. Streaks of silver ran through his Celtic red hair.

"Saints preserve us, we have a beautiful crowd tonight." He wore a face mic and gestured at the auditorium with both hands.

Gerry squirmed. "Is that accent for real?"

"Shhhh." Daisy smacked her well-manicured fingers on her friend's arm.

"Are you ready to be amazed?" The magician walked to the edge of the stage and cupped his hand to his ear.

Cheers and whistles answered.

"Let's heat things up." He clapped above his head, and a fireball shot from his fingers.

"Oh, mercy!" Althea jumped, clutching the front of her shirt.

Seamus looked at the row of Shippers. His focus swept the four ladies, resting a few seconds longer on Gerry, who sat with her arms crossed over her chest. He reached behind his back, and a full-size top hat appeared. Seamus placed the chapeau at a jaunty angle on his head and patted the crown.

"Let me ask you," he said. "What does a magician always require?"

"A rabbit," someone called.

"Can't stand the furry beasts." Seamus shook his head. "No. I was referring to a beautiful assistant." He plucked a microphone from under the cloth on his table, shielded his vision against the bright spotlights, and studied the audience. "Is there anyone willing to volunteer?"

Althea raised her hand and pumped it up and down. "Ooooh. Right here!"

His gaze lowered to the row in front of him. "Wait. I found the perfect lady." He hopped off the stage, stood in the aisle, and held the microphone out to Gerry.

The woman drew herself taut with the austerity of fifty years in the public library system. "I did not volunteer."

"Maybe you were volun-told." Seamus's green eyes sparkled, and the audience laughed and cheered.

"Do it, baby." Althea pushed her off her seat and into the aisle.

Gerry's lips pinched together, but she took the mic and followed the magician, ignoring the hand he offered her at the steps. They reached center stage and stood side by side. She topped him by a full head.

He grinned up at her. "I always did fancy someone taller."

"Me too," Gerry droned into the microphone.

The crowd roared.

Seamus made a dramatic show of wiping his brow. "I think I'll need all the fairies in Ireland to help me with this one."

Emily chuckled at her friend's embarrassing predicament, but her attention wandered as she scanned the room again. Gilded Corinthian columns rose from the ground floor to the balcony. Every seat was full. Staff in white uniforms walked the aisles, serving trays of refreshments to the passengers, but still no sign of Lacey. Was she avoiding them? Emily's conscience prickled. If the girl detested the idea of a relationship that much, perhaps they should leave her alone.

No. Lacey deserved to be happy, whether she wanted to be or not. Emily wasn't sure what had locked the poor girl up tighter than a fortress, but Jon might be the man who could scale the unbreachable walls of her heart.

"Don't act so pained, my darlin'." Seamus beamed at Gerry as he waved to a stagehand behind the curtain. "One trick to go."

Two crew members wheeled out a tall black box with a window cut out of the front.

Gerry glared at the massive prop. "You don't expect to lock me in that thing, do you?"

"Only if I can climb in with you." He elbowed her. "Two's company."

"Company," Emily murmured from the front row. She smacked a fist against her palm. "That's it."

Althea shuddered beside her. "The last time I saw that look, they almost made us walk the plank."

Emily stole a glance at her watch. How much longer till the show ended? She had to return to HQ and draft the new mission.

This one would be groundbreaking. Every bone in her body confirmed it.

CHAPTER 12

"I FOUND A NEW LEAD."

Collins waggled his eyebrows twice as he smirked around the giant wad of gum in his mouth. People promenaded the deck in everything from sequins to Speedos. An older couple approached from the left in formal clothing, and Jon held up a hand.

"Yes, sir." He patted Collins on the back. "I'd be happy to show you where the gym is."

"Gym?" Collins blanched.

Jon shoved him around the corner. They walked down the hall until they came to a recess in the corridor that led to a stairwell. He pushed the detective inside. "What did you find?"

"While you were keeping an eye on the little old ladies in Punta Verdad, I overheard a couple of kitchen workers talking in Spanish."

"You speak Spanish?"

"A few words. Anyway, they repeated *lechuga* at least ten times."

"*Lechuga*?" Jon paused. "You mean lettuce?"

"Exactly. Are you fluent?"

"No, but I grew up in Florida. It's easy to learn a little— Never mind. What does lettuce have to do with anything?"

"It's street slang. Lettuce can mean marijuana."

Jon waited for more, but Collins stood silent. "It can also mean 'lettuce.' They work in the kitchen. They might've been talking about the dinner salads."

Collins pursed his lips and shook his head. "Trust me. They weren't talking about dinner. They had that tone in their voice, if you know what I mean."

Jon censored his first response before answering. How did this guy get recommended? Did the general manager owe Collins a favor? "That's not much to go on. Even if they were talking about weed, it might have nothing to do with the case. We just left a Mexican port where the government decriminalized marijuana use. Perhaps they made poor recreational choices on their afternoon break. Every major drug bust on Monarch ships involved cocaine."

"A store can sell more than one product." Collins stopped smacking his gum and held it between his teeth. "I'm not saying these are the guys, but at least it's a lead. You got anything better?"

Jon ran a hand through his hair. "No."

"So we dig into these two and keep our radar on. Agreed?"

He nodded without conviction. He was beginning to think they should hire more detectives. Collins's less-than-stellar performance gave him little hope for cracking the case. If it were only a few grams of weed, the company wouldn't call for a full-blown investigation. Someone died. A Monarch Cruises employee. And it was Jon's job to make sure it never happened again.

Lacey lifted her foot out of the navy pump, then twisted her weary ankle in circles. The massive front counter hid her toes from the customers as she stretched them. In many ways, the MS *Buckingham* was a giant, floating hotel. And tonight, she was on desk duty. It wouldn't have been half as bad if she hadn't just spent the afternoon rehashing the past with Jon.

"Thanks again for filling in, Lacey," her coworker Malaya said for the second time that evening. "Something's going around the ship, and Francine spent half the morning puking her guts out."

Lacey made a face. "Don't worry about it. It's hard enough to stand for ten hours a day without adding a fever on top of that. You two must have feet of steel."

"But still, you're losing time off by helping me. I promise I won't forget it."

"How about you do a load of laundry for me this weekend, and we'll call it even?" Lacey checked a card and typed a new spa request into the computer.

Malaya didn't answer.

"Deal?" Lacey looked up.

"There he is." Malaya's hands fluttered to her hair and smoothed the sides.

Lacey pointed her attention to the computer screen. She didn't have to ask who Malaya meant. The arrival of the gorgeous new cruise director had caused a stir akin to what a celebrity would among the female staff. New shades of lipstick and padded bras abounded. It seemed the MS *Buckingham* was hosting its own personal beauty pageant.

"How are you, Malaya?" A familiar male voice approached.

Lacey ignored the cream-coated baritone and typed away on her keyboard.

"Hi, Jon," the woman simpered. "I'm wonderful."

"Glad to hear it."

Out of the corner of her eye, Lacey saw him place a hand on the counter.

"Can you do me a favor?" he said. "This envelope is addressed to the home office. Will you mail it, please?"

"Of course. It's no trouble. My pleasure. I'd be glad to do it. I'll take care of it right now."

Lacey refrained from rolling her eyes. Her fingers tapped the keys a little harder. How many different ways could Malaya say yes?

Jon patted the shiny wooden counter. "You're a lifesaver. Thanks."

Lacey's gaze rose when he walked away. What a relief. He hadn't even spoken to her. Although, she *was* standing two feet from his nose. Someone else might consider it rude. The man could've at least said "hello." She'd made a point of saying they were friends during their trip to Punta Verdad. Come to think of it, he hadn't spoken to her since they reboarded the ship. Was that any way to treat a friend?

Malaya's upper half flopped onto the desk, her face pressed against the wood, and her body shuddered with a sigh. She switched cheeks so she was pointed at Lacey. "He talked to me."

"Congratulations," Lacey muttered.

Perhaps Mr. King had finally gotten the hint and backed off. No more surprise lemonade deliveries. Her life would be a lot easier going forward.

"He flat-out ignored her." Emily paced in between the Shippers. Her feet reached the end of the bed, and she spun around. "Didn't even say 'hello.'"

"That's a bad sign." Althea stuck a straw in her mouth. "He's always been the eager one." She took another swig of her chocolate raspberry smoothie.

Daisy passed Althea a tissue when a splotch of ice cream dripped on her dress. "The male ego can only take a certain amount of rejection."

"I agree." Emily swerved around the bed and poked at a chart on the wall. "Ladies, we need to do damage control. It's time for plan B."

"Plan B?" Daisy recoiled. "But it's so . . . so . . ."

Gerry finished her thought. "Illegal."

Emily waved away their objections. "If they won't speak to each other, we throw the one trick at them they can't ignore."

"Which trick is that?" Althea dabbed at the stain.

"Proximity." Emily's eyes glinted. "After all, two's company. A ship full of people is a crowd. We isolate them somewhere nice and quiet and lock them in until they talk things out."

Gerry's lips twisted. "Talking things out in Cozumel made their relationship worse. What makes you so sure this plan will work? What if Lacey has a key to the door? What if an employee walks by as we lock them inside? What if one of them pulls out a cell phone and calls for help? Are you going to pick their pockets before you put them in there?"

"Don't be silly." Emily pointed at the large paper. "I've made an operation plan that includes every contingency. I chose the lost-and-found storage for a reason. Deck zero is the least populated place on the ship. The storage door is usually kept propped open because no one has a key to the room but the head steward, the maintenance man, and the members of the cleaning crew. We'll make sure to distract anyone who tries to go down that hallway so they can't hear any shouting."

"And the cell phones?" Gerry asked.

Emily let out a slow breath as if the question were a waste of time. "Lacey will most likely call someone close to her, right?"

"Right," the other three chimed.

"And who is Lacey's closest friend on board?"

"Her roommate," Daisy said.

"Exactly! We monitor Abigail O'Brien." Emily flipped her right hand. "And then we block her from helping them if she gets a call." She flipped her left hand.

"How do we do that?" Althea asked.

"By whatever means necessary." Emily studied her battle plan and smoothed a curling piece of tape back on the wall. "The plan is foolproof. They'll be locked in tighter than Alcatraz."

Gerry cringed. "Remind me never to get on your bad side."

CHAPTER 13

Lacey yanked a sweatshirt over her head and left her hair trapped under the collar. Her polka-dot-pajama-clad legs sprinted down the passageway. She pressed her cell to her ear.

"Why on earth are you in the lost-and-found storage?"

"To find something that's missing, dear." Emily's voice faded in and out like she wasn't talking directly into the phone. "But it's pitch-dark in here." A crash sounded. "Oooops. I hope that wasn't valuable."

Lacey kicked it up a notch. "Go out in the hall and wait for me. I'll be there soon."

She hurtled through the empty corridors. Most passengers were smart enough to be asleep by 3:00 a.m. But not Emily Windsor. That woman could cause trouble in a mausoleum. Lacey reached deck zero, where the crew stored any unclaimed items. She sped by utility spaces and workrooms. No sleeping cabins on this floor. Or people, for that matter. She saw the storage room, skidded to a stop outside the open door, and stuck her head in.

"Emily?"

No answer.

What if she was hurt? What if a heavy object had fallen on her? Lacey entered the unlit room and waited for her eyes to adjust. She barely made out the rows of shelves, stacked to the ceiling with indistinguishable items of all shapes and sizes. Her fingers skittered along the wall, but she couldn't find the switch. Lacey pulled up the flashlight app on her phone and shone it around.

Empty golf bag. Teddy bear. Piñata.

But not a sign of Emily.

Heavy footsteps sounded behind her. Lacey turned and spied a tall, familiar silhouette in the doorway. She aimed the light his direction. "Jon?"

"Lace?" He recoiled as the beam hit his retinas.

She pointed it away from his face. "What are you doing here?"

"Emily texted and said she was poking around in the dark. I came before she hurt herself. What about you?"

"Same." Lacey swung her arm, and the flashlight illuminated the semiorganized chaos. "I don't see her. She must have given up."

"That's a relief." Jon crossed the threshold. He wore sweatpants and a T-shirt with his favorite basketball team's logo. "I've heard about this place, but this is my first time visiting." He pointed at a pair of antlers on a top shelf. "Is that a mounted moose head?"

"Believe it or not, that isn't the weirdest thing in here." Lacey waved at a shelf. "I saw a—"

The hallway door banged shut. Darkness enveloped them, broken by the tiny circle of light from her phone.

"Hey!" Lacey rushed to grab the knob.

Locked.

She pounded on the door. "Hello? There are people in here." She rattled the knob again. "Help!"

Jon stepped behind her and hammered a fist above her head. "Hello? We're locked in."

Lacey tried to ignore the heat from the masculine body hovering a centimeter from her back. She inched forward and knocked louder. Between the two of them, they made enough noise to raise every sleeping passenger on the ship, but no one appeared. Lacey rapped until her knuckles ached.

She trained her phone on Jon. "You're strong. Can't you break it open?"

"That door is made of metal." He squinted against the light and pushed her hand down. "A fractured shoulder might hinder my work performance. Why don't you call somebody?"

"Right." Lacey laughed while she pulled up her favorites list. "I'm not thinking straight. I'll call my roommate. She can come let us out."

"Does she have a key?"

Lacey paused. "No. I'm not sure who does, but Abby can find out." She punched the name and drummed her finger against the side of the phone as it rang.

"Pick up," she muttered. "Pick up. Pick up. Pick— Abby? Can you come to the lost-and-found storage? We're locked in here. Hello, Abby?"

Jon moved around in the darkness while she talked. "Can you point your phone over here?"

Lacey switched her phone to speaker mode and shone the light on the wall. Jon located the switch and flicked it. Nothing happened. He tried again.

Down. Up. Down. Up.

Still nothing.

He flicked it one last time. "They must not have changed the bulbs in a while."

Lacey tapped the speaker off and held the phone to her ear.

"Abby, wake up!" She stomped her foot against the tile floor and spoke very slowly when her roommate answered. "Jon and I are locked in the lost and found. Find someone with a key and get us out . . . Of course we didn't do it on purpose. It was . . . we were . . . it's too complicated to explain. Please come get us."

Lacey ended the call and held the flashlight at eye level. "Abby's pretty useless after eleven o'clock. Even she admits it." She explored the contents of the room. "Maybe there's a spare key inside here for emergencies."

She traced the walls and racks with the beam from her light, but no key appeared. The scent of mildew and aging leather filled the room. Her throat tightened as the towering shelves of junk closed in on her. She grabbed a red-and-white-checkered tablecloth and waved it around.

"Who would bring this on a Caribbean cruise?"

Jon shrugged. "Someone who wanted to go on a picnic?"

How had she wound up locked in a glorified closet with Jonathan King? It was as if someone wanted to—

Her confusion at the unexpected imprisonment cleared as the puzzle pieces snapped together.

"Wait a minute. Why did Emily text you if she'd already called me?" Lacey pinched the bridge of her nose, and the air rattled in her throat as she exhaled.

"You mean they—" Jon laughed out loud and slapped his hand against the door. "I think I've watched this scene in one of those cheesy holiday movies my sister adores."

"Emily and her accomplices must've bought a ticket for the same movie." Lacey threw the tablecloth on a shelf and sank to one of the few empty spaces on the floor, right next to the entrance. "They. Will. Pay."

"Why do you always assume the Shippers are doing it on purpose?" Jon sat next to her in the darkened room, leaned his head back too hard, and banged it against the wall. "Ow!"

"Are you okay?" Lacey stirred beside him.

"Fine. I misjudged the distance."

Lacey half-heartedly thumped on the door once more. "Help! Anyone there?"

"Give it a rest, Lace. Who's going to be checking the lost and found at three in the morning?"

The light flickered and disappeared.

"What—" She checked her phone. "No. No. No!"

"What's wrong?"

"I'm out of battery." She hissed in a long, frustrated growl. "It was almost dead when I plugged it in to charge before going to bed. Let's use your phone."

Jon squirmed. "I didn't bring it."

"Why wouldn't you—"

"I was in a hurry."

They sat in silence, the forced intimacy of the darkened space pressing in on them. Their arms rested side by side against the wall. Lacey sensed his body moving with each breath. She shifted away and hunched her shoulders.

He cleared his throat. "If it really was the Shippers, they should've left us a few snacks. I'm starving."

"The world could be ending, and you'd still be searching for a taco truck."

He laughed. "The lady knows me too well. I'm so hungry I can smell those cherry tarts the chef was cooking earlier."

Lacey sniffed. "I don't smell anything."

"No. I'm sure I smell them." Jon's body leaned toward her.

"We're on the opposite side of the ship from the kitchen. There's no way."

He drew closer to her shadowed figure and inhaled. "It's coming from you. Did you smuggle some tarts without telling me?"

"Stop being stupid." She shoved him, but he came even closer. "Are you planning to frisk me for pastries?"

"I can smell them. You ate one without telling me, didn't you?"

"What are you— Oh." Lacey put a hand to her lips.

"Ready to admit it?"

"No. I just remembered." She rummaged in the front pocket of her sweatshirt, pulled something out, and waved it under his nose. "Is this what you're smelling?"

Jon grabbed her fingers. "I knew it." He tried to wrestle it from her, and she smacked him on the back of the head with her free hand.

"It's my lip gloss, you idiot." She popped the plastic cap off. "Cherry Surprise."

Jon plucked the tube from Lacey's fingers but didn't let go of her hand. He held the gloss under his nose. The sweet, fruity scent filled his nostrils. He looked at Lacey, or what he could distinguish. The crack of light under the doorway helped him make out her shape but not her expression.

He loosened his grip, and his thumb slid down to rest on her palm. Lacey jerked her hand away and smoothed her hair. She tugged at the strands trapped under the neckline of her sweatshirt.

"What's taking Abby so long?" she said.

He passed her lip gloss back. "I imagine she had to wake up whoever has the key."

The sliver of light between the door and the floor vanished. Lacey's faint outline disappeared, and total darkness engulfed them.

"W-what happened?" Her voice trembled.

She fidgeted beside him. Jon moved and bumped into a soft object at face level. The downy skin of her cheek grazed his as she turned. A puff of air told him they were pressed nose to nose. It was a miracle she didn't pull away.

He withdrew a centimeter. "Are you all right?"

"It's really dark in here," she whispered.

Her breath grazed his mouth. Jon closed his eyes, not that it mattered in the windowless room. He swallowed. The sweet cherry scent beckoned him.

Focus.

What if Emily wasn't behind this? What if the drug runners were onto his investigation and locked him in here on purpose? He had to stay alert and not get distracted by anything or anybody. That's what he kept telling himself even as he leaned forward. His lips found hers easily, as if the room were lit by a thousand candles. He'd dreamed of kissing Lacey again many times. But never in a crowded storage closet.

A full three seconds later, she eased away.

"Sorry." Her voice sounded unnaturally high. "It's hard to see anything in this cave."

He froze. That's how she was going to play it? An accidental collision. Her lips had moved against his for the briefest moment. He was sure of it.

"Forget it." Jon slid over and folded his arms in front of him. He flopped back, and his head hit the wall for the second time.

"Are you okay?" Lacey brushed his arm with hers.

He scooted to the left. "Fine and dandy, *friend*."

The scent of cherries hovered under his nose, and he scrubbed at his lips. When would he learn? Romantic progress with Lacey was like sailing through the Bermuda Triangle.

A person was capsized before he knew it.

CHAPTER 14

EMILY TWISTED THE FLUORESCENT GLASS bulb in her hand before tucking it into her purse. She checked her watch. "I hope they're making progress. Let's give it another twenty minutes. It takes time to settle things."

Daisy tsk-tsked. "Aren't you ashamed of lying to the poor girl?"

"How did I lie?" Emily raised one finger. "I told her I was looking for something in the lost and found. Which is true. I was looking for an excuse to get her and Jon together." She added another finger. "I told her it was dark. Also the truth."

"It's dark because you took the bulb and switched off the hallway light. Wasn't that a little harsh? It must be black as chicory coffee in there."

"They'll be fine." Emily peeked around the corner, but no one entered the shadowy hall on deck zero. "Lacey has her phone with her. That will help. All I know is there's nothing less romantic than fluorescent lighting." She lifted her walkie-talkie and pressed the call button. "Gerry, are you and Althea in position?"

The receiver crackled.

"Roger that. We followed Lacey's roommate to the steward's office. If she goes to the storage, we'll head her off."

"Maintain your post. We'll join you soon."

Emily and Daisy rode the elevator to the deck where the crew's cabins were located. The doors opened, and a commotion sounded to their right. Emily rushed out to find Althea moaning on the floor, with Gerry crouched beside her, cradling her head. Lacey's roommate, Abby O'Brien, stood next to them, her hands frozen on either side of her ears like she was being held up.

Emily knelt beside the pair. "What's wrong, Althea?"

"Oh . . . oh, my gallbladder." She pressed her fingers into her stomach. "Oh, it hurts so bad!"

Abby leaned over her. "Don't worry, Mrs. Jones. I'll go for help."

Althea grabbed her arm, her eyes rolling under her lids. "Don't leave me, baby," she gasped. "I . . . don't wanna . . . die . . . alone."

Daisy slipped a handkerchief from her purse and wiped at nonexistent tears. "Please don't leave her."

"Thank you, Daisy." Althea reached with trembling fingers. "I can always count on you in my hour of need."

Gerry shook her head behind Abby's back, and Emily clenched her lips. Althea was going for the Academy Award.

The tension of the death scene heightened as the woman's voice faded to a whisper. "Don't. Leave. Me."

"Oh no, Mrs. Jones." Abby's red cheeks almost matched her hair. She grasped Althea's hand. "I won't leave you."

"If only"—Althea coughed—"I could have found the love of my life before I kicked off."

"For the fourth time?" Gerry droned.

Althea glared at her before she squeezed her eyelids shut with a groan.

Abby cast a panicked glance at Emily and Daisy. "Can one of you get the doctor? I'll stay here with her."

Emily tapped her foot. It had been long enough. They shouldn't make Lacey too mad. Emily knew there'd be a reckoning when the pair escaped the closet.

"Althea, I doubt it's your gallbladder. It's probably the salmon you ate for dinner. You know fish doesn't agree with you."

Althea's eyes popped open. "You think so?" She sat up and held out a hand. "Help me, Gerry. I'll muster the strength to stand."

Gerry grabbed one elbow and Abby the other. Together, they hauled the patient to her feet. She dusted off her rear end and fixed her hair.

Emily motioned with both hands. "Come on, Althea. We'll take you to your cabin."

"I'm gonna get me a hug right quick." The tiny Abby disappeared as Althea's arms engulfed her. "Thanks for looking out for me, baby."

Daisy hovered behind them. "I apologize for the bother we caused, Abigail. Come and find me tomorrow, and I'll treat you to a cup of tea."

Althea let go and entered the waiting elevator. The other Shippers followed.

"Are you sure you're okay?" Abby stood outside the car, her brow puckered.

Emily pressed the button for their floor. "Right as rain. Go ahead and do what you need to do. Don't mind us."

The doors closed, and the Shippers let out a collective sigh of relief. Daisy and Althea started to giggle, and Gerry pulled her notebook from her pocket.

"Nice work, team," said Emily.

She hoped the frazzled Abby remembered to let Lacey and Jon out of the lost and found. A still small voice deep down in her soul warned her they'd gone too far, but she batted it away. When she was younger, Emily had almost made the mistake of living a life without love, and she refused to let Lacey choose that lonely path. All the plotting and prevarication would be worth it in the end, when Lacey and Jon realized they were meant for each other.

CHAPTER 15

LACEY RUBBED HER EYES AS the glare from the endless white walls stretched in front of her. After Abby had rescued them from the lost and found, sleep had been impossible. She lay awake until sunrise, then put in a good eight hours at the front desk. It was better than reimagining Jon's soft breath against her lips.

Again.

She plodded down the long corridor that spanned the length of the ship. Only accessible to staff, the plain-Jane hallway was dubbed Route 66 since it stayed busy twenty-four hours a day. Lacey took a right into the staff mess. The red vinyl booths, chrome tables and chairs, and checkered floor tiles resembled those of an old fifties diner. Her coworkers' conversations buzzed like bees in a hive. Faces turned her way as she grabbed a salad from the buffet and wound through the diners to an empty table in the corner. It appeared the scuttlebutt of last night's escapade had already made its way around.

She didn't blame Abby. Her roommate had woken the head steward, Mr. Gozar, to borrow the lost-and-found keys, and he'd wanted to know the reason they were required at three-thirty in the morning. A logical question. But even her roommate's short explanation was ample fodder for the rumor mill. Why did the keeper of the keys have to be the biggest gossip on the ship?

Lacey clunked her plate on the table and sat with her back to the room. The Argentinian housemaids congregated to her left, and their words tumbled over each other as the women talked in their native language. With three years of high school Spanish and four years' interacting with international coworkers on a cruise ship, Lacey understood most of it. Salacious suppositions about why she and Jon had been in a closet in the middle of the night. She leaned on one elbow and picked at her uninspiring but healthy lunch, poking the wilted lettuce with her fork.

"It is not good?" asked a deep voice with a thick, charming accent.

She looked up into the sparkling regard of Ricardo Montoya, the pastry chef on the MS *Buckingham*. His curly black hair spilled over his forehead, giving him a boyish, innocent quality. He sat down across from her with his food.

His hand motioned to the dish in front of her. "The salad is not good?"

Lacey shrugged a shoulder. "Not as good as your cherry tarts."

He beamed and sucked in a breath, his chest expanding. "I will save some for you."

Ricardo made the motion of the cross and said a silent prayer. When he finished, he cut into his ground sirloin, took a bite, and gagged. "The person who made your salad also made my steak."

She pushed her plate away. "Someone in the kitchen was having a bad day."

"It is an epidemic. The head chef bit on my head this morning."

Lacey tried not to chuckle at his unusual twist on the old cliché. "Why?"

"He told me to make three hundred extra cherry tarts for the captain's special reception. I did not hear him right and made a few too many."

"How many?" She lifted her water glass and took a drink.

"Three thousand."

Lacey choked and wiped the dribble from her chin. "Three . . . three *thousand*?"

Ricardo grimaced. "You are making the same face as Chef did when he found out. I spent hours making those tarts. He should recognize my hard work. But all he does is worry I wasted the ingredients. Too much flour! Too much sugar!"

"He has a point. Resources are limited. If a cruise ship runs out of food, the customers will mutiny."

"We will not run out." Ricardo sawed off another piece of over-cooked meat. "I am arranging for more to be delivered with the fresh produce when we dock in Puerto Limón. It was supposed to be my afternoon off, but I will spend most of it coordinating with the pro-vision master about the new supplies." He shoved the steak in his mouth. "At least I will still have time for dinner. My good friend runs a restaurant there. He grills a red snapper with lemon and basil"—he kissed his fingertips—"so fresh, like it jumped out of the ocean onto the plate."

Lacey laughed. "Sounds delicious."

"Come with me. I can pick you up after I supervise the delivery, and we will eat together." His warm perusal of her promised more than friendship if she was interested. "It will be my treat."

Lacey hesitated. She enjoyed Ricardo's company but wasn't sure a date was a good idea. The housemaids stirred beside her, and their volume rose. Faces pointed in the same direction—at the tantalizing cruise director who'd walked in the room. Jon's gaze found her, along with just about everyone else's. The employees scrutinized them both with whispers and smirks.

Lacey looked away. She hated being the center of a cheap scandal. None of it was true. Jon was her friend. Period.

"Lacey?"

Ricardo's voice broke into her musings.

"Yes?"

"Tomorrow? The snapper?"

She made a split-second decision. "I'd love to eat dinner with you."

Ricardo smiled so big his upper lip disappeared. He dropped his silverware and grabbed the edge of the table. "What are your favorite flowers? I will bring them for you."

"You don't have to do that."

"It is my pleasure."

Lacey had received so few bouquets in her life, she had to think a moment. "How about something unique and colorful?"

Ricardo winked. *"Claro."* He took Lacey by the hand and stroked her fingers.

She fought the urge to see if Jon noticed. Her attention stayed fixed on Ricardo.

"I will be counting the hours," he said.

"Me too." She was a very punctual person.

Ricardo released her hand, held his drink for a toast, and tilted it her way. "Until tomorrow night?"

She clinked her glass against his. "Tomorrow night."

"Mind if I join you?"

Lacey's nerves jumped at the new voice. Her water sploshed onto the table as Jon towered over them with his tray. She wiped the renegade drops and kept her head down. "What?"

"Is this seat occupied?" He motioned to the empty chair beside her.

"Please, sit." Ricardo scooted his things to make more room at the table.

Lacey stayed where she was and said nothing.

Whoever he is, he's friendly.

Jon vaguely recalled the man's face from studying the employee profiles. He placed his lunch on the spot the stranger made for him and sat, his eyes automatically swerving to Lacey. No one would guess she had done a brief stint locked in a dingy storage space. Her hair glowed like a ray of golden sunshine in the industrial-lit cafeteria. She avoided his eyes, which wasn't surprising. They'd left on an awkward note when Abby liberated them from their unconventional prison. But the touch of her lips still lingered on his own, making him reckless. Why not risk rejection one more time?

He held out his hand to the other man. "I don't believe we've met. Jonathan King."

"Yes, the new cruise director. Mucho gusto." He shook his hand. "I am Ricardo Montoya, pastry chef."

Jon picked up his fork and pointed the blunt end at him. "Are you the one who makes those seven-layer chocolate cakes?" He nodded at Lacey. "I bet you love those."

She fished a piece of lettuce with brown edges from her salad and didn't answer.

Ricardo raised his chin. "Guilty. I add a touch of chili powder as my mama used to do."

"Your mother was a wise woman. I must've gained five pounds on this ship." Jon tasted his food and winced. "But not from this. Monarch should feed its staff better."

"I agree. Maybe you should tell them."

"Maybe I will." He grinned and turned to the silent Lacey. "I was looking for you. Have you confronted Emily yet?"

Her head jerked. She cut her gaze to the pastry chef and back to Jon before she answered. "I haven't discussed that particular matter with her. It's an uncommon situation."

"That's one way of putting it. It's not exactly normal to lock—"

Lacey smacked the table. "Trust me. She and I will have a heart-to-heart soon."

"Don't be too hard on her." Jon reached over and touched her hand. She withdrew it and glanced at Ricardo again.

Jon tamped down the same old sense of rejection. He wished Lacey would have a heart-to-heart with more than just Emily. When would it be his turn? If she'd only be honest with him and reveal the real reason she left all those years ago. Had God brought them back together for reconciliation or closure? Neither was happening.

He took a drink of his water and dived in again. "Have you got any time off in Puerto Limón? I thought we might have dinner."

"You are a few minutes too late, Jonathan." Ricardo waved a finger at him with a good-natured smile. "I already claimed this beautiful woman for tomorrow evening."

Jon's eyes shifted between the two, and he resisted the impulse to break that waving finger. "My mistake."

Lacey stabbed her fork in her salad and left it there. "Would it kill them to serve us fresh food?" She pushed her chair back and stood with her tray. "I can't eat this. If you gentlemen will excuse me, I should go check my mail."

Jon watched her beat a hasty retreat from the dining room. The other diners clocked his reaction. He focused on his plate, took a bite from his meal, and chewed.

This was no time to be drawing attention to himself. The investigation required discretion. And it's not like his clumsy romantic overtures made the gamble worth it. Every time he chucked his metaphorical pride out the window, it landed with a thud. Why did he keep expecting Lacey to catch it?

She'd friend-zoned him. Rejected his kiss. And made a date with another man.

It took his hard head a while to get the message, but he finally admitted the truth. The answer was no. He had to move on.

I might need a little help, God. But I can do it. Right?

CHAPTER 16

LACEY STEPPED ONTO THE LIDO deck with a small pile of mail. The first thing to catch her eye was a bubble mailer with a new shirt she'd ordered online. A flyer from her alumni association came next, probably asking for money. At the bottom of the stack was a pink envelope. She studied the return address.

Home.

Lacey slipped a finger under the flap, tore the envelope open, and withdrew a birthday card with a teddy bear on it. Only one person would send her such a childish thing. She opened it and read.

> *Dear Lacey-bell,*
> *No matter how big you get, you'll always be my little*
> *girl. Happy birthday. I hope it's full of many surprises.*
> *Love,*
> *Dad*

A bitter lump rose in her throat. It tasted all too familiar. She'd experienced it countless times throughout her life, whenever her father consistently proved how little he knew her. She hated being called Lacey-bell. She hated pink. And most of all, she hated surprises. Thanks to her dad's impulsive, immature decisions, she'd experienced way too many of them.

Routine, stability, safety. Those were the things that gave her comfort.

The floodgates threatened to crumble. She drew in a deep breath and wiped the moisture from her lashes. That's when she saw them. Five feet away, Gerry and Emily stretched out on deck chairs overlooking the ocean. Lacey walked to a nearby trash can, pitched everything but the new shirt in, and advanced toward the women.

Emily spotted her and hopped up. She darted between the chairs and scuttled in the opposite direction. Gerry sat with a novel in one hand and a red pen in the other, so she didn't see Lacey's approach.

Lacey stopped in front of the chair and crossed her arms as Emily disappeared through the double glass doors in the distance. "Your fearless leader is avoiding me." She stared down her nose at the remaining older woman.

Gerry's shoulders jumped, but her voice remained calm. "Wouldn't you run, if it were you?"

"So you admit it?" Lacey crowded closer. "You admit it was a setup."

"I admit nothing." Gerry raised her slender chin and turned a page.

"Whose idea was it to lock us in the closet?"

"Someone locked you in a closet?" A guileless expression shone through her reading glasses. "You poor thing."

Lacey eyed her, but Gerry's attention reverted to her book. The CIA could use a tough cookie like her for covert ops. An undeniable fondness surged for the quirky ladies.

She leaned over and saw red markings on the pages. "Are you highlighting the steamy parts?"

"I'm editing." Gerry clicked the top of her ballpoint pen and tossed the book in the bag at her side. "Four misspellings. What kind of proofreaders are they hiring?"

"Do you do this for fun?" Lacey sank onto the chair beside her and reclined. "Or do you actually send your edits to the company?"

"I send them. When they reprint it, they can fix the mistakes. Making me a laughingstock to all my former coworkers. What kind of librarian can't utilize proper spelling in her own book?"

"Wait." Lacey sat straight. "Her own book?" She reached into the bag, grabbed the novel, and checked the author's name. "This says it was written by Dina La Rue."

"Otherwise known as Geraldine Paroo."

Lacey flipped to the back cover and saw quotes from reviewers praising the story. "Is this your first one?"

"Sixth."

"What? Were the others published?"

"Yep. Last three hit the New York Times Best Sellers list."

"Wow." Lacey returned the novel to her. "All this time, I thought you were working on the same book."

Gerry laughed as she stuffed it in the bag. "Everyone does. Althea teases me daily about my unfinished masterpiece."

"Why write under a pen name? If I published a book, I'd brag to anyone who'd listen."

"That's a little complicated." Gerry squirmed on her lounge chair and pulled off her spectacles. "Can you guess what the first advice they give in writing class is?"

Lacey shook her head.

"Write what you know." Gerry blew her lips out with a noisy puff of air. "How can I explain to my readers that their favorite romance author is a dried-up old spinster who's never been in love and only ever kissed a man once?"

The mere mention of a kiss transported Lacey to the dark storage room. Her pulse quickened as her body relived the touch of Jon's gentle lips on her own. She'd wanted to stay there forever, but that nagging voice in the back of her mind had whispered the same word over and over.

Run.

Lacey inhaled and forced her mind back to the conversation. "One time? How was it?"

"I have no idea." Gerry snorted. "I squeezed the juice out of that kiss for five novels until there was nothing left. No flavor. No pulp. Just a crumpled rind of a memory." She pounded a fist against the arm of her deck chair. "What else can you do when that's the sole experience you have? It's a mercy I don't write the books with the racy covers. I'd be stumped." She chuckled. "I could always ask Althea."

Lacey laughed with her, but Gerry's smile faded away as she raised her face to the clouds stretching overhead and sighed.

"Don't be like me, Lacey. Make more memories."

Lacey was supposed to be mad at the Shippers, but the plaintive note in Gerry's voice tugged at her heartstrings. "Hey." She swung her legs between the two chairs and grasped the woman's arm. "You've still got plenty of time to make some of your own."

"I suppose so." Gerry continued to stare at the afternoon sky. "But it's not as much fun making memories alone."

"You're not alone. You have your friends."

"That's true."

"And me."

"Do I?" Gerry glanced her way. "Thank you, Lacey. Friends make the loneliness bearable."

"If you're lonely"—Lacey nudged her—"I recall a certain redheaded magician who'd be happy to help."

"Oh . . . button it." Gerry clicked her pen and yanked another book from her bag.

Lacey considered the romance novelist in front of her who'd admitted she knew nothing about real love, and the unwelcome thought occurred that she was looking at her future. If she continued on her current trajectory, she'd end up independent but alone. Would answering to no one but herself be too high a price to pay? There'd never be anyone to share the good moments or the bad.

Could Gerry be right? Was it time to throw caution away and make new memories?

CHAPTER 17

TWO CHILDREN COVERED IN STREAKY sunblock squealed at the splash pad while their mother worked on her tan and scrolled through her phone. Jon passed rows and rows of empty deck chairs as he tracked down the hired detective who was, once again, missing. The ship was easier to maneuver with most of the passengers enjoying the tropical pleasures of Puerto Limón. He spotted Collins wandering near a bevy of bikini-clad coeds playing volleyball. The investigator had traded his messy Hawaiian shirt for a tank top molded so tight it revealed the man's outie belly button.

Jon caught his attention and waved him over to a pair of adjustable recliners. "You said you were going to follow those kitchen workers if they got off the boat. Did you get their names?"

"Not necessary." Collins stretched out on the chaise and propped up his feet, his customary wad of gum missing. "It was a dead end."

"How so? What made you cross them off the—"

"They were talking about salads. You were right."

"Excuse me, Jon." One of the college girls bounced beside them. "Our team is desperate for another member. Do you happen to play volleyball?"

"Not today I don't." Jon pointed at a trio of guys in the hot tub with their tongues practically hanging out. "But I bet one of those gentlemen will be happy to accommodate you."

She peered their direction, gave an unenthusiastic grunt, and left. Collins's elbow jabbed him in the lower leg.

The detective waggled his eyebrows. "Must be nice having every beautiful girl on the boat calling your name. Wish I'd become a cruise director instead of an agent."

Jon pushed away the horrific mental image of Collins in thigh-high white shorts. Every past and current cruise passenger should count their blessings the man had chosen the FBI and their suits. Though Jon shuddered to think what damage the lackluster detective might have done to the bureau.

He straddled the chair across from Collins. "I asked the main office to cross-reference our passenger list with everyone who's sailed on a Monarch ship this year. If we find a person with multiple trips in a short period of time, they might be a likely suspect."

"When do you expect the results?"

"Today, I hope. Tomorrow at the latest. The computer can generate the names quickly, but I asked a friend at corporate to organize them in specific groups. It depends on how long it takes him."

"What kind of groups?"

"Various factors. Age. If they're traveling with children. Do they have a criminal history? We'll focus on the most logical suspects first and then work our way through the list. In the meantime, we monitor everybody as best we can."

Collins made no effort to move. The so-called professional appeared to be more concerned with his tan than catching the criminals.

Jon ground his teeth. "Why don't you station yourself by the gangplank and keep an eye on people returning to the boat? Take note of anyone with a suspicious amount of luggage or shopping bags."

"Couldn't hurt." Collins checked his watch and stood. "But first, I'm gonna hit the head. Who knows when I'll get a chance if I start tailing someone."

The detective took the long way to the restroom—which included a complete circle around the volleyball bunnies. Jon rubbed his left temple. No time for a headache. He needed to make a circuit of the downtown shops. If any passengers were involved in the smuggling, they wouldn't travel far to make a pickup. But once Jon returned, he'd make an urgent call to corporate. When the MS *Buckingham* pulled into home port, he wanted a replacement for Collins. Fast.

"I wish I were you." Abby's upper half hung over the top bunk as Lacey prepared for her night out with Ricardo. "I haven't been on a date since I can't remember when."

"Why not?" Lacey buckled a pair of strappy stilettos on her feet. "I bet plenty of guys would jump at the chance."

"Who has the energy for romance after taking care of a hundred kids all day?" Abby flopped on her mattress and moaned. "Why did I think being a childcare worker on a cruise ship was a great way to use my teaching degree?"

"Why did you?" Lacey applied one more spritz of hair spray to the silky French twist at the back of her head.

"I planned to spend my free time dating handsome crew members, like you're doing." Abby thumped her alarm clock with a forefinger and yelped. "Oops! I was supposed to be at a water balloon fight five minutes ago." She scrambled down the ladder and raced to the door. "Have enough fun for both of us."

Lacey blew a kiss at her exiting roomie and spun in front of the mirror. Her cranberry vintage-style pantsuit skimmed her curves in all the right places. It reminded her of a costume from an old black-and-white movie. She felt glamorous and mysterious, so unlike her normal, starchy self.

Lacey reached for her lip gloss but paused. She stared at the Cherry Surprise and then her reflection. A soft pink tinge infused her cheeks. She placed the tube in her bag and pulled out a vibrant red lipstick instead. It'd been two and a half years since her last date. Two years and seven months, to be exact. Might as well make the most of it.

She finished primping and checked the clock on her dresser. Time to go. Lacey hurried to their meeting spot as fast as her high heels allowed. The gangplank was empty as most of the passengers had disembarked hours earlier. She walked down the metal ramp, leaning forward on her toes to keep her stilettos from catching in the grated floor. Ricardo stood on the pier, hiding something behind him. He wore white slacks and a black silk shirt. His thick curly hair gleamed in the sunlight. The perfect picture of an exotic Latin suitor.

Lacey tottered as she hit the pavement. "Sorry I'm late."

"It was worth the wait." Ricardo scoped her out from head to heels. He presented a bouquet from behind his back with a flourish.

Lacey's smile faltered at the dozen white roses. Not exactly unique. Or colorful. But what kind of wretch was she to be disappointed? Most women would faint dead away over the beautiful flowers.

"Thank you very much." She took them and held the roses in front of her bridal-style. Was there a less conspicuous way to carry them? Lacey tried laying them in the crook of her arm. More awkward.

"I'll go put them in my cabin."

"No, no. I made reservations. We should leave." Ricardo placed a hand at her waist and urged her down the pier. "You will love this restaurant. The owner is a friend of mine."

Lacey wobbled like a baby deer taking its first steps as she tried to keep up in her sky-high stilettos. Ricardo held out his arm, and she grabbed the offered lifeline. New memories were waiting to be made.

Four pairs of eyes pointed at the departing couple. The Shippers lined the deck railing, watching the date unfold. Emily observed each interaction with her binoculars, and Gerry took notes in the binder. When the couple was out of sight, the women turned and sat at a shaded table.

"I didn't see that coming," said Althea. She dug around in her fanny pack and unwrapped a *tortue*. Her granddaughter bought the special candies in the French Quarter and mailed them to her at regular intervals. Althea bit into the creamy mix of chocolate, caramel, and pecans and talked around the gooey mess. "We should've stuck with Ricardo in the first place. It's obvious Lacey prefers him."

"Do we change our target again?" Daisy asked.

"Perhaps." Emily drummed her fingers against the tabletop, running the options in her mind. "Gerry, read me the information we gathered on Ricardo."

Gerry flipped through the binder and scanned the page. "Ricardo Montoya. Twenty-six years old. Born in Juárez, Mexico. Youngest in the family, with four older sisters. Graduated culinary school three years ago and—"

"Please stop," Emily moaned. "Dry and boring, like his relationship with Lacey would be. No sparks. We vetted Ricardo before Jon came. He seemed a good choice at the time, but now . . ." Her fingers restarted their beat. "Something feels off. We should follow them. They were on foot. If we grab a bicycle taxi, we can catch up."

"Why don't we take the path of least resistance?" Daisy asked. "Lacey likes Ricardo. Ricardo likes Lacey. Easy."

Emily slammed her fist, and the glass tabletop rattled. "Easy isn't always better. Can't you see that?"

Silence.

Gerry and Althea averted their gazes.

Daisy blinked twice. She placed her oversize sunglasses on her trim nose and rose from the table. "I'm a bit tired. Perhaps I'll lie down for a spell."

She glided away, and tension took her place. The distant noise of children playing in the pool accentuated the awkwardness. Emily brushed at a loose thread on her shirt.

Althea crossed her arms in front of her generous bosom. "You're going to apologize for that, right?"

Emily deflated. "I'm sorry. This case has got me all twisted. I'll be sure to make it right with Daisy." She leaned back and glared at the bright Mexican sky. "Lord, why won't Lacey cooperate? Did you have to put so much stubborn in that girl?"

"Takes one to know one," said Gerry.

Emily cut her eyes over, but her friend's face hid behind the usual romance novel. No use denying the statement. Once she accepted a mission, it was full speed ahead. Emily prided herself on her stick-to-itiveness. But her impatience was another story, a chronic flaw that caused her to hurt the people she loved.

The chair legs scraped against the deck floor as she stood. "At least one of you stay here and report when Lacey returns. If you get tired, call me, and I'll relieve you. I need to find Daisy."

Althea grabbed her hand and gave it a squeeze. "Try the art gallery. She wanders around there when she's upset."

Emily left them on guard duty. She wanted to race down the gangplank and keep tabs on Lacey. But friendship was more important than matchmaking. Time to do something she had plenty of practice at—apologizing.

CHAPTER 18

LACEY AVERAGED A COMPLIMENT A minute from her date during dinner. He declared her hair shone in the candlelight. The color of her outfit made her skin glow. Every man in the room wished she were at his table. One thing was certain, Ricardo knew how to treat a lady.

Saturated with praise, Lacey floated out of the restaurant. Almost. Her screaming toes kept intruding on the fantasy.

She tried not to hobble as she walked, her purse and flower bouquet clutched in her arms. Her attentive date pointed out local landmarks and made her laugh with funny stories of his restaurant-owner friend and himself. They wandered through the city streets without a set destination. Exuberant mariachi music floated out of a café, and locals and tourists bustled around in a talkative, noisy herd. The sweet smell of fresh-cooked churros wafted from a vendor's cart.

Lacey pointed at the sugar-coated sticks. "How about I buy us dessert?"

"I would lo—" Ricardo froze when he saw the time on a large neon clock in a store window. "Is it eight?"

"Yes, I think so."

Ricardo smacked his forehead. "This is when I am supposed to be in the kitchen. We must go."

He grabbed her wrist and towed her down the sidewalk. They stopped at a four-way intersection, but all the taxis were taken. The traffic light shone red. No cars crossed in front of them.

Ricardo muttered in Spanish and tapped his phone against his leg. He looked from right to left and thrust a finger at the other side of the road. "Go now." He jetted into the street without waiting for a response.

Lacey hurried to follow. She tripped off the curb, and her right heel caught in the wide hem of her pantsuit. Her arms flailed as her body propelled forward. Her left knee hit the hard pavement, followed by her hand. The roses scattered on the asphalt. Her skinny purse flung open, and the contents spilled across the street. A tube of lipstick rolled past her nose.

Ricardo raced to her. "Are you hurt? *Pobrecita.*"

He reached down, and Lacey scrambled to retrieve her things, ignoring the throb in her left knee. The humiliation hurt worse. She didn't dare make eye contact with the drivers waiting at the stoplight, sure they were laughing at the spectacle.

"I'm fine." She shoved the items in her purse and staggered to her feet.

It wasn't really a lie. She *was* fine, compared with starving people in impoverished countries. Tripping in her high heels on the way to a luxury cruise ship was a first world problem.

Ricardo took her by the elbow. "Let me help you. These terrible streets. Why don't they time their traffic lights better?"

He helped her onto the sidewalk. Lacey dared a quick glance at the cars and met a familiar pair of eyes as she scanned the road. Jon stood on the opposite corner, a blank expression on his face.

"Of course," Lacey murmured.

"What did you say?" Ricardo asked.

"Nothing. Let's get back to the ship."

The two ran through the crowded streets and along the lengthy pier. Lacey's knee throbbed, but she kept pace with Ricardo. They reached the entrance to the ship as a large group of passengers was making their way aboard.

"Can I leave you here?" Her date bounced on his toes as he tipped his head at the boat. "Chef hates it when I'm late."

"Go. I'll be fine."

Her knee called her a liar, but Ricardo bought it. He bolted up the gangplank, pushing past the people in his way. Lacey's shoulders sagged, and she grabbed hold of the railing as she hauled her way on board. Her feet hobbled, the tiny heels sticking in the grated metal floor. She bent and yanked the torturous stilettos off. Her pants legs dragged along the incline. Once inside the ship, she limped her way to the nearest sitting area, tossed the shoes to the floor, and sank on a velvet-cushioned bench with a whimper. She surveyed the hallway to be sure no one was around and pulled her pants leg to her knee. An angry red patch with jagged gashes stared back at her.

"At least it's not bleeding." She poked the scrape and winced.

"Bleeding?" Jon appeared out of nowhere and knelt. "Let me see."

"No, no." Lacey lifted off the cushion and waved both hands like a pair of frenetic windshield wipers. "I'm fine."

"Your knee disagrees with you." Jon gently pushed her onto the bench and squinted as he grabbed one of her waving hands. "Your palm disagrees too." He examined the skin and pointed to the deep welts left by the unforgiving road. "Is this your definition of *fine*?"

"It's no big deal." Lacey averted her eyes.

Jon hovered in front of her, but she studied the golden carpet. He dropped her hand, rose to his feet, and left without another word.

Lacey watched him disappear around the corner. "That's it?" She pulled her drooping pants leg back up to inspect her wound. "It's not like I'm dying or anything, but you could at least say 'goodbye.'"

She searched in her purse for something to dab at the scrape but didn't find so much as a tissue in the tiny clutch. Lacey jumped as a white plastic box dropped on the bench beside her.

Jon bent to open the first aid kit and pulled out several items. Cotton balls, disinfectant, and bandages formed a sterilized pile. "Let's start with the hand." He knelt once again.

"It's fine. You don't have to—"

He ignored her as he tore open an antiseptic wipe, grabbed her palm, and dabbed it with the wet cloth.

Lacey stared at his glossy brown hair as he worked.

He tugged the pants leg a little farther past her knee and scrutinized the ugly spot, which was already developing a purplish tinge around the vivid red center.

"This might sting." He took a small brown bottle of hydrogen peroxide from the bench and covered a cotton ball with the pungent mixture.

Lacey sucked air through her teeth as the medicine hit her skin and burned the open wound. The liquid bubbled into a tiny white foam over the cut. Jon rested his free hand on the side of her calf, leaned forward, and blew softly. His breath hit the fiery patch and cooled the tingling sensation.

Too bad it couldn't cool the full-blown blaze his lean fingers on her leg caused. It was like someone poured cooking oil on a gas range. The flames leaped up and threatened to toast her insides.

"I . . . I think it's okay now." She brushed his hand away and stood. Her trouser slid to her ankle, covering the still-stinging wound on her knee.

Jon rose from his kneeling position, his trademark smile missing. "You're sure?"

"Mm-hmm. Thanks to your quick attention. I didn't know you had medical training." She tried to joke away the awkwardness hanging between them.

"Vacations with my nieces." He concentrated on packing the supplies in the first aid kit. "There's always plenty of skinned knees when those three get together."

"Three? I thought you had two nieces."

"My sister added another one since the last time we worked the same ship." He turned to her with the kit at his side.

The awkward silence returned while they stared at each other.

"I forgot things change," Lacey said.

"Some things." He tilted his head and eyed her French twist. "You never wear your hair down anymore."

Jon took a step closer until he was standing near enough she had to raise her chin, and he ran a finger across the silky roll. The gesture set her inner radar on high alert.

Warning! Warning!

If she wanted to keep him at a distance both physically and emotionally, she needed to move. That's what her head told her. But her body wasn't cooperating. She'd swear she was leaning forward.

She swayed, tilted back, and cleared her throat. "Thanks for your help."

Jon held something up to her face, and she looked cross-eyed at the bandage in front of her nose.

"Put this on your knee when you get to your room."

She took it, and he moved away.

"Thanks again," Lacey said.

"No problem. See you at early-morning staff meeting." He walked away, unaware of the fire he'd stoked inside of her, and Lacey raised a fist at his back.

Why couldn't sweet, gorgeous, ex-almost-boyfriends keep their bandages to themselves?

CHAPTER 19

A SLIVER OF SIDEWAYS MOON smiled at Jon like it was mocking him. He stood on an outside deck and watched the parade of weary passengers trudging to the MS *Buckingham*. The once-bustling shops along the pier stood in eerie silence, deserted by the tourists. There could have been tumbleweeds blowing across the sidewalk.

A man in hot pink shorts approached. He threw his arm around the woman with him. "I feel like I'm in the last half of a marathon."

"When did you ever run a marathon?" She placed her palm on his back and propelled him up the slanted gangplank.

A mother with a crying child at her side and a sleeping toddler in her arms followed. "I gotta regroup myself here." She shifted her baby onto one hip and held the collar of the weeper. "What a day, what a day."

Jon observed the vacation drama unfolding before him with fondness. This was cruising. Not the handful of criminals trying to make a fast buck. The treasured memories these people made on a brief voyage would long outlive their aching feet.

His call with corporate hadn't produced the results he wanted. The general manager insisted Collins might seem a little dense but had cracked numerous high-profile drug cases. For the life of him, Jon couldn't understand how. He whispered a prayer in his mind.

Lord, I feel like I'm rowing against the current. Please don't let these criminals ruin a good thing.

A picture of Lacey shuffling behind Ricardo flashed through his brain. His fist clenched, and he banged it against the metal bar in a slow, deliberate rhythm.

"Pardon me."

Someone tapped him from behind. Jon pasted on his cruise-director smile and turned to a young couple in matching heart-covered T-shirts. Honeymooners. It didn't require coordinated outfits to identify them. Their goofy grins said it all.

The husband's arm wrapped around his new wife's waist. "Is there any way we can take a picture in the very front of the boat? You know. The movie pose." He stretched his arms out like a pair of wings and warbled a line from the film's famous soundtrack. His bride cooed her approval.

"I know where you mean." Jon nodded. "That part of the ship contains the helipad and is only open at certain times, but there are special photo ops every day at eleven o'clock. You can sign up at the front desk."

They thanked him and canoodled away, wrapped against each other too tightly for it to be called walking. Jon dropped his professional demeanor. Once he'd imagined that would be Lacey and him. A long time ago.

"Aren't they precious?"

Jon jerked to the side. A decidedly unmanly yelp escaped his lips. Emily Windsor stood at his elbow. She wore a floral-print windbreaker over her T-shirt and jeans.

"Emily"—he clutched at his chest—"how can you move without making a single noise? Have you got any ninjas in your family tree?"

She cocked her head with a chuckle. "My late husband was fun to scare. He always gave such huge reactions. I perfected my talent for sneaking up on him."

"What a cruel woman."

Emily's grin faded, and she stepped back. "Not really. I may be pushy, but it's because I care."

He reached out to her. "It was a joke. A bad one, obviously. You're a lovable sweetheart."

She stuck her hands in the pockets of her windbreaker and faced the dock. "I admit I'm surprised to hear you say that—after our extended lighthouse excursion and . . . other activities. Aren't you a little put out with me?"

Jon turned the same direction. "I heard some hard truths, which weren't fun to listen to, at the lighthouse. And your closet scheme didn't do Lacey and me any good." He held up his hands when she looked like she'd argue. "You haven't admitted you're behind the lost-and-found thing yet. But *if* you were, I don't think it produced the result any of us wanted. She's dating Ricardo." Jon ruffled the hair at the nape of his neck. "But I'm actually grateful to you. Lacey and I hashed out our differences. Now we can both move on."

Emily slumped. "My husband scolded me for what he called my 'confounded meddling.' Said it did more harm than good. He must've been right."

"What did you say his name was?"

"Bill." Emily's voice dipped. She lowered her gaze and coughed. "I'm afraid he's partially to blame for my meddling. He complained, but he was quite the enabler—always did anything and everything I asked, no matter how far-fetched. He was my perfect partner in crime." She laughed. "I could tell you stories."

"I hope you'll share them sometime." Jon noted her downturned lips. "You must miss him."

"Like I'm walking around with half of me gone." She took her hands out of her pockets and slapped them on the railing twice. "But I've found a group of friends who are almost as good, if not nearly as handsome, as Bill. They keep me in plenty of trouble."

"Are you sure it isn't the other way around?" Jon bumped her shoulder with his arm.

"You're calling me out." Emily bumped him back. "Since you realize what an old troublemaker I am, I'll speak what's on my mind. What are you going to do about Lacey and Ricardo?"

Jon clenched his molars. "Nothing. Lacey and I are just friends. She's free to date whomever she pleases."

"I've known that girl a while now. One thing I've noticed—she rarely does what she pleases. She's too busy taking care of other people, me included. Lacey needs someone who will take care of her for a change." Emily pulled on his sleeve until he looked her in the eye. "I believe that someone is you. If you agree with me, then you shouldn't accept her rejection. Do something about it."

"Like what?"

"Lord, help this boy." Emily closed her eyes. "He got all the looks and none of the smarts." She squinted at him. "You said you talk to God on a regular basis. Ask him for some wisdom. I can't come up with the answers for you. You probably know Lacey better than I do. What are her favorites? What drives her crazy? Put that hard-earned knowledge to good use."

Jon studied his hands as he rubbed them together. "And if she still says no?"

"Then you lose a little pride. Trust me on this one, dear. I regret the times I didn't do something more than the times I did. Don't let that be you."

"You're pretty good at pep talks. Are you going to charge me for this coaching session?"

Emily pinched his arm.

"Ow." He rubbed the tender spot and grimaced.

"Fewer jokes. More action. Got it?"

"Yes, ma'am," Jon automatically agreed to the order, but his spirit wasn't convinced. Lacey rebuffed every attempt he made to draw closer. Besides, his investigation left no time for romance. Better to focus on the job and save them both some pain.

CHAPTER 20

LACEY GRABBED HER DIRTY-CLOTHES basket and carried it next door. When you had an hour lunch break and no clean underwear, living by the laundry room came in handy. She placed the load on a long counter in the middle of the room, opened two of the washers, and threw the colors in one and the whites in the other at hyperspeed. After dumping the soap in and slamming the lids, she chose the quickest setting. Maybe she could get a meal before they finished.

"*Hermosa!*" Ricardo loped into the room, dragging an overflowing netted bag. "You are also doing laundry?"

"It's now or never. I have to be at the jazz concert in"—she checked her watch—"fifty-seven minutes."

Ricardo hauled his load onto the counter beside her basket. "It is so hard to make space for all the work." He drew a soiled apron from the bag. "Chef wants extra pastries for the evening buffet. I have no time." His mournful eyes turned to Lacey.

Water whooshed in the machine beside them. A click sounded as the lid locked in place.

"If you need to leave"—Lacey motioned to her own things—"I'll be here awhile. I can switch your wet laundry to the dryer."

"You would do that?" Ricardo clasped his hands. "You are an angel. I promise to make it up to you." He advanced, but she scooted to the side and sneaked her basket between them.

"Don't mention it."

Ricardo slid his laundry along the counter and pulled a bottle of detergent from under the pile. "Separate the lights from the darks and put one cup of this in with each load. You are the best." He leaned over her basket, kissed the air near her face, and rushed off.

"Wait, I didn't mean—"

He was gone.

"Right." Lacey stared at the bottle. "This is payback for dinner last night."

She tugged the bag in front of her but hesitated at the silk boxer shorts on top. She liked Ricardo, but they weren't *that* close. Lacey headed next door to her cabin. Perhaps she had a pair of cleaning gloves under the bathroom sink.

Jon checked the staff schedule on his computer and compared it with the roster on his desk. He scrolled through the names. There was one musician who was infamous among the crew for borrowing money. Never seemed to have enough. A ripe target for drug runners and worth inspection. The man was scheduled for an outdoor jazz combo performance in ten minutes. Jon noticed Lacey's name on the list. She was overseeing the setup for the mini concert.

He opened a desk drawer and eyed the tube of ointment inside. Was her knee still sore? It wouldn't hurt to check. He logged out of his computer and shoved the medicine into his pocket. After walking to the office door, Jon took hold of the handle and stopped. His index finger tapped against the knob.

What if she gave him that look again? That no-entry, go-away, roll-up-the-welcome-mat look. Was it worth trying to help? The door swung in before he decided. Jon stumbled and almost toppled onto Emily Windsor. He grabbed the doorjamb to prevent a collision.

She smiled at him, not the least bit startled. "Good afternoon, Jon."

"Hello, Emily." He righted himself. "To what do I owe the pleasure of your visit?"

"Could you spare a second?" She grasped the strap of her large black purse.

"For you?" He waved her in. "I can even spare two."

Emily entered the small office. Jon made sure she was comfortable on the chair facing his desk. He sat, folded his hands together, and rested his chin on his fingers.

Emily settled her pocketbook on her lap. "I wanted to show you my gift." She unzipped her purse, pulled out a small paper bag, and set it on his desk.

He picked it up and shook it. Something rattled inside. "What's this?"

"Dark chocolate–covered almonds."

"For me?"

"No." Emily swiped it from his hand. "For me. Lacey bought them." She swung the bag. "I locked the girl in a closet two days ago. She's still mad as fire at me but purchased these in Puerto Limón because they're rich in fiber and antioxidants. Lacey didn't even say anything when she gave them to me, just shoved them in my hand and stalked off."

"Why doesn't that surprise me?"

They grinned at each other, and Emily fussed with the collar of her shirt.

"I have a little . . . arrhythmia, now and then. Lacey's always giving me heart-healthy foods."

"Is it serious?" Jon reached across the desk, but she swatted him away.

"Nothing to worry about. The doctor told me to be careful with what I eat, and to exercise."

"And do you?"

She shrugged. "Getting around this floating metropolis keeps me active."

Jon dragged his keyboard in front of him and logged into the computer. "We offer a senior aerobics class twice a week. I'm going to sign you up."

"I hate aerobics, and that's not why I'm here." Emily shoved the chocolates in her purse and stood. "The reason I came was to bolster your get-up-and-go. Lacey may fret and fume at the first sign of commitment"—Emily bent her head and lowered her voice as if sharing a secret—"but she's soft mush underneath."

Jon smiled at the sweet face with the frizzy gray halo hovering over his. "Like someone else I know."

Emily placed a tiny hand on his cheek. "Don't lose heart." She straightened and ran her fingers through her flyaway curls. "I saw Lacey on the lido deck a few minutes ago. In case you were wondering."

"How kind of you to inform me." Jon rose from his seat. "I think I'll take a stroll that direction." He didn't mention his motive had nothing to do with romance. Better to let Emily believe her efforts weren't in vain.

She held up a finger. "One last thing. Don't mention our talk to Lacey. She wouldn't appreciate it."

Emily left without a goodbye, and Jon sank onto his desk chair. He reached into his pocket and pulled out the medicine. Twisting the tube in his fingers, he considered her advice. He should be concentrating on the investigation, not romance, and pursuing the beautiful but prickly hostess guaranteed more scrapes and dings on his already battered ego. But the little matchmaker was right about one thing.

Lacey was worth it.

CHAPTER 21

FOUR MINUTES UNTIL THE BAND arrived. Lacey checked the strategically placed tables to make sure no one swiped the chairs. The glossy wooden dance floor gleamed in the sunlight, waiting for the twinkle-toed tourists.

"Someone was asking for you." Abby sidled up with a mischievous expression.

Lacey's breath caught, and she searched the deck for that familiar pair of broad shoulders. Passengers milled around in various stages of undress, from shorts and T-shirts to string bikinis. But no handsome cruise directors.

"Here he comes," Abby singsonged and pointed.

Lacey looked to her right. Her breathing returned to normal. Ricardo bounced across the deck with a small paper box.

"Hermosa!" He slid to a stop and held out his gift with both hands. "We did not get the churros you wanted on our date. I baked these for you."

"That's so nice." Lacey took the box and peeked under the lid at the skinny, sugar-covered treats. Why did she feel more excited about the churros than Ricardo? "I hope you didn't use all the flour again."

Ricardo's smile wavered, then he laughed. "No. We have enough now."

A six-piece band tromped onto the small stage beside them and unpacked their instruments. Passengers wandered over and settled on chairs to enjoy the show. A not-so-shy couple dashed onto the dance floor in front of the musicians and launched into a rumba before the music even started. The piano player churned his arm like a windmill for the others to hurry. The guitarist plugged his instrument into the amp, and the band gave the dancers a lively beat to show off their moves to.

"It's crowded here." Abby grinned at Lacey like a kid with a secret candy stash. "Later, alligator."

Ricardo placed his palm at the small of Lacey's back and urged her past the crowd to stand at the railing. He balled two fists at chest height and wiggled his torso. "Would you care to dance?"

"Pass." Lacey shook her head.

Ricardo put a hand on either side of her and rested them on the deck rail. He leaned close enough to pierce her personal-space bubble. Lacey blinked and settled her gaze on the mouth that drew ever closer to hers.

"Your assistance with my laundry was so sweet." A smattering of black stubble covered his upper lip.

"I'm glad I could help you out." Lacey cleared her throat. "This one time."

He tilted his head to the right and moved in. Her fingers tightened on the churro box. Lacey jerked away. Ricardo's mouth grazed the side of her cheek as her eyes connected with a pair of dark ones on the balcony above. Jon stood overlooking the lido deck, near enough she saw the muscle jumping in his jaw. His easy smile was absent. Lacey stiffened. Ricardo bent to nuzzle her neck, and she squirmed from his arms.

"I don't . . . that is . . . there's somewhere I have to be." She tottered to the side in her haste to escape. "See you later."

Lacey took off toward the elevators without another word. Not that she was running from Ricardo—or Jon. She spared a quick glance, but he hadn't followed. An elevator was closing, and Lacey hurried to catch it. She pressed the call button, the doors parted again, and she stepped inside—right next to Emily Windsor. Lacey's first instinct was to run back out, but that would be cowardly. She stayed put, and the two faced the doors as they shut.

"Hello, Lacey."

She saw Emily's reflection in the shiny metal doors, watching her. "Hello."

"Isn't it a beautiful day?"

"Lovely." Lacey smoothed the front of her hostess jacket and tucked a stray hair in place.

The matchmaker's reflection contemplated every movement. "I heard you're dating Ricardo Montoya."

"Yes."

"Wasn't that a hasty decision?"

Lacey observed Reflection Emily. "Ms. Paroo told me I should make more memories."

Emily met her head-on. "There's a difference between memories and mistakes. Make sure you know which is which."

Lacey squared her shoulders. She had just opened her mouth to answer when the elevator paused. The doors slid open, and a group of teenagers walked between them. Emily and Lacey stared at each other through the group of kids silently texting on their phones. The teens got off at the next floor, leaving an awkward chasm between the two remaining riders.

Lacey stopped the door as it began to close. "We need to talk." She held it open and motioned for Emily to go first.

"I agree." Emily exited and led her to an outside deck along the side of the ship.

A breeze hit them as they walked through the double doors. The older woman moved to the railing and rested her arms on the top. Lacey started to speak, but Emily interrupted her.

"Save yourself the lecture, dear. I'm interfering in your life. You want me to butt out. Is that about the gist?"

Lacey's lips twitched. "I approve your choice of words."

"Message received." Emily tilted her head and let the wind whip her gray curls.

"It's supposed to turn chilly today." Lacey joined her at the railing. "Should I get you a blanket?"

"I'm wonderful. Enjoying the smell of the sea." Her eyelids drooped, and she inhaled.

Lacey recognized the look. She'd seen it on Emily's face many times when she'd stood at the rail. "You love it, don't you?"

"It reminds me of home. I grew up by the ocean."

"Do you miss your friends and family?"

"There's not much family left to speak of since my husband passed away. And I have plenty of friends right here." She leaned over and nudged her. "Present company included."

How could Lacey help but love this frustrating, adorable lady? Would it be unprofessional to wrap her arms around the frail woman beside her?

Emily smiled. "Besides, who'd help rescue lonely cases like yourself if I returned home?"

The hugging urge evaporated.

"You can stop helping." Lacey scooted to the right. "I'm dating Ricardo."

Emily's hands slid across the metal railing as she moved closer. "You may require more help than you realize."

"Ricardo is a great guy. He's sweet."

"Yes, he is."

"And attractive."

"Bottle his looks, and you'd make a fortune."

"And . . . and he cooks well."

"Especially his cherry tarts."

"He's"—Lacey searched for a new word—"sweet."

"So you said." Emily stared out at the ocean. "But I can't give him the unconditional Shipper stamp of approval. I admit we used to think Ricardo was a viable match, but now we've witnessed you with Jon . . ." She turned to Lacey and shook her head. "Ricardo isn't right for you. Jon is the one."

"The one?" Lacey scoffed. "Do you really believe there's only one somebody for each person in the world?"

"No." Emily smiled. "I believe there's only one somebody for *some* people in this world. And you're one of those people."

The words dropped into Lacey like a coin in a fountain. Plunk! They floated deep down until they rested on top of her soul.

But she'd be older than Emily before she'd admit how the romantic declaration affected her.

Lacey steeled herself against the sentiment. "What makes you think that?"

"Because I'm one of those people too." Emily's eyes wandered, looking into a distant past. "I dated a surplus of boys—first, in high school. Then college. The navy kept a fresh crop of fun-loving sailors floating through town. We went to parties and dances and movies. I was quite the belle of the ball."

"Why am I not surprised?" Lacey imagined a young, vivacious Emily holding court over a besotted group of admirers.

"Dressing up for a date gave me butterflies in my tummy, but the butterflies never reached my heart. Not until I met my husband. Bill walked into church one Sunday morning in his dress whites, cap in hand. I was sitting in the choir loft, so I had a good view. One glance, and that was it."

"Did he feel the same way?"

"He asked me to marry him two weeks later."

A jumble of emotions flitted across the older woman's face. Pride. Happiness. A tinge of sorrow. Nostalgia softened the lines around her mouth and hinted at the girl she used to be.

Lacey hoped her own life would boast such sweet memories one day.

But how can it if you never allow yourself to love? A voice whispered inside of her with a salient but disagreeable point. She tried to ignore it by focusing on Emily.

"How long before you said yes to your eager suitor?"

"A year."

"What?" Her eyebrows snapped together. "I thought you said he was the one."

"He was." Emily's gaze sharpened on Lacey. "I knew it, and he knew it. But the reality of marrying him scared me. Living in a navy town, I knew what it meant committing to life as a military wife—always shuffling around every few years, planting roots in a new place, then having them ripped up at the government's whim. I wanted stability and routine."

Stability.

Routine.

Two of Lacey's favorite words.

"What changed your mind?"

It wasn't a casual question. She truly wanted to know. *Needed* to know. How did a person develop the courage to trade the familiar for the uncertain?

"Bill got orders for a two-year stint in Japan and gave me an ultimatum. Either I went with him as his wife, or it was the end. Life without him sounded worse than any instability imaginable. So I put my faith in God and took the leap." Emily placed her hands together and mimed diving into the water.

Lacey envied the woman who'd already jumped into the scary ocean of love and lived to tell about it. "Did you sink or swim?"

"The Lord has a sense of humor. I grew to love our many adventures around the world. Bill and I saw places other people only read about in books. He was my somebody." Emily smacked the railing. "And Jon is yours. Running doesn't work, Lacey. You have to accept the truth."

"The truth?" Lacey wrapped her arms around herself. "The truth is, I don't want to entrust my life to somebody . . . anybody. I'd rather keep control, even if it means being alone."

"But you said you're dating Ricardo. Does that still count as *alone*?"

She broke eye contact and polished the gold buttons of her uniform jacket with her sleeve.

Emily bent her body until her eyes met Lacey's. "Besides, the one you should really turn control over to isn't Jon. It's the Good Lord up there." She pointed to the sky. "Do you ever pray about the things that bother you?"

"Of course I do." Lacey straightened. "But I just . . . I get busy."

"Talking to God is never a waste of time. Why don't you ask him what he thinks of Ricardo?" Emily placed a cashmere-soft palm on Lacey's cheek. "I'm not sure what locked you up inside, dear. But don't waste your time on a man with no key." She walked back inside, leaving Lacey with her thoughts and the wind. It tore her hair from its carefully styled bun and lashed her cheeks with the flyaway strands.

It was true.

Dating Ricardo was the same thing as being alone.

CHAPTER 22

JON JABBED AT HIS NOISY phone, hoping for five more minutes of sleep, but the snooze button wasn't working. His tired brain cleared enough to register it was a phone call and not an alarm making the sound. He grabbed his cell and answered.

"Hello?"

"Mr. King? There's an emergency in the lobby."

Jon bolted out of bed and started dressing before he even heard the details. "Give me five minutes. I'll be right there."

Four minutes and thirteen seconds later, Jon skipped the poky elevator and raced down the stairs. His shoes squished against damp carpet as he passed by the marble columns and went into the main lobby. Puddles of water gathered on every surface. An army of crew members filled the room, moving furniture and mopping. He slowed enough to keep from slipping and located the head manager, who was overseeing the group.

"What happened, Mr. Kapoor?"

The balding man wiped his shiny head with a tissue. "A sprinkler malfunctioned. Soaked everything. It's wet as a kiddie pool in here." He stuffed the crumpled tissue in his pocket. "At least it happened after most passengers were asleep. I called the maintenance crew and asked for volunteers from our best workers to help clean the mess before the customers wake up."

"Are the sprinklers fixed?" Jon avoided three men pushing a grand piano out of the waterlogged lobby.

"Yes. It's just a matter of cleanup. Move the couches. Dry the carpets. Then swap the furniture with replacements. It will take all night."

Jon pushed his sleeves to his elbows. "Tell me what to do."

Mr. Kapoor pointed at a huge mountain of towels. "Try to soak up what you can. We'll bring in wet vacuums to help and also position fans at the worst areas. Hopefully, that will be enough."

Jon grabbed a stack from the pile and searched for an empty spot to start. People crawled around the lobby on their hands and knees. A golden head caught his attention. Lacey knelt in a corner pressing a cloth along the baseboards. Her long hair was barely contained in a lopsided ponytail. She wore flannel pants and a baggy T-shirt. When she stood, the motion revealed long wet stains along the legs of her pajamas. She loaded her arms with sodden towels and carried them to a plastic trash can sitting in front of him.

"Are you waiting for an invitation?" She dumped the soppy mess in the bin and took another armful of towels. "Get to work."

Was it weird he found her high-handed orders endearing?

He chose a location near Lacey. They pushed and soaked and cleaned and dried until the rays of morning sunlight crept through the windows. By the time early-bird passengers wandered in at six o'clock, the transformation was complete.

Lacey dragged herself out of the room and into the service elevator, Jon at her heels. As the car descended, he stretched and rubbed his spine with a groan. "I think I'll skip the gym today. That was a workout and a half. Are you going to grab a few hours of sleep?"

Lacey pulled her phone from her pants pocket. "I have a staff meeting in twenty-two minutes. Barely enough time to get ready."

"I'm sure they'll give you a break after working an extra shift."

"No thanks. I'm wide-awake."

The elevator stopped at her floor, and she sprinted down the hall toward her cabin. Jon shook his head as the doors closed. How could anyone keep up with that kind of passion?

Lacey's chin drooped. Her head tilted forward, and she snapped it back before it hit the plate in front of her. She scrubbed her hands over her cheeks and scoped out the staff dining room. It was easy to pinpoint the employees who'd been part of the flood patrol by their haggard faces. They looked as bad as she felt.

"I have been searching for you." Ricardo slid onto the seat beside her and placed his breakfast on the table. "Would you like to have sushi after work tonight?"

Lacey was glad he sat at her side instead of opposite her. Easier to avoid his eyes. "No thanks. I'm exhausted after dealing with the sprinkler mess. I plan to go to bed the minute I get off."

"My roommate told me about that." Ricardo took a drink of his juice. "It is so wrong you had to clean it up."

"Where were you?" Lacey peered at him.

"I had to wake early to prep the breakfast pastries." He poured salsa over his scrambled eggs. "My sleep is important. The maintenance crew handled the job. It is shameful Mr. Kapoor made you help."

"He didn't make me help. I volunteered."

"Such dedication." He applauded before taking a bite of his toast. "Your parents raised you well."

Lacey forcefully stabbed a piece of pineapple with her fork. "I learned about hard work from my mother's example."

"The cruise line should give you a raise. Do you have an easy schedule today?"

"Not even close. I'm escorting a group of passengers on an island tour. We probably won't return to the boat until sunset."

Ricardo placed his hand on top of hers. "It hurts me you are overworked. Perhaps tomorrow we can eat sushi?"

Lacey slipped her hand from under his and grabbed her tray. Time to break up and run. She slid her chair away from the table and placed one foot to the side, ready to propel herself upward.

"I'm sorry, Ricardo. My life is too complicated right now." She started to rise. "We should keep our friendship simple without any dating."

He cocked his head to the side. "I do not understand you."

"Let's be friends." She stood all the way. "And nothing else."

His lips turned downward. "No sushi?"

"No sushi." Lacey grimaced. "Sorry."

She spun on her heel and speed-walked to the clean-up area. The different bins waited for silverware, dishes, and scraps. Her posture relaxed when she realized Ricardo wasn't following. She sorted her items and sighed.

One more mess cleaned up.

Jon collapsed onto the desk chair, stretched his arms above his head, and moaned. It was the first time he'd rested since the unexpected sprinkler emergency.

Staff meeting, morning announcements, and half a dozen other things he couldn't remember had kept him running. Maybe cruise director wasn't the best cover for ferreting out a drug ring.

A pen rolled to one side, and Jon caught it before it fell off the desk. He twirled it in his fingers as he stared out the window. The water swelled in angry, white-capped waves. Charcoal-gray clouds filled the sky. Splotches of rain hit the glass in front of him.

The Caribbean island of Nevis allowed small cruise ships to dock in port, but large vessels such as the MS *Buckingham* had to anchor offshore and transport passengers to land in small ferries called tender boats. That meant a bumpy ride and a boatload of seasick passengers.

Jon rubbed his head. He opened his laptop, clicked on an email, and spotted the information he'd been waiting for from corporate. "Finally."

The list was surprisingly short. Eighteen people out of the entire passenger list raised a flag in the criminal background checks. Twelve were minor offenses such as shoplifting and speeding tickets. He wrote the remaining six names on a piece of paper. A married couple on deck six had been convicted of real-estate fraud. A VIP member on the diamond deck spent eleven months in jail for insider trading. A couple of men had served short sentences for drug possession in the 1970s. And the final name had a star by it.

Luca Amante.

Three different stints in prison for robbery, money laundering, and aggravated assault. Corporate included details from the assault case. Jon's teeth clenched as he read. This was a nasty character by anyone's definition.

Where was he now?

Jon accessed the man's record in the MS *Buckingham* database. Monarch Cruises required every passenger to take a photo for the ID card they carried around the ship. People used it to enter their staterooms, make purchases at onboard shops, and scan with security whenever they embarked or disembarked. Amante's picture showed a hard mug with deep-set eyes, puffy lips stretched to one side in an unpleasant smirk, and thinning brows that didn't quite match his jet-black hair. The most recent entry showed he'd boarded a tour-bus excursion of Charlestown and had been on the island for five hours. Plenty of time to make contact with a supplier. The confusion that would be caused by multiple tender boats returning in the bad weather provided a perfect cover to smuggle narcotics aboard.

Someone knocked.

"Come in."

The white-blond head of the first mate poked around the door. "Hi, Jon."

"Peter, what's up?"

He winced as he entered. "The weather's horrific. Captain says it isn't safe to bring any more tenders back from the island. He wants you to arrange accommodations for the passengers. They might be stuck there overnight."

Jon's gaze switched to the window. "How many are there?"

"One busload. Sixteen people who took the Charlestown tour." Peter wobbled from side to side with the lurching ship. "Stinks for Lacey. She's the lone employee with that group. I'd hate to be the person to break the news."

Jon stood and shoved past him. "I need to talk to the captain. Now."

CHAPTER 23

A TORRENTIAL DOWNPOUR PELTED THE large windows of the tour bus as it wound through the streets of Charlestown. With a placid smile on her face, Lacey rode on the seat behind the driver. She tucked her purple polo shirt into the waistband of her khaki pants and rested her hands on her stomach. But inside, her brain was biting its nails. Would the tenders still be running? The covered ferries worked great in calm waters, but rough weather sometimes stranded passengers ashore.

"Excuse me, ma'am." A polite young man wearing an *I Love Oklahoma* T-shirt tapped her on the shoulder. "Is this rain going to affect our ride to the ship?"

"No need to worry." Lacey hoped she wasn't bamboozling him. "The ferryboat drivers are used to this island's weather patterns."

He nodded and sat back across the aisle with his bride.

Please, God. Her brain stopped biting its nails and prayed for a miracle instead. *Let the boats be running.*

Her cell phone rang, and her nerves tightened.

Please, God. Please, God. Please, God.

"Hello?" She tried to keep the anxiety from her voice as the honeymooners eavesdropped from the opposite side. Her hostess smile reappeared. "Yes. That's correct."

Mr. Oklahoma tilted his head.

"I understand." Lacey kept her tone calm and even. "Please let me know."

She ended the call and whispered to the driver. He put on his signal and made a sharp left at the stop sign. Lacey stood and faced the people in the bus.

"Ladies and gentlemen." Sixteen pairs of eyes pointed at her. "I'm sure you've noticed the unfortunate storm outside. I regret to inform you that the heavy rain makes it impossible for our tender boat to return to the ship at this time."

Exclamations of disbelief and a few colorful words she wouldn't be repeating answered her announcement.

"It doesn't seem that bad," a woman in the last row called. "Can't we give it a try and turn around if it doesn't work?"

Lacey tried to look sympathetic instead of scoffing at the idiotic question. "Your safety is our utmost priority. We won't risk your lives to stay on schedule. The ship will wait for us."

"Where do we go in the meantime?" Mrs. Oklahoma asked. "Do we stay on the bus?"

"Oh, no." Lacey grabbed the headrest of a seat and held on as the vehicle made another sharp left. "The company has already arranged for a resting area near the dock."

"Are we sleeping in a hotel?"

Lacey wished she could ignore the question, but they'd find out soon enough. "Passengers from other cruise lines are also stranded on the island, and there were no vacant hotel rooms. I'm afraid we'll have to rough it a little."

Thunder crashed. The storm increased both outside and inside the bus. Voices rose in a crescendo of discontent. Lacey braced herself for a mutiny.

"How exciting!" A frizzy gray head popped up among the turmoil. Emily stood and braced herself between the seats as the bus swayed along. "We'll have something to brag about to the people who stayed on the ship."

"I wish I was one of them," Mrs. Oklahoma grumbled.

"And miss the adventure?" Emily shook her finger at the grumpy honeymooner. "Didn't you come on this cruise to get away from the routine?" She sat. "Trust me, my dears. I've lived a long time, and there's one thing I know for sure. The best adventures happen off the schedule."

Lacey mentally retracted every complaint she'd ever made about Emily Windsor. The woman was an angel. Her phone rang as the bus stopped in front of an unidentified building. The dark outline loomed in the pounding rain. She lowered her voice while the caller on the other end informed her of the unattractive details.

A school gymnasium. Army cots. Cold sandwiches. And no one to take care of the passengers but her.

The bearer of bad tidings hung up without a word of sympathy.

Lacey continued to hold the phone to her ear to buy extra time. How could she put a positive spin on this? She sent another silent request heavenward, lowered her cell, and walked down the aisle.

"Would it sound too cliché to say I have good news and bad news? The bad news is, we'll be staying in a school gym."

Gasps and protests ensued, and Lacey raised her voice.

"The good news is this rain is supposed to end in a short while. Once the sea calms, we'll head straight to the ship. It shouldn't be more than a few hours."

"Hours!"

The home-kit dye-job, earring stud–wearing man from orientation day rose from the back row like an angry Grim Reaper. She'd avoided him all day on the tour, but there was no escaping now. There would definitely be no umbrella drinks for him in this place.

Emily slid from her seat with her purse on her arm. "What a relief. Just a few hours." She stepped into the aisle and blocked the angry man from a clear view of Lacey. "Lead the way, dear." She shooed her with both hands.

The bus driver jerked the lever, and the automatic door whooshed open. Lacey sprinted through the rain and reached an awning that stretched from the side of the gymnasium. She turned the dented knob at the entrance and pushed. The rusty metal door creaked as she crossed the threshold. A cavernous room lay before her, and a musty smell emanated from the peeling paint. Battered wooden floorboards reflected the flickering fluorescent lights. Rows of army cots with blankets piled on top lined the far wall, and a cafeteria table was set with sandwiches, chips, and drinks.

Emily appeared at her side, brushing a soggy gray curl from her cheek. "What can I do to help?"

Lacey pressed wet fingers to her overheated forehead and resisted the urge to bury her face in the woman's neck. "Honestly, I don't even know where to start."

Horrified passengers filed into the cold, dreary room. Disgruntled murmurs rose. People held their cell phones high, checking for a signal. Were they planning to leave scathing reviews on every website available?

A woman wearing a damp sundress and holding a small child by the hand stared at the last-minute accommodations. "Is this the best they could do?"

Lacey approached her. "I'm so sorry for this inconvenience. We hope it will only be for a short time. As soon as the weather clears, they can come and get us."

Emily scuttled up. "Think of the great anecdotes we'll get from this. I can hardly wait to tell my friends."

"That's one way to look at it." The woman shrugged. "At least my husband kept the other two kids on the boat with him. I should consider this a mini vacation."

"How old is your daughter?" Lacey waved at the little girl beside her. The strawberry-blond stuck her thumb in her mouth and hid behind her mother's skirt.

"Four."

"Four and a half," a tiny voice behind the woman's legs corrected her.

"Yes." The mom rolled her eyes at Lacey. "How dare I forget those extra six months?"

"It's a good thing you told me." Lacey crouched. "We have a special spot for big girls. I don't want to put you in the four-year-old section."

A blue eye peeked around her mother, and a lopsided smile appeared.

An expletive exploded from the gym doorway, and the little girl's smile disappeared. Lacey saw her black-haired nemesis stalk into the room.

"You got to be kidding me." He dropped a large black bag, pitched his jacket on the ground, and swore again.

A mere sixteen customers were stranded because of the rough waters. Why did Mr. Online Review have to be one of them? Lacey considered her chances if she were to try swimming to the boat.

No.

Even if she made it, she'd be in trouble for deserting the passengers.

Emily stood on her toes and whispered. "We're going to have trouble with that one."

Lacey showed the mother and child to an empty cot and spent the next hour comforting people. Emily served food and tried to bolster morale, and Lacey left her as a lookout while she scrubbed the locker room showers and toilets.

"Finally," Mrs. Oklahoma said when Lacey emerged with her bucket and cleaning supplies. "How long does it take to get a shower here?"

"I apologize for the wait." Lacey swept her arm to the door. "The bathroom is clean. There's soap and a stack of towels on a table by the stalls."

"Great," the young woman grumbled.

Lacey noted the rough white lines on her own palms and hid her hand. Her skin cracked like a desert floor in July from prolonged contact with the harsh industrial cleaner. She wandered through the cots, checking on everyone and offering bottles of water. Most had accepted their sorry lot and were posing for pictures to post on social media. She hoped their comments wouldn't be too harsh.

A clang sounded from the entrance.

"Good evening, ladies and gentlemen!"

Heads turned toward the cheerful voice.

Jonathan King stood in the main doorway, soaked to the skin. He searched the crowd until he found Lacey, gave her a nod, and swung a waterproof knapsack off his arm. His rain poncho dripped a puddle of water on the floor, but his smile filled the gymnasium.

"We missed you on board! So I commandeered one of the tender boats. Trust me, you don't want to make that rough ride just yet." Jon clutched his stomach with an exaggerated scowl. "I'm here to make sure everyone is taken care of until it's safe to travel to the ship." He strode through the room to the very center. "I realize this is a far cry from the dream vacation you imagined, but I promise I'll have the chef whip up an exclusive meal for you the second we get back to the MS *Buckingham*." He ran his fingers through the wet strands of hair hanging over his forehead.

"Wow!" A twentysomething with black lipstick giggled near Lacey. "They sent the cruise director for us."

Impressed whispers volleyed around her. It didn't hurt that Jon looked as if he'd stepped out of a shower-gel commercial. How had he convinced someone to let him take a tender?

Passengers crowded around him, and he listened to a catalog of stories and complaints. The peevish expressions dissipated under the charismatic force of his goodwill. He pulled gourmet chocolate bars from his bag and distributed them while he moved through the room. When he reached the little girl, he lowered himself to her height.

"I brought a friend to keep you company." Jon set the knapsack on the floor and drew out a small teddy bear with a crown on its head and the Monarch logo on its right paw.

The child shyly accepted the gift and hid behind her mother's dress again.

Jon stood and raised his voice. "These accommodations can't compare to the MS *Buckingham*'s, but I packed a little music from home to help us relax." He retrieved a small speaker from his bag and connected it to his phone. Before long, a soothing instrumental orchestration flowed through the gym.

Lacey recognized the mix. The ship played it in the early-morning hours, when they wanted the passengers to calm down and go to bed. She marveled at his thoroughness. He'd planned for every contingency. It would be a shame if he grew tired of his position and switched jobs again. This one made use of his many talents so well.

She shook her head as Jon joined her. "Do you happen to have a popcorn machine and a movie screen in that Mary Poppins bag?"

His eyes swept over her. "You look terrible."

Her urge to swoon dissipated. "Thanks a lot." She smoothed the bedraggled hem of her polo.

Would a kind word kill him? She'd been in a silent state of panic all afternoon. Her appearance had been the last thing on her mind. Until now.

He pulled a dark-blue sweatshirt with matching pants and a toiletries kit from the pack and passed them to her. "I'll handle the situation here. You go take a shower."

She wanted nothing more. But how could she leave him alone with the cranky passengers? "You don't have to—"

Jon grasped her shoulders and spun her around. "Go." He gave her a gentle push and turned to focus on the customers.

Lacey hugged the clean, dry sweats. They smelled of fabric softener and Jon. She'd never read a fairy tale where Prince Charming carried a miraculous backpack, but a change of clothes was better than a glass slipper any day of the week.

And the shower rivaled a European vacation. She allowed herself nine whole minutes of bliss under the hot spray before worries about the passengers prompted her to cut it short. The wet concrete chilled her bare feet while she dressed. She wrung the ends of her hair in a towel as she exited the locker room.

Jon waited for her outside the door. He grinned as he gave her the once-over. "My clothes fit better on you."

Lacey tugged at the loose neckline. "Thanks for bringing them. It's such a relief to be dry." She peeked around his side at a welcome scene. The worn-out travelers stretched on their cots as a tranquil piano piece drifted through the air. A noisy snore sounded from the corner. "Where's Emily?" she whispered.

Jon pointed at a slumbering figure near the sandwich table. "She's a trouper. Helped tend to everyone else before she crashed."

He took Lacey by the hand and led her to a small office off the main room. Inside were a single cot and blanket shoved against the wall. A sandwich and drink sat on a nearby table. Jon motioned to the food.

"You eat and get some rest. I'll keep watch."

Lacey sank on the floor next to the cot. She wrapped the towel around her thick mane of wet hair and squeezed. "I don't think I could sleep. I'd be too worried the call would come that the storm's over." She stopped wringing the moisture out. "Speaking of which, how *did* you get here?"

"It's too dangerous to risk the passengers' lives, but I convinced the captain to let me drive one of the boats from the ship. I have the proper training and promised not to sink on the way."

Lacey combed her fingers through her tangled locks. "Still, I'm shocked he allowed you to—"

"It won't dry the way you're doing it." Jon sat on the floor across from her. He took the towel away and dropped it over her head.

The terry cloth shrouded her. She debated how to react, until two large hands settled on her scalp and began a furious massage.

"Ow." Lacey peeked from under the cloth. "Are you trying to peel the skin off?"

"Sorry." Jon tugged the towel over her face and took the rubbing down a few notches.

She sighed as the gentle pressure relaxed her. The tension drained from her body, and she sank into a hypnotic state as Jon's fingers pushed the worries from her mind.

"Lacey?"

The voice called from far away.

"Lacey?"

She jolted awake as Jon's face poked under the towel. It draped over both of them, providing a private, fuzzy refuge. He stopped an inch from her nose, close enough his breath grazed her skin. Lacey's fatigue vanished. The outside of her body froze, but the inside was hopping on one foot, squealing like a toddler in a bouncy castle.

Jon's gaze wandered from her eyes to her nose to her lips. "If I kiss you, will you start dating someone else again?"

Lacey gulped. Her mouth refused to form the word. All she could manage was a slight shake of the head. He leaned forward, closing the distance between them. Tilting his chin to the left, he looked in her eyes once more as if checking for permission.

She nodded.

His mouth lowered and drew near. Lacey's lids drooped shut as she waited for that first, searing contact her body still remembered so well.

An ear-piercing scream jerked her back to reality.

CHAPTER 24

JON YANKED THE TOWEL FROM their heads, threw it on the end of the bed, and scrambled to his feet. He held out his hand for Lacey and pulled her up. She ran for the door. Jon followed. They entered the chaotic gymnasium to find a group of passengers circling a hysterical woman.

"Get it off! Get it off!" she shrieked. Her jerky hand waved at the cot, where a spindly-legged spider skittered.

"Aw, is that all?" A heavy-lidded man clinched a blanket under his chin. "I thought you found a corpse." He crossed the gym and plopped on his own cot.

Others wandered away, but a few stayed with the woman.

Jon approached, flicked the spider off the bed, and squashed it with his shoe.

"What kind of cruise line is this?" Of course it was Amante asking. "We paid for luxury accommodations, and you put us in this dump."

Lacey cringed. "I deeply apologize, sir. There were no other lodgings available. The bad weather still hasn't cleared, but the moment it does, the ship will send a boat with a certified driver for us. We hope it won't be more than a few hours."

"That's what you said hours ago." He lowered his head and waved a fist in the air. Words poured from his mouth like dirty water from a sanitation hose. If he were on television, the censor's finger would tire of pressing the bleep button.

Lacey flinched but kept her expression neutral. Jon bit back the lecture the man deserved. That wouldn't help the situation. Instead, he slid in front of Lacey. He couldn't stop the raging tirade, but he could shield her from the brunt of the man's fury.

The apoplectic customer swung his arms with all the grace of a dancing inflatable figure outside a grand opening. People around him scattered, and Jon weighed his options. What if this escalated? Luca Amante had served three prison sentences. He couldn't be trusted to stay levelheaded.

Passengers stood at a distance, phones out, recording the blazing fit. Amante's verbal attack continued with no end in sight. Did this guy swallow a four-letter dictionary? Jon spread his legs into a wider stance, and his right hand clenched into a fist, preparing for battle.

"Stop it this instant!" a voice demanded.

Jon's gaze swung. Lacey peeped over his shoulder.

The crowd parted to reveal Emily, her curls pointing every which way. She marched to the unruly passenger and stood toe-to-toe with him. "Just because you're unhappy doesn't mean the rest of us have to listen to obscenities."

"Who are you to stop me?" Amante punctuated his question with a few more curses.

She slapped his arm. "I'm someone who was sleeping peacefully until your potty language woke me. Calm down and go to bed. Your mother would be ashamed of you."

The irate man's mouth hung open as Emily about-faced and walked away. Other bystanders nodded and returned to their cots, leaving Jon and Lacey alone with the contrary passenger.

"She . . . she hit me." He pointed at the spot. "That's assault."

Jon tensed, but Lacey stepped around him. "You're absolutely right, sir. If you want to file a complaint, I'll accompany you to the local police station. You can tell them a seventy-eight-year-old woman beat you up."

Amante's crooked jaw jutted out. "Well, I wouldn't go that far."

Jon took a candy bar from his pocket and held it out to the man. "Your blood sugar must be low from the excitement. Why don't you have a snack and rest? I'll wake you as soon as the reinforcements arrive."

"Don't treat me like a child!" He advanced and poked an aggressive finger. "If I don't receive a full refund, I'll scream my head off to any news channel that will listen. This line's reputation will be"—he squinted in Emily's direction and censored his word choice—"in the crapper." The petulant man snatched the candy and stomped off to his cot.

Jon exhaled. Crisis averted with no injuries. He leaned toward Lacey and murmured from one side of his mouth, "Should we sing him a lullaby?"

She rubbed her temples. "Pass."

He put his arm around her back and steered her to the office. They entered the private area, but Jon made sure the door stayed open so he could keep an eye on Amante, whose bed was a few feet away.

Lacey plopped on the floor in the corner. She released a tired sigh and stared at her chapped hands. "Will this night never end?"

"The rain should quit anytime now." Jon snagged the blanket from the cot and spread it around her. He sat to her left and stretched. "We'll get a call from the ship when it's safe for them to send the tender. Until then—"

"Aaaaah!" She pressed against the wall.

"What?" He raised up on one knee. "What's wrong?"

Her trembling finger pointed to three feet away, where an enormous spider scurried across the broken plaster. Lacey grasped the blanket tight.

Jon observed her cower with a quirk of his lip. "Still hate spiders?"

"With every fiber of my being."

He really shouldn't find her obvious distress adorable. But he did. "Want me to kill it?"

"With *every* fiber of my being." Her eyes pleaded with him.

He pushed off the floor and grabbed a tattered magazine from a nearby table. Rolling it, he walked to the far wall and swatted the bug. Jon dropped the magazine on the floor and returned to her side.

Lacey clapped. "My hero."

"Wish you meant that."

She readjusted the blanket around her body, avoiding the obvious hint. That was nothing new. He was used to it by now. But Lacey sitting beside him of her own free will might even be considered progress.

Incessant rain drummed against the roof in an angry rhythm that Noah of old might recognize. Lacey's nose twitched at the pervasive scent of mold. Her rear end ached from sitting on the hard floor, and even a stiff army cot sounded tempting. But she didn't want Jon to suffer alone. Someone should help keep watch. Who knew when another crisis might arise?

She tapped her fingers against the concrete. Something moved. Lacey looked down and shrieked. Her body vaulted forward. She barreled to the window.

"What?" Jon pushed to his feet.

"Spider." Lacey shuddered. "Another one."

Jon crushed it under his heel. "It's an old building. Probably a lot of them in the walls."

Lacey whimpered.

"Sorry. Not the best thing to say, under the circumstances."

"You think?" She bracketed her face with her hands, trying to shut out the room. "This is a nightmare. I won't get any sleep tonight. I might as well stand with my nose in the corner."

"Spiders can crawl up." Jon ducked as she seized the discarded magazine from the floor and hurled it at him. "Okay. Sorry. But you're so appealing when you freak out."

"I'm not freaking out." She crouched in the middle of the room and wrapped her arms around her legs. "I'm exhausted. I haven't slept in thirty-six hours. First, the sprinkler crisis, and now we're marooned on Arachnid Island with a bunch of litigation-happy passengers." Her body hovered above the floor, only the soles of her shoes making contact with the grimy tiles.

Jon shrugged out of his jacket. After laying it on the ground behind Lacey, he gently pushed her to a sitting position and settled beside her. Patting his shoulder, he nodded.

She scrunched her eyebrows at him.

He thumped his shoulder again. "You can borrow it awhile. I'll protect you from any creepy-crawlies."

"Yeah right." She frowned. "You'll fall asleep the minute my eyes close."

"I promise, not a wink." He tweaked her chin. "Have you ever known me to break a promise?"

She couldn't recall a single time. "You swear you'll stay awake?"

"Cross my heart." He made the motion over his chest and held his hand up like he was taking an oath.

Lacey bit her lower lip. A quick nap. What could it hurt? She inched her head onto the broad shoulder beside her, and Jon slumped a little to make it more comfortable.

Her head lifted. "Wake me if you see a spider."

He blew out a ragged breath and pushed her head onto his shoulder. "Go to sleep."

"Don't tell me what to do," Lacey murmured.

She had to give him credit. Jon showed up when it mattered—when it wasn't even his responsibility. What other man on the MS *Buckingham* would drive a tiny boat through a dangerous storm to babysit a bunch of outraged passengers? Who else would stand between a raving maniac and her? How many guys would—

Her eyelids drooped no matter how hard she tried to keep them open, and she sank into a sweet, spiderless dream.

CHAPTER 25

JON'S SACROILIAC COMPLAINED LOUD AND long. His lower back didn't appreciate remaining stock-still for an hour. He should have laid his jacket against the wall so he had a brace to lean on. Too late now. Moving might wake Lacey.

His location offered a clear view of Amante's cot through the open doorway. The man hadn't budged since he fell asleep. A large black bag rested under his head instead of a pillow, the strap wrapped around his right arm. Was there a reason why he wanted to keep it close? The security guard better take a look inside the moment they boarded the ship.

Jon eased his cell phone out of his left pocket. No messages. Not surprising since it continued to sound like a tropical depression outside.

Lacey shifted against his shoulder. He craned his neck to check on her. That tiny crease between her eyebrows had finally disappeared. Her still-damp hair pressed against his neck, and the flowery scent of her shampoo tickled his nostrils. Jon stared at the stained ceiling tiles above his head.

God, help?

Not his most eloquent prayer, but one of the most heartfelt. Back to square one. Longing for something out of reach. He wanted to be much more than a friend to Lacey, but she always ran away. How could he prove his sincerity?

Thunder boomed like someone had shot a cannonball through the room.

Lacey jerked and rose to her knees. She blinked. "How long was I asleep?"

"Not long enough." He tapped his opposite shoulder. "If you want to catch a few more winks, use this side. You've got a red mark the size of Tampa on your cheek."

She covered the spot with her fingers, walked to the doorway, and surveyed the gymnasium.

Jon stood, and his back cracked. He rubbed his spine as he wandered behind Lacey, peering over her head.

Sleeping bodies filled the cots. Peace reigned. Except for the garbage-disposal snoring of the person in the corner.

"They're fine, Lace. The ship still hasn't texted me. No one's coming to get us yet." He gently tugged her into the office and led her to the empty cot along the wall. "Rest here. It'll be more comfortable than my shoulder." Jon placed his hand on top of her head and pushed her down. Reaching to the nearby table, he grabbed a bottle of fruit punch, twisted off the cap, and passed the drink to her. "Try this and get some more sleep."

Lacey reached for the bottle but fumbled. It tilted between them, and the punch splashed the right sleeve of her sweatshirt. "Oh no!" She shook the bright-red liquid onto the floor.

"Here." Jon grabbed the towel she'd used on her hair. He bent and dabbed at the sleeve. "You were supposed to drink it, not wear it. This isn't a good look for you." He smiled. It faded when he saw the tears welling. "Hey, I didn't mean it." He tossed the towel aside and took her by the arms. "You can wear anything. Fruit punch. Orange juice. Spinach smoothie. I bet you'd start a new trend."

She shook him off and covered her mouth and nose with her hands. Muffled words squeezed out from behind her fingers.

Jon backed up with his arms held high in surrender. "I have no idea what you said."

Lacey brushed the tears from her face. "I said, 'Stop being so nice.'"

She rubbed her sleeve against her nose. "It's hard enough to keep my distance when you're pestering me. When you act like this, I can't resist."

Jon lowered his arms and spread them out. "Then don't." He held his breath.

Her eyes darted back and forth, panic-stricken. Her chest heaved in short, desperate puffs. She rose from the cot, shoved by him, and headed for the door. He watched her leave. Again. Like they were stuck on a sick, twisted carousel, going around and around but never getting anywhere. What were the secret words that would make her stay?

"Please?"

Lacey stopped at the threshold, facing away from him.

Jon remained where he was. He couldn't force her to love him. It had to be her choice.

"I don't know why you're scared of us being together again." His hands twitched at his sides. "But I promise I won't let you down. Like with the spiders. I keep my word."

Her body swayed forward, but her feet stayed in one spot. She wavered, and Jon's mind whispered the same prayer from earlier.

God, help?

Lacey turned. She moved one step closer. Then another. Her eyes fixed somewhere around his chin. He fought to stay where he was, wanting to make it easier, but telling himself he couldn't rush her. Was she trembling? Her vulnerable expression scraped at his heart. She drew near enough that her two feet nestled between his as she stood with her nose a centimeter from his chest.

Jon wrapped his arms around her body so tight his elbows almost met in the middle. He bent his head and buried his nose by her neck, breathing in the smell of shampoo, fruit punch, and Lacey—that indefinable scent that had haunted his dreams for two and a half years. What if he woke and found it was all a fantasy?

Lacey's hands crept around his waist and stretched up his back. Her soft frame pressed against his.

No. His imagination wasn't this good. If the moment was for real, he'd better have her sign on the dotted line while she was feeling amenable.

"Does this make it official?" He raised his head. "Are we a *them*?"

"A what?"

"No longer a *him* and *her*. A *them*. A pair. A couple. Have we finally crossed the dreaded just-friends barrier into an honest-to-goodness romantic relationship?"

"I admit, I'm scared. But I don't want to be. I want to be"—she took a breath—"with you." Lacey pulled away—not out of his arms but far enough to look up at him. "I'll agree on one condition."

"Name it."

The corners of her mouth rose. "Don't tell the Shippers."

He laughed and checked over her shoulder, half expecting to see Emily gloating in the doorway. "They might have us under surveillance as we speak."

"No. We managed to sneak this one by them."

Jon studied her playful expression. "And why don't you want to tell them?"

"Payback." Lacey smirked. "Don't forget, they stranded us in Cozumel and locked us in the lost and found without so much as a candle."

"As I recall, we managed to stay warm."

"Regardless." She smacked his arm. "They deserve to suffer a little."

He shivered and snuggled her close. "I'm glad you're on my side."

She laid her head on his chest. "Me too."

Definitely not a dream. More like a dream come true. He rested his cheek against the top of her head. Maybe he shouldn't push it. But . . .

"Do you think . . . we could continue the conversation we were having under the towel . . . before the spiders invaded?"

"Conversation?" She stayed in his arms but leaned to the right and met his eyes.

"You know." He tilted his head from side to side.

Lacey squinted at him. "Nope. I'm drawing a blank."

"Oh." Jon cleared his throat and looked away.

She reached up and directed his face to hers. "How about you re-fresh my memory?"

Her fingers traced his jawline as he grinned. "I'd be happy to, ma'am."

CHAPTER 26

"I PEEKED IN THE DOORWAY, and there they were." Emily pressed her hands together as she filled her friends in over a midnight supper. "Cuddled like a pair of puppies."

"Doing what?" Gerry seized her notebook from the table and lifted her pen.

"Lacey was sleeping away on his shoulder, and he was sitting there on the floor, grinning like a besotted fool. My poor heart almost burst from joy."

"What happened next?" Althea leaned so far forward her pendant necklace slipped into her soup bowl.

Emily motioned to it with her finger while she continued her story. "Nothing much. The weather calmed, and the tender boat was there before we knew it. We loaded up and returned to the ship."

"Awww." Althea's lower lip stuck out. "What a wasted opportunity."

"But progress." Emily shrugged. "Count the small victories as well as the big ones."

Daisy reached to pull the necklace out of Althea's tomato bisque and cleaned it with her napkin. She picked a piece of lint off her own bolero jacket and eyed a family two tables away. Every member from the dad to the toddler wore baseball caps. "Why do people insist on wearing sports attire in a formal setting?"

"The days of dressing up are gone." Gerry set her notebook on the table and grabbed her fork.

"Yes." Daisy nodded. "Proper cruise attire is all too rare these days."

Each Shipper sat in her own version of dressed up. Emily wore a beaded gold blazer with matching pants. A vintage-style faux fur wrapped around Gerry, and a knit beret with silver sequins tilted on her head. Althea filled out a shiny red spaghetti-strap number with a flowered silk shawl. And Daisy wore her requisite black. Underneath her bolero jacket, ruffles spilled from the neckline, and the billowing sleeves of her poet blouse never once dipped into the food as she dined.

Gerry took a bite of her salad. "If Lacey is warming to Jon, then perhaps we should back off. Let nature take its course, as they say."

"Who says?" Emily scoffed. "Whoever 'they' are haven't met Lacey. I've analyzed that girl for over a year. The only way she'll fall in love is if we give her a good, hard push."

Daisy tipped her bowl forward by the rim and scooped the last bit of soup with her spoon. "But pushy people can also push others away."

"I'm with Emily." Althea took her second dinner roll from the basket, broke it in half, and slathered butter on each piece. "Lacey requires . . . encouragement."

Emily placed both hands on the table and observed her colleagues. "Consider Jon's feelings. The poor man has been pining after Lacey for years."

"He doesn't look to me like he's pining." Gerry pointed across the room with her fork.

Jon's head bent back as he laughed with a large group of passengers at the entrance. His dark-blue suit jacket accentuated his tapered build. He noted the women tracking him and made his way to their table.

"Hello, my lady Shippers." His smile was fully charged. "What a lovely picture you make."

Althea preened as she smoothed her shawl. "Thank you for noticing."

"Are you here alone?" Emily glanced past him.

He walked around the table and stopped at her chair. "Worried about me? Don't be. I've already eaten, and I'm making a few goodwill rounds before I turn in for the night."

Gerry elbowed Emily and motioned with her chin to where Lacey had entered. The young woman wove through the dining area, coming close to their table. When she noticed their group, she took an abrupt left and wandered around the pockets of diners, staying as far away from the Shippers as possible.

"That's strange." Emily's eyes narrowed at Jon. "You two seemed pretty friendly on Nevis."

He dropped his gaze and fiddled with a button on his sleeve. "Crisis draws people together." He waved at a couple who were gesturing to him. "If you ladies will excuse me, a guest is trying to get my attention. We return to Galveston tomorrow, but I assume I'll see you all on the next cruise. Be sure to check out the revamped evening show. They've added a rap number."

"Thanks for warning us," said Gerry.

He nodded and left to greet the passengers at a nearby table.

"Did you hear what he said?" Emily shoved her chair back. "We need a new crisis to throw him and Lacey together."

Daisy dabbed her lips with a napkin. "Somehow I doubt that's what he meant."

Emily placed one elbow on the table and cupped her chin in her hand. "Lacey won't fall for another fake emergency. It has to appear completely coincidental. Where should we start?"

The group fell silent. Cutlery clinked against fine china. Other diners chatted and enjoyed the meal, but the Shippers' supper had transformed into a strategy meeting.

Daisy sighed. "Why is romance so difficult?"

Althea peered over Gerry's shoulder, and her full red lips lifted. "It's not so difficult for some. Here comes romance now."

"Do my Irish eyes deceive me?" a thick brogue exclaimed.

The other ladies' heads turned to find Seamus O'Riley dressed in the same style of white tie and tails he wore for his show. He walked round the table until he stood by Gerry.

"Ah, it's herself—the fairest flower in this floating MS *Buckingham* garden."

Gerry grimaced. "That metaphor makes no sense."

Daisy cringed and whispered, "Gerry, be nice."

"Think nothing of it." Seamus clasped his hands behind his back. "Every word she speaks to me is a point in my favor. I'll win the fair lady yet." He rocked on his heels. "Will y'be coming to my show when the new cruise starts?"

"We have work to do," said Emily. "Perhaps another time."

"You're crushin' me poor spirit." Seamus patted his chest. "But I'll hold you to that promise, and I'll say good night till it be morrow." He left with a twinkle.

Althea swooned. "That was poetic."

"Shakespeare probably thought as much when he wrote it," said Gerry.

"I know it's from *Romeo and Juliet*. I'm not an idiot. But I'm not sure about you. Why don't you date him?"

"He looks like he's part leprechaun."

"I think he's cute." Althea's eyebrows dipped. "Snatch him up while he's still interested."

"He's shorter than me." Gerry pulled a book from under her napkin, snapped it open, and blocked her face.

"Too bad he didn't take a shine to me first." Althea lifted a little from her chair as she watched the magician cross the room. "I'd like to go international for husband number four. Get a little Irish cream in my diet."

"You do that." Gerry lowered her book. "I'll be your bridesmaid."

Emily ignored her friends picking at each other as she calculated their next move in Operation Ambush. Her bones told her success was imminent. She stabbed a russet potato with her fork, sliced it down the middle, and smiled. "Ladies, we may be close to clinching another satisfied match. If we can devise a good scheme, one more voyage should do it."

CHAPTER 27

THE GALVESTON DOCK BUSTLED WITH workers maneuvering fresh supplies onto the MS *Buckingham.* Jon dodged to the right as a forklift barreled past. The provisions master, in his bright-yellow safety vest, took out a thermometer and checked the temperature on a pallet of oysters. Shrink-wrapped skids of perishables waited to be loaded off a delivery truck.

Collins wandered up with his hands in his pockets, and Jon struggled to keep his temper in check. No matter how much he argued with the corporate office, they refused to replace the incompetent buffoon. He'd been tempted to go over their heads and fire the man himself, but ultimately decided to follow protocol a little longer for the sake of workplace harmony.

Collins yawned. "Security checked Amante as he got off the ship. You already know they didn't find anything but souvenirs in that duffel bag he had on Nevis. He's still clean. Sniffer dogs didn't find anything either."

Jon thumped his fist against a wooden crate.

"Take it easy." The detective unwrapped a stick of gum and folded it into his mouth. "You can't hit a home run every time." He stumbled back as a cartload of luggage almost ran over his foot. "Is it always this crazy?"

"Turnaround day?" Jon nodded. "Disembarking thousands of people, cleaning their rooms, restocking the kitchens, and ushering on a whole new batch of passengers in a mere ten hours is like conducting a giant, noisy orchestra with suitcases." He pushed the hair away from his forehead. "And for all we know, one of those suitcases leaving the ship has millions of dollars of cocaine stashed in it."

"Don't get frustrated. It's possible there weren't any narcotics this time."

"Or we missed them because I was searching in the wrong place." Jon scrubbed a hand across his face.

"Amante fit the profile. It was a natural mistake. Did you get any new information from the FBI investigation?"

"They found threatening emails on our former cruise director's personal laptop that confirm he was involved in something nefarious but wanted out."

"Must be why they killed him. Do you think they switched their operation to a different ship?"

"It's possible. But my gut tells me Newberg wasn't acting alone. Someone else on the MS *Buckingham* must have helped. Maybe multiple people. This voyage, let's focus our energy on the crew."

"What is that, a thousand employees?" Collins blew a bubble with his gum and popped it. "Do we each take five hundred?"

"Don't worry. I know a woman who can help. She's smart and recognizes every person on this ship."

But even as he said it, Jon's nerves snapped like a piece of Collins's gum. Was he roping Lacey into a dangerous undertaking? This drug business already cost one Monarch employee his life. But there were too many secrets between Lacey and him. He wanted to be as honest as possible, even if he couldn't tell her all the details.

"We must ward off disaster." Mr. Kapoor, the head manager, walked down the row of hostesses, giving his pre-board pep talk. "Be the front line of Monarch Cruises. As our great founder, J. P. McMillan, said in his last company memo, 'Make them wish they didn't have to go home.'"

Lacey waited with her posture stiff as a board. When he finished, the doors between the ship and the waiting passengers opened, and the noise from the pier floated into the room. She straightened the gold crown pin on her lapel and adjusted the purple scarf around her neck. Suitcase wheels rattled on the outside gangplank as a new round of passengers streamed into the main lobby.

"Welcome to the MS *Buckingham*." She repeated the phrase over and over as she pointed people to the elevators and answered the same old questions.

"The buffet opens as soon as the lifeboat drill and orientation end."

"You can ask the front desk about a room upgrade."

"The golf instructor reserves any course you wish to play ahead of time."

Her shoulders ached from holding them ruler-straight, but she remained at attention. The first impression these passengers received came from her greeting. She refused to disappoint them.

"Lacey-bell!"

Her head whipped to the receiving doors, and her vision tightened like one of those eerie camera shots in a horror movie. A handsome older man walked across the threshold, dressed in a cream linen suit and a straw safari hat. He held open his arms and waited as if he expected her to rush into them.

Lacey took a step back. "Dad?"

Women cast admiring glances at Ronald Anderson, still striking at fifty-eight, as they walked around him.

A frail woman stood at his side, grasping the handle of a carry-on bag. "Hello, honey."

"Mom?"

Lacey's father breezed over and picked her up around the waist, twirling her in a circle. "How's my little girl?"

The ostentatious chandelier spun above her head. The front-desk workers whizzed past, and the musky scent of her father's expensive cologne enveloped her. The last remnants of Lacey's breakfast churned. She pressed her lips together in a tight line. Vomiting in the lobby was not an attractive option.

"Please put me down." She wriggled in his grip. "People are staring."

He dropped her to the ground and pushed his hat up his forehead. "Can't a man be happy to hug his own daughter anymore?"

Her mother joined them, and she stroked his arm. "She's surprised, is all."

"I *am* surprised." Lacey tugged the hem of her jacket and touched a hand to her hair, then tucked a protruding pin into her bun. "What are you doing here?"

"I told you in the birthday card I sent to expect a surprise." Ronald tucked his thumbs through his belt loops. "We got tired of waiting for you to come visit. So we used those cruise vouchers you sent us last Christmas."

"That's wonderful." Lacey's customer-service mask was in place. "Why don't you relax in your cabin, and I'll come visit you when I finish here?" She held both hands to the left. "You'll find the elevators in that direction."

"It's good to see you." Her mother bent forward but hesitated.

Regret surged through Lacey. *I'm the meanest daughter on the planet.* She gathered her mom in her arms. Her heart cracked a little at how fragile her mother felt. "It's good to see you too. I missed you."

Her father wrapped his arms around both of them. "About time the family got together again. Good thing I came up with the idea."

Lacey's throat ached. Pressure built behind her eyes, and she breathed deep before releasing her mother. "What's your room number?"

They told her. She walked them to the elevators, and her parents entered the car. Her dad waved, and Lacey waved back with a smile. It lingered on her face when the doors slid shut. She returned to her duty station in the lobby and welcomed more passengers.

Always with a smile. Her mouth formed the expected pose without hesitation. She'd perfected her disguise a long time ago.

Jon pressed his lips together and rolled them inward as Lacey peeked out the skinny window by his office door. She lowered the blinds and sat on the chair facing his desk. A paper bag with the food she'd sneaked in sat on top.

"We're having lunch," he said. "Not holding a secret conference."

Lacey pulled out a couple of hamburgers, handed one to Jon, and unwrapped the other. "Our lost-and-found escapade got the rumor mill spinning. Any public interaction adds more fodder. Besides"—she took a bite of her sandwich—"the Shippers probably have spies everywhere."

"Now *that* I can believe. But there's an easy way to fix it. Reveal our relationship."

Lacey choked. She set her burger down and pounded a fist against her chest. "Are you"—she coughed—"are you crazy?"

Jon grabbed a bottle of water, twisted off the cap, and passed it to her. "What's crazy about wanting to brag about my beautiful girlfriend?"

Lacey drank a sip and wiped her mouth. "Give it a little more time."

Her eyes begged him to understand. He wanted to try, even if it hurt. Jon sat back on his chair and picked up his burger, his fingers playing with the wrapper. He'd planned to tell her about the drug smugglers at lunch and ask for help, but the relationship issue derailed his plans. Now wasn't the opportune moment.

They ate without talking. Only the rustle of food interrupted the silence. Voices passed in the hallway. Even if a coworker walked in on them, it looked more like a business meeting over lunch than a date.

He stared at the clock on his computer. Five more minutes before she had to leave. How could he fix this?

"My parents came aboard this morning," Lacey said in a quiet voice, face pointed at the floor.

"Your parents? That's great. I'd love to meet them."

"No." She jerked her head from side to side. "That's not a good idea."

"Don't worry. I won't say we're together. I'll introduce myself as the cruise director and—"

"Jon." She reached across the desk and grabbed his hand. "I don't want you to meet them."

He stilled. "We can't reveal our relationship to the crew. And I'm not allowed to meet your parents. Are you sure we're really dating?"

"Of course we are." Lacey avoided his gaze. She let go of his hand, opened a bag of potato chips, and shoved one in her mouth.

"Is this truly about teasing the Shippers?"

She finished crunching and swallowed. "What else?"

The hum of the air conditioner filled the room.

Jon passed her a cookie. Better to let it go. It was early days in their relationship. There was plenty of time to meet her family later. He bit into his lukewarm burger and tried to ignore the gnawing sensation in the pit of his stomach.

Was that feeling because he hadn't told her about the investigation? Or something deeper? Because of something that came between them two and a half years ago?

He wished he knew what that something was.

CHAPTER 28

Smooth jazz played through the sound system as the art deco sconces cast a cozy amount of light. Lacey sat with her parents in the MS *Buckingham*'s exclusive steakhouse. She toyed with her entrée while her dad relished every bite of his filet mignon and lobster meal.

The waiter held out a large bottle. "Would you care for more wine, sir?"

Her still-chewing father tapped the stem of his glass with a finger.

"Are you sure you want another one, Ron?" her mother asked. "Remember your health."

He swirled the dark-purple liquid and downed it in one gulp. "It's fine. I'm on vacation."

A lifelong vacation.

Lacey pushed a mushroom around her plate. Nineteen minutes remained, and then she reported for work. She could make it.

"Are you dating anyone?" asked her mother.

Lacey's fork froze. "I . . . Work keeps me busy—"

"'Course it does," her father interrupted. "These big companies squeeze the lifeblood out of their employees. They probably don't give her time to breathe, let alone date." He grabbed the lobster claw and used the crackers to split its shiny red shell. "I'm willing to be your advocate. Want me to talk to your boss? Give me the signal."

"No!" Lacey sat a little straighter. "I like my job, Dad. They treat me very well."

"This is a classy setup." Her father motioned around the room with his fork. "I'm glad you got in with such a fancy operation. It's way better than the dumps I used to work at before I got sick."

She concentrated on her plate and slicing her coq au vin. "Monarch is a wonderful employer."

"We're so proud of you, honey," her mom said. "But I feel guilty that you keep sending money home. We're doing okay now. I should be able to pay the mortgage on my own. You don't have to always—"

"What do they have for fun on this boat?" Her father refilled his glass and took another swig. "I hear cruise ships are jam-packed with entertainment."

Lacey stabbed the chicken leg with her knife. "There are nightly shows in the main auditorium. A comedy club. Bingo."

"Just bingo? No casino?"

"No." Lacey dropped her silverware with a loud clink. "Monarch Cruises is a family-oriented line. They never have casinos on their ships."

"Pity." Her father cocked his head. "I was mighty good at poker back in the day."

Lacey shut her eyes and silently counted to ten. A gentle buzz rattled the table, and she reached for her vibrating phone. She read the message from her coworker Nadia, lifted the cloth napkin from her lap, and tossed it on her plate. "I'm sorry. There's an emergency at the dining room. I need to go."

"Why does it have to be you?" Her father frowned. "You're not the captain."

"Don't worry about us." Her mom waved her off with both hands. "We'll be fine."

Lacey stood. "Enjoy your meal."

"Monarch ought to let you eat in peace," her dad grumbled as he sawed at his steak. "That's no way to treat employees, disturbing them during dinner."

Lacey clamped her lips in a tight smile and beat a hasty retreat from the restaurant while thanking God for the delightful disturbance.

She ducked into a staff hallway and pounded up the stairs to one of the main dining rooms on deck eleven. Exiting into the passage behind the galley, she swerved out of the way as a server in a black uniform with purple buttons zoomed past, holding a tray of food above his head. Staying close to the wall, Lacey walked toward the door that led into the eating area.

A colorful print caught her gaze as she passed a connecting hall where two people stood. Ricardo waved his hands at a large man leaning against a cleaning cart. The stranger's pineapple-and-lime cotton shirt partially stretched over his belly. He'd buttoned the top half. She guessed the lower buttons no longer met in the middle.

Lacey paused. "Good evening, Ricardo."

He spun around. "Lacey?"

"Is there a problem?"

"I was . . ." Ricardo straightened the white bandanna covering his hair. "This man . . . he is not supposed to be here."

The clatter of plates and silverware sounded from the kitchen entrance at their right. A chef called out an order, and several voices answered in chorus.

"Hello, sir." Lacey's practiced smile grew bigger as she directed her attention to the passenger. "Can I help you find something?"

"No thanks, cupcake." He scribbled on a small black notepad.

"You might not realize, but passengers aren't permitted here. This is the kitchen area. I wouldn't want you to get sideswiped by a racing waiter."

He flipped his notepad shut and smirked. "I'm not lost. Just doing my job."

"Job?"

"Check with the cruise director if it bothers you." He shouldered past her and exited into the main area.

"Do you know him?" she asked.

Ricardo gave a violent shake of his head. "No. Please excuse me. Desserts. I must finish them."

He hurried from the hallway as Lacey took her phone from her pocket. The dismissive trespasser provoked her. His suspicious behavior went far beyond that of the typical nosy cruiser sneaking a glimpse of the backstage process. Maybe Jon could solve the mystery. Before she dialed, a text appeared on the screen.

Nadia!

Lacey had forgotten her latest mission in the confusion. She bolted for the door. One emergency at a time.

CHAPTER 29

"Is this writing in yellow marker?" Lacey bent and studied the scrawls on the light walnut paneling of the bathroom stall. "Who brings a highlighter on a Caribbean cruise?"

"Sorry to call you here before your shift starts." Nadia wrung her hands. "I know it's not that important, but I wasn't sure whether to show Mr. Kapoor or clean it off without saying anything."

Lacey placed an arm around her and squeezed. "Your message came at the perfect time." She pulled her phone from her jacket pocket and took several pictures of the cuss words. "Did you check the other stalls?"

Nadia's eyes rounded like life preservers. "I didn't. Do you think there's more?"

It was a small restroom, three stalls total, on the far side of the dining room. Each was fully enclosed with a slatted wooden door. Nadia took the stall in the middle, and Lacey checked the one by the wall.

"Oh no," Nadia wailed.

Lacey hurried to the middle stall. Nadia pointed to the bottom half of the wall near the toilet. A tiny smiley face leered at them with a speech bubble containing a rude phrase. Lacey took another picture.

"Go ahead and clean it off." She tucked the phone in her pocket. "I'll report this to Mr. Kapoor. It may have been a fluke. Let's wait and see if it happens again."

Nadia nodded. "Sorry."

Lacey shook her head. "If anything else pops up, and I mean *anything*, call me."

She exited the bathroom and wound through the tables. If there was one place that guaranteed customer satisfaction, it was here. Diners talked and laughed as they enjoyed the MS *Buckingham*'s world-class culinary offerings. The scent of roasted duck with savory garlic mashed potatoes drifted by her nose. She hadn't eaten much at dinner.

"Lacey-bell!"

Lacey's gaze snapped to the entrance. Her father and mother stood in line at the front doors, waiting to be seated.

"What are you doing here?" She hurried over. "We already ate together."

Her father rubbed his stomach. "It's not often I get to eat this good. I want to enjoy it while I can."

Lacey glanced at her mother. "Are you still hungry, Mom?"

She looked at her husband. "I can drink a cup of coffee while your father eats."

The man at the front desk approached. "Are these your parents, Lacey? I'll give them a table by the window."

"Thank you, Dennis."

"Good evening, sir." He bowed to her father. "I don't know what we'd do without your daughter. She makes sure everything on this ship is perfect, whether it's in her job description or not."

"I expect nothing less from my little girl." Ronald Anderson nodded. "Don't you take advantage of her."

Jon's voice came from behind them. "Did I hear these are Lacey's parents?" He approached the group—impressive in his dress white uniform with black-and-gold epaulets on the shoulders.

Dennis introduced him. "This is our cruise director, Jonathan King."

Jon reached out. "It's an honor to meet you both." His warm tone welcomed them. He shook hands with Lacey's father and mother.

Lacey stiffened from her knees to her earlobes. Her brain spun. How could she separate them before it was too late?

"You're the cruise director?" Ronald leaned forward. "I had a question about the entertainment."

"Not now, Dad." She jumped in. "I need to discuss a matter with Mr. King. You and Mom enjoy your second dinner." Lacey grabbed Jon's arm and hauled him away from the pair. Dragging him from the dining room, she whispered, "I told you not to meet my parents."

"They don't know who I am," he whispered back. "To them, I'm simply the cruise director."

Lacey steered him to the elevator and pressed the button. The doors opened, and a noisy group spilled out of the car. She stepped aside to let them pass.

A man with a head-to-toe sunburn spotted them. The space where his sunglasses had sat gleamed white. "Hey, buddy." He slapped Jon on the back. "I'm loving this cruise."

"So glad we're doing our jobs." Jon returned the slap. "Be sure to use real sunblock, not the spray-on kind."

The sunburned man guffawed. "You got me. I'll remember that next time."

Lacey and Jon entered the elevator. She pressed the button and then crossed her arms, her body angled away.

He ducked his head to see her expression. "Why is this such a big deal? All I did was introduce myself."

She turned to him. "Do you have a good relationship with your father?"

One side of Jon's mouth twisted in a bemused smile. "He's my best friend."

"Then you can't relate." Lacey drew closer and took his hand in both of hers. "Take my word for it—the less time you spend with my dad, the better. Please avoid him for the rest of the voyage."

"Can you at least tell me why—"

She let go and faced the doors. "I don't want to talk about this anymore."

The elevator dinged and opened. A woman in a burgundy sequined dress stumbled in. The smell told them she'd been enjoying the open bar for a while. She met them with a wide-mouthed grin. "Hi, y'all." The lady grasped a box of popcorn as she swayed. She giggled at Jon and held out the box. "You want some?"

The popcorn tottered back and forth with its owner.

"Sure." He grabbed a couple pieces and tossed the kernels in his mouth. "Thanks."

"Don't mention it, cutie. How 'bout you?" She waved the box at Lacey.

"Um . . . sure. Thank you." Lacey grabbed a single piece of popcorn and raised it to her lips.

The elevator dinged again, and Jon and Lacey got off on the promenade deck. He pointed at a trash can as the door closed behind them.

"What?" she asked.

"You can throw it away now. I know you didn't eat the popcorn."

"You must think you've got me figured out." Lacey hid her arms behind her.

"Ah-ah." Jon grabbed at her hand. "Don't try and get rid of the evidence."

She spun around, but he enveloped her body and grabbed her fist. They feinted and dodged, and the weight of their earlier conversation dissipated. Teasing was easy. Family problems were hard. Better to put them off until later.

The Shippers watched with glee as their favorite couple bickered good-naturedly. Jon grabbed Lacey in a headlock. He received an elbow to the gut as they made their way out of sight.

Emily gave a thumbs-up to her crew. "This looks promising."

"Good ol' roughhousing." Althea chuckled. "Definitely an improvement."

Gerry agreed. "Their mood is friendlier."

"My second husband and I were friendly like that a lot." Althea nudged Daisy as the Shippers started down the hall. "That's why we had six kids."

"Althea, please." Daisy's cheeks colored, and she fiddled with the brooch at the neckline of her black lace blouse.

"Nothing wrong with a little horseplay. Keeps the relationship spicy."

The ladies walked to a side lounge at the end of the deck and settled at an empty table.

"I agree with Althea." Gerry slid her laptop out of her tote bag and opened it. "Every good romance novel throws in the PC when things start to heat up."

Daisy's smooth brow wrinkled. "Politically correct?"

Gerry locked her fingers together and whispered, "Physical contact."

Emily laid her hand on the table near the computer. "It's about time we saw forward movement. Gerry, make a note of this in the log. We'll observe them for the next few days and see if this flirtatious atmosphere continues."

"I wonder what changed." Gerry typed away. "Did anyone notice a catalyst? We might be able to use the same tactic in future cases."

Emily tapped the spot between her eyebrows with a finger. "He played the rescuing knight on Nevis when we were stuck in that gymnasium. But Lacey appeared colder than ever on the ride to the ship the next morning. I doubt she said two words to him."

"I can't figure our girl out." Althea fluffed the hair around her ears. "If a man did that for me, I'd melt at his feet in a puddle of goo."

"When you love deep and hurt deeper, it's hard to let people in." Emily pulled her fuzzy knit cardigan tight as the air-conditioning kicked on. "That's why our help is so crucial."

"She appears to be thawing," Althea said. "I hope it lasts."

"What if it doesn't?" Daisy asked. "Suppose they have a falling-out again?"

Emily leaned back on her chair. "Then we'll find another closet to lock them in."

Daisy cringed.

Althea laughed.

And Gerry took out her book.

CHAPTER 30

THERE SHE IS.

At the sight of Lacey, Jon's heart sped up and slowed down at the same time. Was that even possible? Excitement and calm flooded him.

It had taken twenty-five minutes to locate her, which was equivalent to a couple of hours in a busy cruise director's schedule. He wanted to fill her in on the drug-smuggling investigation and ask her to keep a sharp lookout. Jon stood at a distance while his lady love faced off with a manager.

"But, Mr. Kapoor"—Lacey's shoulders snapped straight, and her eyebrow rose—"we've found graffiti four times. It's making extra work for the cleaning crew, and it also undermines the standard of respectability of our cruise line. If other passengers see writing on the bathroom stalls, it makes us no better than a bus station."

"I agree with you, Lacey." The short man backed up a little. "But what can we do about it? Throw whoever it is off at the next port? I doubt she's traveling alone. Imagine the complaints from her spouse or family, the angry posts and vicious internet reviews. We have to let a few things go."

Lacey's breath hissed out between her teeth. "I'm not good at letting things go, Mr. Kapoor."

Jon chose that moment to interrupt. "She's *not* good at letting things go, Mr. Kapoor. I'm a firsthand witness."

"Have I got a tracking device on me?" She gave him a death glare, and he smiled.

"Regardless," the manager said, "we can't be sure who did it unless they're caught in the act, and we're not going to punish our passengers for such a small infraction as if they were a bunch of kindergarteners. Remember what our founder, J. P. McMillan, says: 'Treat the customer like your best friend.' Please turn a blind eye in this instance. We can't bother the guests."

The man walked off, and Lacey stomped her foot on the floor.

"It isn't fair. My 'best friend'"—she made air quotes with her fingers—"does whatever she pleases without any consequences, and the rest of us clean up the mess."

"I agree." Jon stood at her side and placed a hand on her elbow. "But I'm also inclined to agree with Mr. Kapoor. There isn't much we can do. People play pranks."

She rolled away from his touch. "Those people should be stopped."

"Laaaaace. What are you planning?"

"I'm not planning anything." She pivoted on her heel. "I'm doing my job to the best of my ability—making sure the MS *Buckingham* is a luxurious, graffiti-free place for our passengers to enjoy."

"Lace, I wanted to—"

She marched on without pause, and Jon shook his head. How could he fault her passionate attitude when it's what made him fall for her in the first place? But he almost pitied the bathroom scribbler. Once Lacey set her course, not even an iceberg would stop her.

A passenger pounded out a tone-deaf version of "Chopsticks" on the grand piano as Lacey hit the lobby. Two women in full-length evening gowns passed on the way to the main theater. Right behind them came a gentleman in a T-shirt and shorts with a clown-sized sparkly bow tie. Lacey caught one of the desk clerks laughing and glared at him.

Formal-dining night always brought out the comic relief, but no matter how ridiculous the costume, a good employee held it in.

"Hello, honey," her mother's voice called.

Lacey searched for her parents. They entered from a connecting hallway. Her mom wore a simple knee-length dress of pink chiffon. Locks of graying blond hair waved softly. Her hand was tucked in the crook of her husband's arm. He strode through the lobby in a fully decked out tuxedo, with shiny dress shoes that squeaked on the marble tiles.

"We've barely seen you since we arrived," he complained.

"I'm sorry." Lacey met them at the center of the room. "It stays crazy busy on a cruise ship. I don't get a lot of free time." She turned to her mother. "That's a great color on you."

"Yes, it is." Ronald patted the hand on his arm. "Reminds me of our wedding day. You wore pink then, didn't you?"

His wife flushed and nodded. "Thirty years ago."

He bent and kissed her cheek. "You look like it was only yesterday."

"What a lovely thing to say," a voice behind Lacey trilled.

Emily walked up in her gold blazer and matching pants. She stopped in front of Lacey's parents and studied their faces.

Lacey gestured to the new arrival. "Mom and Dad, this is Mrs. Emily Windsor."

Emily nodded. "I see the resemblance." She rested her fingers on Lacey's back. "You two must be proud of this beautiful girl here."

"Very proud." Mrs. Anderson smiled. "How do you know our daughter?"

Emily and Lacey looked at each other and laughed.

"That's a long story, Mom," Lacey said.

"Suffice it to say"—Emily patted her—"she helps watch over me while I live on board the MS *Buckingham*."

"You live here?" Lacey's mom blinked.

"Sounds heavenly." Her husband's eyes closed. "People to cook and clean and entertain you. What a genius idea."

Emily adjusted the front of her jacket. "I enjoy it. But it's thanks to people like Lacey—caring, compassionate, hardworking."

"She got that from me." Mr. Anderson's chin rose.

"I'm trying to find someone to take care of *her* for a change." Emily pinched the side of Lacey's sleeve and tugged. "But she's fighting me."

"I can take care of myself, Mrs. Windsor." Lacey brushed off Emily's fingers.

"Certainly you can." She nodded. "But that doesn't mean you have to do it all the time."

"My thoughts exactly." Her father gave Emily two thumbs up.

Lacey inched away. "I should get going. There's a delicate problem on the ship requiring my attention."

"Is it dangerous?" her mother asked.

"Oh, no." Lacey took another step back. "Just a sensitive matter which requires special oversight. I'll see you later."

She left her parents with Emily, although she knew it was risky. Lacey hoped the little matchmaker behaved herself. But it couldn't be helped. She had a bathroom vandal to catch.

CHAPTER 31

Silverware rattled as diners lurched on their seats. The dining room listed to one side, and Emily's water sloshed over the rim of her glass. She grabbed the edge of the table.

"My word! Peter must be driving tonight. I hope he's using the stabilizers."

Gerry nodded. "How did that boy ever make first mate? He drives like a teenager who just got his permit."

A light-green tinge colored Daisy's countenance. She shoved her pasta aside and pressed her fingers between her arched brows. "I discerned the water was a mite choppy. He must be doing his best."

"Baby, you don't look so good." Althea speared a truffle with her fork and popped it in her mouth. "Do you want me to walk you to the room?"

"No thank you." Daisy grasped her teacup. "Perhaps a sip of Earl Grey will settle my stomach. How many voyages must I make to fully conquer the motion sickness?"

Althea reached out and rubbed her arm. "I can grab you a seasick bag. Just holler."

"Back to what I was saying." Emily held on to her water glass with one hand and gestured with the other. "I met Lacey's parents in the lobby. They were both as nice as could be. Her mother was a quiet little thing, and her father was all that was charming. I'm glad Lacey came from a good home. Of course she would, seeing how kind and conscientious she is."

"Do you think they've met Jon?" asked Althea.

"Knowing Lacey, I doubt it." Emily sighed. "She's made progress, but having him meet the folks is a big leap for anyone."

"We should introduce them." Althea waved at their server. "Isaac, can you get us a plate of saltine crackers please?" She put down her fork and scooted closer to Daisy. "Those'll help the nausea."

"I'm sorry, dear." Emily patted Daisy's white knuckles. "I'm completely ignoring your health. Forgive me for being horrible."

"No such thing." Daisy waved her hand. "I always get this way on rough-weather days. I'll be fine as soon as the floor stops rocking." She stood on unsteady feet as the ship rolled. "But perhaps I *will* visit the powder room."

Althea hopped to her side and took her by the arm. "Here, I'll go with you. I wanted to touch up my lipstick anyway."

Emily squinted. "I saw Jon walk that direction. Pin him down if you get the chance. Find out anything you can."

The two headed off with their new assignment, and Gerry quirked her lips at Emily. "What exactly are they supposed to talk to Jon about outside the bathroom?"

"You never know." Emily took a sip of water. "Every conversation is an opportunity."

Lacey stood near the staff entrance to the dining room. Her pen was poised above a pad of paper. From this position, she could observe anyone entering or leaving the restrooms. Her feet stood ten inches apart, braced against the jerking of the ship. It had been a rocky evening, and more than one customer had walked by cradling their bellies. The women's bathroom boasted a line of people out the door.

"Hey, Lace." Jon walked up, but she was busy writing. "Isn't this your free shift? I'd like to tell you something."

"I'm busy." She barely acknowledged him.

"Doing what?" He peered over her shoulder.

A list of times followed by boxes filled the sheet. Some contained a check mark, and some didn't. Lacey froze as Jon's face drew close to her own. Her pulse stuttered, and her cheek tingled when he brushed against her. She tried to act natural as she updated her notes.

"I've been systematically checking the stalls in the ladies' bathroom whenever I get the chance." She kept her voice low so the women in line didn't hear her. "This is the only location with writing. That tells me it's a guest who's been eating in this dining room. The words are always written in print and far too neat for it to be done by an inebriated passenger. The culprit is fully aware of their actions."

Jon's nose was close enough to her neck that his breath warmed her skin, but she continued.

"I've checked this restroom five times a day for the past three days and always found writing in the evenings. Last night, I spent my break monitoring the stalls every fifteen minutes and was able to narrow down to a specific window when the writing appeared. When I checked at 8:30 p.m., the stalls were clean. At 8:45 p.m., there were scribbles in the last stall by the wall."

"Impressive, Miss Sherlock." He reached around and turned her body. "But how do you plan to discover the right person?"

"I already have." She savored his shocked expression as she tucked the notepad in her pocket. "I visited the security team and had them show me the footage from that specific time. Five people used the restroom during that period. Two of them were Shippers. I know they'd never do something so childish, so that leaves us with three suspects."

Lacey grasped his waist in her excitement, oblivious to the people around them. True, this vandalism came at an opportune moment, when she appreciated a distraction from her parents. But even on a good week, she'd be livid at the casual destruction. No one messed with her ship.

Jon enjoyed the proximity of Lacey clutching the sides of his shirt. Her eyes sparkled as she explained her methods. His fingers slid farther down her arms. Could she be any cuter? He noticed Althea and Daisy watching them from the line at the bathroom. They'd report this physical contact to Emily for sure.

"Judging from the language used," Lacey said, "I'm inclined to think it's a younger person, and a single suspect fits that description. Going from my gut, she's the one."

"Even if that's true, what can you do about it?" He studied a freckle near her right ear. "Mr. Kapoor told you not to bother the guests."

Lacey's gaze sharpened as she focused behind him. "Go with me on this."

She dragged him by the arm to where the line of women stood near the restroom. It was a popular place at mealtime, and not everyone fit inside as they waited their turn. Two women in sundresses chatted at the front, while a mother and daughter waited behind them. The daughter, a preteen girl, wore a cropped T-shirt, hoodie, ragged jean shorts, and flip-flops—hardly the dress code the cruise line asked the passengers to follow for the dining room. She ignored her mother as she played with her phone.

"Don't worry about me," he said as they neared the facilities. "I went to the bathroom earlier."

Lacey dropped his arm and made a face at him. She leaned in close and whispered, "Follow my lead." Lacey led him directly behind the line at the door and raised her voice. "They're closing in on the person writing on the bathroom stalls."

"Is that so?" Jon matched his volume to hers.

"They've identified the specific window of time one of the incidents happened." She turned her back to the line and pointed at a small black half globe on the ceiling. "When they study the security footage, that will narrow it to a few suspects."

"It shouldn't take long after that." He manufactured an overdramatic scowl.

Lacey rewarded him with a smile and a fervent nod. "That poor lady. You know what comes next when they catch her."

Jon followed her cue, and he saw the preteen's head cock, her ear tuned to their conversation. "How do you mean?"

"I bet she doesn't realize cruise ships have a jail. I wouldn't want to spend even five minutes in that cell. It's cold and dark and right next door to the morgue."

The young girl's head whipped around. Her eyes bulged like two Ping-Pong balls.

Jon tried to remain deadpan, but it took effort as he looked at Lacey's butter-wouldn't-melt-in-her-mouth expression. "The morgue, huh?"

"Can you imagine being locked up right next to a dead body?" She shivered. "A horrific price to pay for a few scribbles, but we can't make exceptions. Young or old, the person responsible will suffer big-time."

"Too bad. I'd rather spend my vacation at the pool than in the brig."

"Oh well." Lacey shook her head. "It's probably too late for her now."

"Poor lady." He copied her head movement and adopted a morose expression.

The girl in line squeaked, "Mom, I don't need to go anymore."

Jon watched her out of the corner of his eye.

"I'll be at the table." She ducked out of line and pulled the hood of her jacket over her head.

He marveled at Lacey, but she wasn't finished. She spun as the preteen attempted to pass by, blocking her way.

"Oh, excuse me." She drilled the preteen with her gaze. "I hope you enjoy your vacation—without any problems."

"Yeah, thanks," the girl muttered and scurried away.

The corners of Lacey's mouth lifted. She stuck her chin out and gave a curt nod at the girl's retreating back. "I bet she doesn't use this bathroom for the rest of the cruise."

Jon shuddered. "You could put frost on an ice cube. Is this how you're going to be with our ch . . . cherished younger passengers?" He bit the inside of his lip.

Almost slipped that time.

"Young or old, we have to keep them in line." Lacey's eyebrow rose.

"And speaking of which . . ." She walked forward to where Althea and Daisy lingered. "Fancy meeting you two here. How are you ladies doing?"

Daisy's hands cuddled her petite frame. "I'm afraid I'm feeling indisposed."

Althea looped her arm around Daisy's waist, supporting her. "She's seasick again."

The suspicious look dropped off Lacey in an instant. "I'm sorry. Can I get you anything, Mrs. Masterson?"

"You wouldn't happen to have some ground anywhere that doesn't rock, would you?" Daisy said.

Jon stepped up. "My mother used to suffer from the same problem and spent many an ocean voyage huddled on the bathroom floor. Then a housemaid suggested mixing a dash of green tea with ginger ale, and it worked wonders. Should I have the bartender re-create the concoction?"

Althea jiggled her friend. "Give it a try, baby."

Daisy gave one regal nod as if she were bestowing an honor on him. "Anything would be better than this Tilt-A-Whirl inside of me."

"I'll ask the bartender to mix it and meet you at your table." Jon placed a hand on Lacey's shoulder. "If you ladies will excuse us, Lacey and I have to discuss something important."

Althea giggled. "Don't mind at all. Discuss away."

Jon stopped to speak with the bartender about the ginger ale for Daisy, then led Lacey to a deserted balcony outside the dining room.

The wind blew silky strands from her neat, upswept hairstyle, and she tucked them behind her ears. "My break is ending. Tonight, I'm passing out confetti poppers at the evening show. I can imagine the disruptions when impatient—"

"Lacey." He laid one finger on her lips. "I didn't invite you out here for stargazing. It's important."

She stared at him. "Okay."

He lowered his finger. Now that he'd gained her attention, he wasn't sure where to start. "There's a reason I became cruise director for the MS *Buckingham*."

"You mean it wasn't your overwhelming charm that got you the job?" She quirked her head to the side and grinned.

Jon sucked air between his teeth and scratched his head. "My charisma didn't hurt." He grew serious. "But an unhappy circumstance led to the vacancy. I'm here because Dexter Newberg, the former cruise director, drowned."

"What?" She recoiled. "I didn't hear anything about it."

"The company kept it quiet on purpose. The authorities suspect foul play, and it appears Newberg was involved in a cocaine-smuggling operation that's been using Monarch ships."

"That's been *what*?" Lacey's nostrils flared. "They're using *our* ships to transport drugs?"

Jon took hold of her elbows. "We're attempting to figure out how they're doing this, but it's hard to keep track of a thousand crew members and five times that many passengers. Your help would be much appreciated."

"What do you want me to do?"

"I want you to put those deductive abilities to work for something bigger than a bathroom scribbler." He ran his hands down her arms until his fingers clasped hers. "Lacey Anderson, I've been alone too long. Will you do me the honor of joining forces to catch the smugglers?"

Lacey's thoughts swelled in a giant tidal wave of questions.

Cocaine on Monarch Cruises? Who was behind the operation? How were they getting the drugs on and off the ship?

And why was Jon—

Her eyes narrowed. "Please don't misunderstand my next question. I think you're pretty great, but . . . why did Monarch ask you to investigate?"

"Why?" He looked to the right and let go of her hands. "You don't believe I'll do a good job?"

"That's not what I meant. But you'd never even been a cruise director before our last voyage. Why did they ask you to oversee a crisis this important?"

He wasn't answering. Had she hurt his feelings? But her question was a legitimate one. Was there something he wasn't telling her?

Jon cleared his throat. "I'm sorry, Lace. There are certain details I can't reveal at the moment. This is a very complicated problem. Two other Monarch ships have been involved in recent drug busts. One more scandal, and our reputation as a family line is shot. I'm not the only one involved in the investigation. We beefed up the security team for this ship, and the company hired a retired FBI agent. With your help, we can catch these guys in no time. You know every crew member on this boat and would be the first to notice anything suspicious."

Suspicious. The word rang a bell.

"Jon!" She grabbed his wrist. "I remember one passenger. He was skulking around near the kitchen on deck eleven. There was definitely something off about him."

He straightened. "Did you catch his name?"

"No."

"What did he look like?"

"Late fifties. Mostly gray hair. Wearing an awful Hawaiian shirt that barely covered his potbelly."

"Aw, cupcake." A new voice spoke. "Do you have to be so mean?"

Lacey jerked to the side. The uncooperative man from the galley hallway stood at the entrance, his arms crossed over a different but equally loud printed shirt.

He sauntered onto the balcony and shut the glass door behind him. "That's no way to talk about a guy who's offering you his protection and expertise."

"Lacey"—Jon grimaced—"this is Reid Collins, the retired agent I told you about. He's been working on this case since our last voyage.

Mr. Collins, this is Miss Lacey Anderson. Please address her with respect."

Collins popped a tiny white bubble and pulled the wad of gum from his mouth. He tossed it over the railing and held out spit-covered fingers.

"Pleased to meet you, Miss Anderson."

Lacey stared at the saliva-coated hand and glanced at Jon. If this was the best assistance corporate had given him, no wonder he needed help.

CHAPTER 32

THE BONE-TIRED VACATIONERS STUMBLED onto the MS *Buckingham* as a long day in port drew to a close. Lacey stood at her post in the lobby to offer assistance when necessary and bolster the spirits of the people with bags full of unnecessary trinkets and buyer's remorse. Abby once dubbed it Affirmation Duty. Except this time, Lacey had two motives. Offer the customers moral support. And catch a smuggling ring.

Easy-peasy.

"Welcome back." Lacey greeted the worn-out passengers as they wobbled past her. "I hope you enjoyed yourself."

"You bet I did. Check this out." A middle-aged woman showed off the banana-yellow poncho she'd haggled over with a street vendor.

Lacey oohed and aahed in the correct places. "Fifty dollars? I'm surprised you talked him down so much."

Lacey eyed every bag that came aboard and made a note of anyone wearing clothes baggy enough to disguise something underneath while still performing her normal hostess duties. She answered questions about the after-dinner show, complimented purchases, and directed a pair of cherry-red passengers to the infirmary for sunburn cream. They plank-walked away with their arms pointed straight out to keep any part of their body from touching the rest.

"There you are." Jon appeared at her side. "I've been missing you all day."

She shushed him and answered another person's question. "Yes, sir. You can use the money you exchanged at the next port of call."

"Did you miss me too?" Jon kept his eyes on the passengers and didn't see the glare she gave him.

"Please go away. Do you want everyone on the ship to know we're a couple?"

He shrugged. "I wouldn't mind."

"I would." Lacey stepped a few feet away, but he stayed at her heels.

He tweaked the chignon at the nape of her neck. "I was wondering if we—"

A male voice bellowed, "What a miserable place that was!"

Lacey backed away from Jon.

Her father stalked into the lobby and flung his arms wide. "It's good to be back in civilization."

Her mother followed behind him, carrying several shopping bags.

Lacey avoided Jon's questioning glance and hurried to her parents. "What's wrong, Dad? Didn't you enjoy the port of call?"

"I would have if it weren't full of thieves."

"Excuse me, sir." Jon joined them. "Is there anything I can help you with?"

"You're the cruise director, correct?" Her father tugged his straw hat lower and held out a hand. "Thank you for offering. I would *love* some help."

Jon shook the outstretched hand. "My pleasure."

Lacey shoved in between them, breaking the contact. "What happened? Did a pickpocket steal your wallet?"

"You could say a one-armed bandit robbed me." Her dad collapsed onto a lobby armchair and spread his legs out in front of him. "It's no big deal. I lost a little money."

"Lost it, how?" She suspected the answer but wanted him to admit it with his own lips.

"The beach was blazing hot. Your mom and I decided to go into one of the hotels to cool off. They had a casino in there and—" He pointed his index finger at Jon. "How do I file a complaint to the city? They shouldn't take advantage of tourists."

Lacey blocked her father and pushed Jon away before he answered. "I'll manage this."

Jon studied her parents. "I could check—"

"No." She held up a hand. "I know my dad. Let me deal with this problem."

Lacey recognized the stubborn set of his mouth. He wanted to argue.

"Please," she whispered.

Jon searched her face. He started to say something but stopped. He nodded and left without a word.

She made sure Jon was out of earshot before she sank onto the chair by her dad. "You gambled in the casino?" Lacey's gaze darted around the crowded lobby, and she lowered her voice. "How much did you lose?"

"Not that much." He scooted his legs against the chair and tugged his hat lower. "I got a payout from the little machine, but when I switched to the Big Bertha . . ." His shoulders rose. "I bet they were rigged."

"How much, Dad?"

He ducked his head and mumbled, "Twenty-two hundred."

"Two thousand two hundred dollars!" Lacey sprang from her chair. "How did you spend that much on a slot machine?"

Her father's lips scrunched into a pout. "If they had decent entertainment on this boat, I wouldn't have been so bored. It's not like my daughter is making time for me in her busy schedule."

"But two thousand . . ." Lacey tried not to calculate how many hours of work that equaled. "Where did you get the cash?"

"Your mother had her debit card with her, and . . ." He waved his hand in a circle.

"Mom." Lacey's voice sank. "Why did you give it to him?"

Her mother's chin quivered. "Your father was sure he would hit the jackpot. He wanted to buy you a special present for your birthday."

Lacey covered her face with her hands, the air leaving her nose in tiny, derisive puffs. "Happy birthday to me."

"Are you sick?" her mom asked.

"I'm fine." She looked up, but her mother wasn't speaking to her. She was leaning over her husband.

He slumped forward, his arms propped on his knees. "I think today was too much for me."

Lacey's jaw clenched, and her gaze traveled to the painted ceiling overhead. Angelic cherubs peeked at her from behind flowering trees. She counted the mischievous infants in the pastel fresco.

One.

Two.

Three.

"My chronic fatigue is flaring up." Her father staggered from the chair and swayed.

Lacey's fingers clutched at the sides of her skirt, wrinkling the starched material. A phone rang at the front desk. Laughter exploded from a group entering the side door. A child whined for a snack.

Four.

Five.

Her mother grabbed his arm. "Lacey, help me get your father to our stateroom. The color's drained out of his face."

Six.

Seven.

"Don't bother her," he said. "I don't want to be a burden. She needs to get back to her job."

Eight.

In her peripheral vision, she saw her mother loop an arm around her husband's waist.

"Try to make time for us tonight, honey. We can have dinner together if your father's recovered."

Nine.

"Bye, Lacey-bell. I'm sorry my health ruined your birthday."

Her parents headed for the elevators, and Lacey let out the breath she was holding.

"Ten."

She grabbed the top of a nearby chair and waited for her stomach to get off the merry-go-round.

Emily and Gerry sat on the couch behind where Lacey's family had gathered. A frosted-glass wall blocked them from view. This time, the eavesdropping was truly accidental. Gerry had wanted to observe the passengers, mining the crowd for colorful characters to use in her novel, and Emily joined her on a whim. They'd already taken a seat when Lacey and her parents walked over.

The ladies communicated with their eyes. They argued without words. Should they stay? Should they leave? What if Lacey noticed them? She might get the wrong idea. Their silent debate continued as the parents left. They waited a few seconds for the family to disperse, then let out a mutual sigh.

Until Lacey walked around the corner. She locked on them, and her left brow rose.

Their frames hunched as if they were trying to fold up like umbrellas.

Emily rushed to explain. "Dear, we didn't mean to—"

Lacey held her hand stiff like a Stop sign.

"Lacey." Malaya called from the front desk and waved her arm. "Can you help us, please? This couple wants more information about the ballroom classes."

Lacey squeezed her lids shut for a brief second, smiled, and pivoted. She walked the few yards to the couple. "I'm so glad you asked. You'll love the ballroom classes. I took one myself, and it's better than a thirty-minute workout."

Her cheerful chatter carried to the regretful eavesdroppers. Gerry ducked her head. Emily placed a hand on her shoulder and patted.

Small convulsive shudders shook her stoic friend as she fought for control. Geraldine Paroo might masquerade as a cold, grumpy spinster, but inside, she was a hot spring of empathy.

"It's okay, dear." Emily pressed her lips together.

Lacey finished helping the customer and stalked away.

Emily rose from her seat. "Stay here, Gerry. I'll explain it to her."

She hurried after Lacey's rigid form, but the girl was practically running. She outpaced her by half a hallway and disappeared around the corner. Emily kept on until she also passed the corner. She walked quickly despite the growing ache in her spine, examining each connecting corridor.

Lacey was nowhere.

Emily paused, rubbed at the hollow in her lower back, and tried to imagine where Lacey would go on this deck for privacy. Her head turned to the starboard side. An outer balcony stretched the length of the ship. Right before dinner hour, when the passengers were returning from town, it would be deserted.

Emily made her way to the double doors and pulled on the handle. A blustery wind hit her as she walked outside. She scanned right and left. The wooden floorboards stretched empty in both directions. Except . . . a crumpled white heap by the wall caught her eye. The setting sun hindered her vision.

Emily peered in that direction until she saw the huddle move. Lacey crouched above the ground, not quite sitting, with her arms hugging her legs. She shot up an instant later and stomped her foot against the floor. Her head tilted to the sky, her mouth wide open as if she were screaming. Lacey pushed her hands into her hair and grabbed it like she wanted to tear it out.

Emily considered going inside. The poor girl obviously didn't want company. Emily grasped the knob, but Lacey spotted her. She unwound her hands from her hair. Dead air stretched between them like an awkward chasm.

Lacey spoke first.

"So now you know." Her voice wavered. "I have a loser for a father."

Emily thought it best to stay where she was. "I'm sure he's sorry for his mistake, dear."

"Of course he is." Lacey laughed. "Every time. When he left me waiting in the cold for an hour and a half after my dance recital, he was sorry. When he declared bankruptcy and moved us to a new town during my senior year, he was sorry. And when he blows the money I send them on online shopping sprees, he's always sorry." The fading sun highlighted the wet tracks streaking Lacey's cheeks. She looked out at the water and drew a shuddery breath.

Emily inched near, but the distraught girl didn't move. Emily closed the distance and stood at her side. "Does your father have a gambling problem?"

Lacey's lip quirked. "Not at all. He has a maturity problem."

The correct response eluded Emily, so she remained silent.

"It was like growing up with a ten-year-old for a dad." Lacey stared at the clouds. "If he wanted something, he bought it. If the boss offended him, he quit. My mother worked three jobs to support us, while he did anything and everything he pleased."

Emily whispered a silent prayer for wisdom. She reached out. After taking one of Lacey's hands between her own wrinkled fingers, she held on as the poor girl talked.

"Dad doesn't have a drinking problem. Doesn't smoke. Never cheated on my mom. You might wonder why I'm so hard on him."

"You're exhausted."

"Yeah." Lacey laughed bitterly. "Maybe Dad's illness is catching—not that he's ever been diagnosed by a doctor. I had a friend in high school with a genuine case of chronic fatigue syndrome. Poor Leah fought to live a normal life. She struggled to keep up in classes and refused to let CFS beat her. But when Dad heard her symptoms"—Lacey rolled her eyes as she shut her lids—"he immediately decided it must be the ailment he had. It was the perfect excuse to keep him from applying for any more jobs. Whenever inconvenient responsibilities arose that he didn't want to deal with, he had another *attack*." She yanked her hand from Emily's.

"What made him that way?"

Lacey snorted. "I have no idea. Some people are just born lazy." She scrubbed her sleeve over her face, wiping away the traces of her tears. "At least the cruise ends tomorrow. He'll go home, and I can have peace again."

Emily studied the disillusioned girl in front of her. She doubted any distance between Lacey and her father would bring complete peace. But this wasn't the time to mention it. Let her believe whatever gave her relief.

For now.

CHAPTER 33

Jon grabbed a handful of velvet-soft rose petals and spread them around the polished floor of Cloud Nine, the most exclusive dining venue on the ship. It was an intimate location at the top of everything, far away from the noise and bustle below. Plush red benches lined the circular outdoor deck, and a table for two sat in the center. The staff had created a twinkle-light wonderland complete with a sideboard buffet of the most luxurious dishes in the chef's repertoire. What would his sensible Lacey's reaction be? Delight or disdain?

"You shouldn't have." Collins's voice intruded.

Jon sprinkled the remaining petals on the floor. "This isn't for you."

"Kinda figured." He plopped on a cushy bench and rested his arms on its back. "So what's the big news?"

"I got an email from corporate about thirty minutes ago." Jon straightened and brushed off his hands. "The authorities found another stash of cocaine on one of our ships—the MS *Royal*. While it was in the Bermuda port, police arrested a crew member making a deal on the street. They came aboard with the dogs and found more in his cabin locker."

"What did your bosses say?" Collins leaned forward on his seat.

"They were happy they kept this one out of the news and hope the arrested worker will disclose the whole operation."

"He probably doesn't know much. Drug mules do what they're told for the cash."

"I'm afraid you're right."

"But this arrest might make the smuggling ring switch to a different cruise line, once they realize you're onto them."

"Does it sound terrible to say I hope so?" Jon gave a rueful smile. "I want these guys caught, but I also want them far away from Monarch."

"Perfectly normal." Collins eyed the fancy spread. "Throwing a little party to celebrate?"

"Not exactly." Jon grinned. "But I figured one night off wasn't too much to ask for."

Lacey admired the bouquet of deep-purple orchids as she climbed the stairs to deliver the flowers to Cloud Nine. Was the couple already there? Lacey hoped she wouldn't be intruding. She reached the top and knocked on the door before grasping the knob. It swung open, and she stumbled forward. A strong pair of arms caught her.

"Jon!" She sounded too excited even to her own ears.

"Falling for me?" He tugged on a wisp of hair at her ear.

Lacey noted he was out of uniform, wearing a crisp white shirt that stretched across his wide shoulders, along with black trousers and shiny dress shoes. She struggled to remember why she was there. "Oh, the flowers."

She checked to ensure the orchids weren't crushed. Fluffing the petals with her fingers, she surveyed Cloud Nine.

Table set. Buffet prepared. Chopin drifting through the sound system. Flawless.

Jon took the bouquet and wandered away.

She did one last spot check. "What time does the couple get here?"

"Right now." He retrieved a suit coat from the chair, shrugged into it, and held the flowers out to her with both hands. "Happy birthday."

Lacey paused before accepting the bouquet and looked around. "I'm confused . . . this is all for us?"

"All for you." He waved at the dinner table with its expensive china and twenty-four-karat utensils. "I know you've had a tough day because of your father, and I decided you deserved better than wilted lettuce."

Lacey blinked at hyperspeed to keep the tears at bay. She shifted the orchids to the crook of her arm and picked up one of the golden spoons. "Do cruise directors get a discount?" She put it back. "Never mind. Even if you do, it still must cost a fortune. This is too extravagant."

Jon chuckled. "I admit this isn't the reaction I was expecting, but I should've known. It's why I love you."

"What? You . . . you—"

"Love you?" Jon walked around the table, took the flowers from her, and set them on a chair. He placed his hands behind her back and urged her closer. "I do. Very much. For a very long time. And I plan to keep loving you for even longer. At least a lifetime."

The frozen barricade guarding her heart melted at his confession. Emotion stopped her throat. She tilted forward until her forehead pressed against his chest.

"I'm sorry," she whispered.

He stiffened. "Sorry for what?"

She swallowed hard. "I'm sorry for running away back then. For avoiding you when you showed up here. For . . . for everything."

"Oh, thank God." He laughed as he crushed her to himself. "I thought you were rejecting me. Again."

Lacey sniffled. "Nope. Never again."

A strong gust of wind invaded their private moment, knocking the orchids from the chair. They hit the floor and tumbled from their wrapping. The petals scattered on the deck.

"Oh no!" Lacey knelt by the fractured arrangement. She gathered the flowers and picked at the slender fallen pieces.

"Leave them." Jon bent down. "I'll get you another bouquet."

"I don't want another one." She reached under a chair to snag a petal.

"This is the bouquet I was holding when you said you loved me. Nothing can replace that."

His hands took hold of hers, and she focused on him.

"You're right. I'll do it." He released her and crouched. His fingers gently retrieved the stray petals and dropped them on his open palm. "Why don't you relax? I'll get this."

Lacey straightened and walked to the five-foot-high wall that concealed their hideaway from the decks far below. The ocean glimmered in the early evening, and the fading twilight painted the low-hanging clouds a heavenly array of lavender and coral shades.

Jon moved behind her. He set the rewrapped flowers and petals on the bench seat and folded his arms around her in a back hug, stooping to press the side of his cheek against her own.

She sighed. "It's obvious why they named this place Cloud Nine."

His torso vibrated against hers. "Someone told me it used to be called the Crow's Nest in the beginning."

"The Crow's Nest? Like on a pirate ship?"

Jon nodded against her skin. "Monarch created it as a special frill for passengers who wanted a picturesque dinner spot to get down on one knee, but hardly anyone reserved it. The owner couldn't figure out why no one was taking advantage of the romantic location until his wife called him a fool. She said no woman wanted to be proposed to in a place named after a screechy bird."

"Sounds like a smart lady."

"She is. Are you hungry?"

"A little. Funny, I don't recall hearing that story before." A frigid breeze hit them, and Lacey wrapped her arms around her middle. "I should've brought a jacket."

Jon released her and opened the top of the padded bench at their side. He withdrew a fleece blanket, closed the lid, and wrapped the material around her—followed by his arms.

"There's a gourmet feast waiting. Though I wish I could eat it without letting you go."

She turned in his arms and tilted her chin. "Food is overrated."

Jon's eyes twinkled, and he lowered his head. But she leaned back and raised her gaze. "There's something I should tell you." The ship's stack marred the view and blocked the stars with its white plume of smoke.

The arms around her tensed. As she looked at Jon's face, she saw his smile fading.

"Don't worry. It's not about us. Not exactly. It's about . . . my family."

His muscles relaxed. "I expected there was more to the story."

Lacey bit her lip. "It's not a pretty one. I'm afraid it doesn't have a happy ending. But I'm willing to tell you if you want to listen."

Jon sidestepped with her, never letting their bodies separate, and sank onto the bench, pulling Lacey down with him. He tucked the blanket tight around her. "I've got as much time as you need."

Her heart sprang open at his unconditional acceptance. She took a deep, fortifying breath. "When we had our little talk at the lighthouse, there were embarrassing details I left out."

Jon's arms loosened, but he didn't let her go. Lacey peered up at him. She had his full attention.

"Two and a half years ago, I flew home for a visit and found a foreclosure notice taped to the front door. My dad had taken a second mortgage to finance a 'surefire' investment that flopped. I managed to stave off the bank by signing as his guarantor, but I'm still paying for his mistake on the first of every month." Lacey's cheeks heated as she spread out her family's dirty laundry. "You've met my father. He's a sweet, charming, and, I admit it, sincere man . . . In some ways, you remind me of him." She pulled away far enough that the evening air chilled the empty space between them. "That's what terrified me. I was afraid I'd end up babysitting another loser for the rest of my life."

The hum of the ship's engines and muted voices from the decks below were the only sounds. She waited for him to protest, but Jon said nothing. He watched her, waiting for anything she wanted to give him.

"You're not my father." Lacey bent toward his warmth and placed a hand on his chest. "I know that now. It sounds pathetic to say 'I'm sorry.'

It's not enough for being an idiot back then and hurting you. But I am . . . I am so, so sorry."

His rapid pulse beat under her fingertips.

"I wish we could've had this talk years ago." Jon brushed at the tear sneaking across her cheek. "We've wasted too much time." His irrepressible smile appeared. "But it's going to be a whole lot of fun making up for it."

"That's it?" She studied his expression. "You don't want me to grovel?"

He puckered his lips and wrinkled his brow. "Tempting. But that doesn't sound nearly as enjoyable as my plan."

Something unwound deep inside of Lacey. She bracketed Jon's face with her hands and stared at him. Her soul unlocked its last hidden stronghold and opened to the man in front of her, and she reveled in the freedom of meeting his eyes—no more misunderstandings or secrets between them.

CHAPTER 34

EMILY RAPPED TWICE ON THE door, paused, and knocked three more times. No one answered. She tried again, with the same result.

"They might be asleep," Gerry said. "Like we should be." She tugged the black hood of her jacket onto her head and leaned against the wall.

"I told them three o'clock sharp." Emily raised her knuckles again.

The door swung open before she knocked. Althea stood before her. At least, she assumed it was Althea. The woman wore a black tracksuit, leather gloves, and oversized Jackie O sunglasses. A thick scarf wrapped around her head, obscuring half her face.

With one finger, she lowered the fabric below her mouth and whispered. "Daisy refuses to get up. Once the girl is out, it's easier to wake the Sphinx."

Emily humphed and pushed by her. "I'll take care of this." She marched to the single bed closest to the bathroom and shook her friend's delicate figure. "Daisy, it's mission time."

Daisy moaned and rolled away, tugging the padded white duvet over her head.

Emily poked a finger in her back. "Daisy Mae Randolph Masterson, you're delaying the whole operation."

"Go without me," Daisy mumbled from underneath the covers.

Emily looked at Althea and Gerry in the doorway. They shrugged.

"I think we should leave her," said Gerry.

"We're all in this together." Emily grabbed the comforter and sheets and flipped them to the end of the bed.

Daisy lay there in a black velvet housecoat.

"See," Emily said. "You're already dressed for the occasion. All you have to do is stand on your feet."

Daisy curled in a tight ball and groaned. "What good would I be? It's a crazy idea anyway."

Emily took her hand and nudged her to an upright position. "Crazy or not, it's for Lacey. The poor girl has had a hard week. We have to make sure the rest of her life isn't that way. Don't do it for me. Do it for her."

The sleepy woman released a long-suffering sigh, swung her legs out of bed, and stuffed her feet into her tasseled slippers. Her bones creaked as she stood. She shuffled to the dressing table against the wall.

"Where are you going?" Gerry asked.

"I have to fix my hair," Daisy drawled.

Emily grabbed a black sun hat from a hook on the wall and plopped it on her head. "There you go. You're gorgeous. Let's move." She placed both hands behind Daisy's shoulders and propelled her from the room.

The Shippers padded down the silent corridor. Not a soul in sight—most passengers were sound asleep behind the shiny wooden doors. They reached the bank of elevators and took one to the administration floor, where Jon's office was located. Once they exited the car, they tiptoed to their destination, keeping an eye out for crew members.

Althea pointed to a security camera in the corner and gathered her scarf closer. "If they catch us, we're done for."

"Remind me again why we're doing this," Daisy said.

Emily drew a slow breath and explained one more time. "Lacey broke it off with Ricardo, and she appears much more relaxed around Jon. That's progress. All they need is a little more one-on-one interaction. If we can change her schedule so she's always at the same event as him, I'm sure nature will take its course."

"His office is probably locked," Gerry argued.

Emily slipped a key ring out of her pocket and jingled it.

Daisy gasped. "Did you steal those?"

"Of course not. One of the maids dropped it while she was cleaning this floor, and I happened to pick it up for her. I'll return them as soon as we're finished."

"She stole them." Althea cackled and slapped her on the back.

Emily cringed at the forceful love tap. "Here's his office."

She inserted the key in the lock. It opened easily. The four scurried inside and shut the door.

"I hope we don't regret this," Gerry said.

"I already do." Daisy flopped onto the cushy chair in front of the desk and crossed her legs.

"Oooh, candy." Althea yanked off her sunglasses, dug in a glass container on the side table, and pulled out a gold foil–covered chocolate. "I love hazelnuts."

Emily sat behind the desk, switched on the lamp, and pressed the power button on the computer. The screen lit, and the log-in box waited.

Gerry peered over her head. "Password protected. It figures. Now what do we do?"

Emily hit a few keys, pressed Enter, and she was in.

Gerry backed away and stared. "How did you do that?"

She tilted her nose in the air. "Jon signed in when I stopped by the other day. I spied which keys his fingers were hitting."

Althea grabbed another piece of candy and sank onto the chair beside Daisy. "You missed your calling. You should have been a secret agent. How you ever had the forethought to— What? What is it, baby?"

Emily stared at the computer, gobsmacked by what she saw.

Drugs?

The email popped up the moment she signed in. Jon must have left it open.

She reread the contents and looked at her waiting friends. "Girls, criminals might be using the MS *Buckingham* to smuggle cocaine."

"What on earth?" Daisy raised her palms in horror.

Althea clicked her tongue, and Gerry took out her notebook.

"It says here"—Emily squinted as she leaned—"they arrested a crew member in Bermuda. He had the drugs hidden in his locker, but this isn't the first time they've caught someone. A group is targeting Monarch vessels."

"How dare they use *our* ship to move their filthy junk!" Althea thumped the armrest.

Emily held up a finger and shushed her. "What's that noise?"

She flipped the lamp off, and the Shippers sat in the dark with only the faint light from the computer screen. The sound of footsteps echoed through the hallway.

"Do you think they'll catch us?" whispered Althea.

Daisy clapped a hand over her roommate's mouth.

The gentle whir of the computer sounded like a jet airplane in the quiet office. Four pairs of ears listened as the heavy clomping passed by and continued down the hall. The women exhaled in unison.

"That shaved ten years off my life," said Gerry. "And I don't have much to spare."

"Let's keep the lamp off." Emily maneuvered the mouse and clicked on the Schedules folder. "We can't leave until we change Lacey's assignments to match with—"

The office door flung open, and the glare from the fluorescent bulbs overhead blinded them.

The four women turned in unison.

"What are you doing in here?" A hulking security guard in a black uniform stood with his hand on the switch.

Althea whimpered as she stuck her sunglasses on her face. "Lawd, help us."

"Amen," said Emily.

CHAPTER 35

"How did we manage to talk all night?" Lacey shifted her body against the solid man at her side. "I have to be at work in"—she checked her watch—"three hours."

The twinkle lights cast their romantic glow over Cloud Nine as Lacey sat next to Jon on the plush bench. A blanket was wrapped around them both, providing a soft, comforting barrier against the early-morning chill.

"Do you want me to walk you to your cabin?" Jon asked.

She snuggled deeper in their fleecy cocoon. "What for? I'm already dressed for duty." She twisted her lips at the scuffed navy pumps on her feet and swatted his chest. "Next time, give me fair warning when you're about to pull out the fancy stuff. I'll come decked out for the occasion."

Jon's fingers tugged at the strand of hair by her ear. "You take my breath away no matter what you wear."

She snorted. "That was a little corny."

"But true." He wrapped his arms tight around her waist. "Have I told you how much I love you?"

"I recall you mentioning it." She crossed her legs at the ankles.

"That's good." Jon cleared his throat. "Did you have anything particular you wanted to say in return?"

Lacey stilled. Her ankles uncrossed, and she stared at her sensible shoes.

"Something short?" he said. "Three words long?"

She slowly raised her head. His mouth was smiling, but his eyes held a question. Did she?

Of course she did. How could she not love a man as gorgeous, compassionate, and caring as Jon? Still . . . saying the words was a leap off a cliff. Something she could never take back.

Goose bumps rose on her arms, but they weren't from the cold. She opened her mouth. "I—"

A shrill ring sounded from Jon's pocket. He pushed the blanket off and pulled out his phone.

"Who's calling me at four in the morning?" Jon tapped the screen. "Security. I'd better answer this."

Lacey scooted away.

He wrapped an arm around her hip and dragged her to his side. "Stay here. It only takes one hand to answer the phone."

She giggled and laid her head on his shoulder.

He accepted the call and held the phone to his ear. "This is Jonathan King." He tensed. "What did you say?" Jon withdrew his arm and stood. "I'll be right there."

"What's wrong?" Lacey looked up at him.

"It's the Shippers." The hand holding the phone dropped to his side. "They've been arrested."

Lacey and Jon sped down the narrow hallway. A husky security guard in a black uniform stood at the end, blocking a beige door with Brig posted on it. He moved aside as they approached and then took a ring of keys off his belt. After unlocking the door, he pushed it open and led them inside. They walked through an even smaller hallway with scuffed linoleum flooring and opened the door at the end.

Blue padded walls greeted them as they entered a plain space about the size of a suburban second bathroom. A tangy odor filled the tiny area—magnolia perfume mixed with sunblock and butterscotch. The lone piece of furniture was a single bed, on which sat four senior citizens dressed from head to toe in black—looking, for all the world, like a group of naughty children in time-out.

"They claim they were trying to change two duty rosters to match." The guard stuck the keys in his pocket. "Said it was more romantic or . . . something. Do you suppose they're going senile?"

Jon's breath stuttered. Lacey eyed him as he pressed his lips together and rolled them inward, his chin twitching. She reached behind him and pinched his back.

"This is serious," she whispered.

He nodded his head, his mouth still quivering.

"I'll leave you to it." The guard stepped out and shut the door.

Lacey propped her hands on her hips. "Was it worth it, ladies?"

Althea's and Daisy's lower lips protruded. Gerry hung her head.

But Emily raised her chin and stared Lacey down. "It was for a worthy cause."

"Worthy enough to go to jail?" Lacey flung her arms wide. Her fingertips almost reached the width of the cell.

"You can't prove anything," Althea said. "It's our word against the security guard's."

Jon scrunched his face. "They have camera footage of you entering my office."

Her eyebrows dipped. "That . . . that wasn't me. I might bear a passing resemblance to her, but you can't identify who it was under the sunglasses and scarf."

"I never said what she was wearing."

"Nice going." Gerry gave her the stink eye.

Althea bit her lip and wrinkled her nose.

With her arms crossed, Lacey hovered over Emily. "Since you're the ringleader, it's your fault the Shippers are locked up."

"Pish-tosh." Emily sniffed at the barren room. "It's not so bad. There aren't even any bars on the door."

"We can have some installed if you plan to make this a habit."

"Heavens, no!" Daisy said. "We've learned our lesson."

Althea held up her right hand. "We promise, baby. No more—"

"Don't let her bully you." Emily stood straight and tall. "We know this is all for show. It's normal protocol to lock unruly passengers in their cabins. You must have arranged this to keep us in line. Am I right?"

Lacey gritted her teeth. The woman was scary smart. If only she would use her powers for good instead of matchmaking. "Emily"—she forced her voice to stay calm—"all you have to do is stop these crazy, convoluted plots."

"But we want you to be happy, dear." Emily sat back on the bed with the heartbroken expression of a spanked child.

"Gah." Lacey thrust her hands in the air and curled her fingers. "How can I get through to you?"

"Lacey." Jon captured her elbow. "We should come clean."

"Shhhh!" She jerked her head at the Shippers.

"Look at them." He motioned to the four aging prisoners on the narrow bed. "I'm afraid they'll get in real trouble if they keep going."

Lacey glanced at the Shippers. The obstinate tilt of Emily's chin guaranteed future meddling.

Lacey pursed her lips and flicked a gaze at the ceiling. "You're right. Tell them."

Gerry folded her arms. "Tell us what?"

The hand Jon placed on Lacey's elbow slowly slid down her arm, and his fingers interlocked with hers. He faced the women. "You win, ladies. Lacey and I are officially together."

Emily side-eyed him. "What do you mean by 'together'?"

Jon placed his free hand to his chest. "I offered my heart, and the fair lady has accepted me. We are in a committed romantic relationship."

Five seconds of shock followed.

Then . . .

"Hallelujah!" Althea jumped up and did a Sunday-morning shuffle by the bed.

Gerry slapped the blue padded wall and nodded her head. "I knew something was fishy."

Daisy sneaked a handkerchief from the pocket of her velvet robe and pressed it to her mouth.

And Emily sat silent and still. But her eyes betrayed her happiness. The joy welled and spilled out of them in shiny little drops.

Lacey regretted her churlish behavior at the sight of tears. But she'd make it up to the stubborn old matchmaker, who'd been right all along. It was stupid to run from love. Lacey should have stopped sooner. No more avoidance. Jon was a permanent part of her life, and that meant there was an important task she had to complete.

Whether she wanted to or not.

CHAPTER 36

Lacey stood on the chaotic pier with her mother and father. People milled around them in a sea of stress and clamor. Passengers hauled their suitcases. Crew members rushed up a side gangplank—already in turnaround mode. A thousand things needed to happen in the few quick hours before the next wave of customers arrived—bedsheets washed, food delivered, pianos tuned. Lacey longed to be a part of the mind-numbing bustle, but she had something to tell her parents.

Her mother embraced her in a gentle hug. "When does your current contract end? Will you come home on your break this time?"

"We'll see." Lacey let go.

Her mom sniffled and wiped her nose. "It's silly to get teary about a fully grown daughter, but I can't help it."

"Don't cry." Lacey rubbed her mother's arm. "I'll try to visit in a few months."

"I'll paint your old room for you." Her dad stuck his fingers in his belt loops. "Pick a color."

"You don't have to do that, Dad."

"Of course I don't have to, but I want to pamper my little girl. Any color you desire."

Lacey focused on the disembarking passengers. A woman with a huge sunflower decorating her hat wrestled with a rolling suitcase. "Yellow."

"Yellow it is." He grabbed her in a bear hug. "I promise you won't recognize the place."

"Thanks, Dad."

She didn't much care for yellow, but it hardly mattered. Her father would never follow through. Lacey stopped trusting his promises when she was eight years old.

"Lacey!"

She sagged with relief at the sound of Jon's voice. Disentangling herself from her father's arms, she waved Jon over.

"Dad. Mom. There's a special person I want you to meet."

Jon joined their group and stood beside her.

Her father stared at him. "The cruise director? We met already."

"He's not just the cruise director, Dad." Lacey straightened her spine and looped her arm around Jon's waist. "This is Jonathan King . . . my boyfriend."

Jon stood taller at her words. His chest even puffed out a little. He looked adorably proud as he extended his hand to her father. "It's nice to meet you, sir. I'm sorry we didn't have enough time to get to know each other. I hope we can rectify that soon."

Her mother's smile stretched. She took in all six foot, two inches of attractive male and clasped her hands. "I'm so relieved you've found someone. I admit"—she leaned forward to whisper to Lacey—"I was starting to worry."

Her father studied Jon without taking his hand. "Are you good enough for my daughter?"

"No, sir." Jon kept his hand out. "I doubt anyone is. But I'll try my best to be worthy of her."

The sarcastic side of Lacey wanted to tease him for the old-fashioned speech, but the softer, more sensitive side she buried deep was tempted to swoon. "Dad, he's the best, most honest, and kindest man I've ever met."

Her father's face tightened at the declaration. He shrugged and accepted the handshake. "Can't argue with such a sterling recommendation. But I'll be keeping an eye on you, young man. If you don't treat my little girl right, you'll regret it."

"Rest assured, Mr. Anderson." Jon let go of his hand. "I'll take good care of her."

"I can take care of myself," Lacey said.

One more round of hugs, and her parents left to catch their flight. Lacey watched them walk away. Her mother lugged the suitcase with one hand and swung her purse in front of her with the other. She drew out a piece of candy and offered it to her husband. He took it and passed the empty wrapper back to her. They blended into the crowd of disembarking passengers disappearing inside the marina terminal.

"Whew." Lacey collapsed against Jon's side. "I'm glad that's over."

"Why?" He wrapped his arms around her. "Were you afraid I'd embarrass you?"

"No, it's . . ." She made a split-second decision to chip away at her natural inclination to hide the ugly parts of her life. "It's the other way around. I can't predict what will come out of my dad's mouth, and I spend the whole time holding my breath whenever we're together."

He urged her closer. "Sounds rough."

"Sometimes." She inhaled and exhaled in a melodramatic fashion. "But I'm breathing fine now." She leaned into him. "I wish we could get away and have a real date. A place on dry land where the dinner plates don't rock with the current."

Jon pulled her near as a forklift whizzed by them, stacked high with boxes of toilet paper.

"On turnaround day?" He released Lacey, placed an index finger on her forehead, and pushed her away. "Keep dreaming."

She whimpered.

"No use aiming those big eyes at me." He spun her around, settled his hands on her shoulders, and eased her toward the gangplank. "We have a ship to get ready. The new batch of cruisers will be here in eight hours. If the galley crew can load sixteen thousand pounds of potatoes and ten thousand soda cans in that short amount of time, the least we can do is play our part."

"Since when do you memorize the cold-storage numbers?" Lacey attempted to stop.

He kept pushing. "You know I've worked from stem to stern on cruise ships."

The reminder of his job-hopping dug up old insecurities. A weed of doubt threatened to sprout inside of her, but she stomped it flat. Jon wasn't her father. In fact, Jon was the one prodding them back to work at this very moment. He'd been a little flighty in the past, but he'd matured.

I can trust him now, Lacey argued against the negative voice in her head.

Bodies scurried. Cruise workers carried bottles and bedsheets, towels and toilet brushes. Jon steered Lacey through the ship entrance and into the lobby. A crowd of men in coveralls huddled in front of a giant TV. They groaned as a player on the screen fumbled the ball.

"I didn't realize this game was today." Jon let go of her and joined the group.

Lacey followed. "What happened to 'playing our part'?" She lightly punched his back.

Emily Windsor popped up beside them. "Don't you like football, dear?"

Lacey jerked to the side. The woman walked as soft as a cat. "I used to go to games in college, but it's been a while."

"I was a huge football fan back then." Jon dragged his gaze away from the screen. "My friends and I drove to all the away games. I can just imagine you as a cute coed. I guarantee I'd have asked for your number."

She raised her nose. "If you were wearing the wrong school colors, I would've ignored you."

He shoved a fist in the air. "Go Crimson."

Her mouth twitched, and she tried to keep a straight face. She elbowed him in the gut, and he moaned. "Isn't he—" Lacey turned to Emily, but her spot was empty. "She's gone."

"What?"

"Emily left, and we didn't even notice. She's must think we're so rude."

Jon laughed. "Do you remember who you're talking about? She's probably crossing another satisfied couple off her list."

"You should have seen them." Emily filled in the other Shippers as she took the strategy plans off the wall and folded them neatly. "They flirted like a pair of teenagers at a drive-in. It was too cute."

Gerry relaxed on the couch cushions. "I love a happy ending."

Daisy sat on the desk chair with her hands resting on her lap. "This case kept us on our toes. The drama felt as if it would never end."

Althea yawned and stretched her arms above her head. "I vote we take a short break before we choose a new target. This match took it out of me."

"We're not done yet." Emily paused from her cleanup. "There are still two holes to be plugged."

"Why?" Althea moaned. "Lacey and Jon are together. They're in love. Close the curtains and turn the houselights up. The end."

Emily shook her head. "Hole number one, we couldn't find any background on Jonathan King since we didn't have much to go on. But I gleaned a helpful tidbit today. He said, 'Go Crimson,' when he mentioned his college team. We know he was raised in Florida. I'm assuming he meant the Crimson Tide at the University of Alabama."

"Makes sense he'd go to a neighboring state for college," Althea said. "But what does it matter? Don't you trust him?"

"Jon is wonderful." Emily sat on the edge of the bed and adjusted the crooked afghan. "But we follow protocol. Every couple we've matched received a thorough background check." She stood again. "Gerry, tell your detective cousin to look into a Jonathan King who attended the University of Alabama."

"On it." Gerry retrieved her laptop from a side table. "I'll email him the new information. He's good at getting back quickly."

Daisy raised a finger. "Alabama's not the only school with a football team named Crimson. Harvard claims that too. Now I reflect on it, Jon acts like a Harvard man."

"Fine." Emily picked up her pile of battle plans and placed them in a bottom drawer, where a discarded stack filled half the space. "Gerry can have her cousin investigate both schools. Once we get a few more blanks filled in, we can mark this case closed."

"You said 'two holes.'" Gerry stopped typing. "What do we lack besides the background check?"

"Glad you reminded me." Emily's tone hardened. "Our next match will have to wait awhile. Hole number two, we find the heathens using our ship to smuggle their filthy drugs."

CHAPTER 37

LACEY'S REDHEADED ROOMMATE BIT INTO her buffalo chicken wrap. The iceberg lettuce crunched in her mouth as she chewed with a quizzical scrunch of her brow. "Is it just me, or has the food gotten better lately?"

Lacey shrugged. "Maybe the passengers aren't eating as much, and they're giving us the leftovers."

"Cruise ship passengers eating less?" Abby took another bite. "What are the chances of that happening?"

"I see your point." Lacey cut a corner off her lasagna and pushed it around the plate with her fork.

The staff dining room was almost deserted. Apart from a lone housemaid slurping her soup in the corner, they had the place to themselves. Lacey glanced at the digital clock hanging above the door. Three hours until she'd see Jon.

She took her knife and sliced into the pasta again. They should meet in his office to lessen the gossip. Not that they were hiding their relationship anymore. They'd walked through the lobby with their arms around each other on turnaround day. Half the ship must have heard by now.

"What's wrong?"

Lacey's head snapped up. "What did you say?"

Abby motioned to Lacey's lunch. The lasagna was cut into tiny, bite-size pieces. "If it doesn't taste good, order a different dish."

"The food is fine." Lacey shoved the plate away. "But I'm not hungry."

Abby set her wrap aside, wiped her hands, and placed her elbows on the table. She steepled her fingers in front of her face and perused Lacey.

"What?" She squirmed under the scrutiny.

"You don't look sick. Or unhappy. You look like something good happened."

Lacey schooled her features into a passive mask. "I don't know what you mean."

Abby placed a finger under Lacey's chin and tilted her head. "I'd say your eyes are sparkling, but that would be too cliché. You look . . . lighter."

Oof. Good friends knew which emotional buttons to push. The tide rose inside Lacey. She gave Abby a watery smile. "I feel lighter."

"Is this because your parents left?"

"Of course not." She dropped her gaze. "Okay, a tiny bit that, but mostly something else."

Abby balled a fist. "Am I going to have to beat it out of you?"

Lacey laughed and raised her hands. "I surrender. The truth is—"

"Hello, sweet potato." Jon slid onto the chair beside Lacey and kissed her on the cheek.

She quirked her eyebrow at him. "Sweet potato?"

"I'm trying out endearments. What do you think?"

"I think you better keep thinking." She jabbed him in the rib cage.

He doubled over and moaned. "Oh, the woman is cruel."

Lacey brandished both index fingers and poked him again.

He grabbed hold of them and swung them back and forth. "If you wanted to hold hands, you should've told me."

"What are you doing here?" Her fingers curled around his. "I thought you were busy until later."

"I'm still busy. That's why I came looking for you. I have a ton of work, but I couldn't concentrate. I missed you too much."

"Oh, really?" Lacey feigned an innocent expression.

"I figured if I saw you, I might be able to focus again."

"How's that working for you?"

Jon tugged on her hands. "Not so good. I can't keep my mind on anything but you."

Lacey cringed at the cheese level of their conversation, but the sound of a throat clearing made them turn their heads.

The neglected Abby sat in the same position. Her knuckle tapped against her chin. "I could be reaching here, Lacey, but I'm guessing you wanted to tell me about you and Jon. Has there been a"—her lips puckered before breaking into a sassy grin—"change in your relationship?"

Lacey slipped her hands out of Jon's. "What gave it away?"

"The fact you forgot I was on the same planet, let alone at the same table." Abby chuckled.

Jon scooted his chair closer to Lacey's and placed his arm tight around her. "Congratulate us. We are officially an item."

"My sincerest congratulations," said Abby. "This is the best news since they told me someone else was assigned finger-painting duty. When did you become a couple?"

"On Nevis," Jon said.

"What!" She pouted at Lacey. "And you didn't tell me till now? I need a new roomie."

"I'm sorry." Lacey reached across the table. "I told Jon not to tell anyone. I wanted to tease the Shippers a little bit."

Abby nodded. "Understandable. Okay, I forgive you."

Jon stood and pushed his chair away. He tweaked Lacey's earlobe. "Now that I've seen you, I have to get back to work. Costumes, music, a midnight chocolate buffet. The plans for the masquerade ball are crazy elaborate."

"Chocolate buffet? Yum," Abby said. "What made the company throw such a big shindig?"

Jon scooted his chair in. "It's a pilot study thing. They're hoping it will attract more customers to Monarch, set it apart from the other cruise lines. People like dressing up for formal night. How much more would they enjoy a masked royal ball, complete with a red carpet and plenty of selfie opportunities?"

"Sounds promising," said Lacey.

Abby grimaced. "Unless you work in the children's area. All I hear is extra hours babysitting the kiddos way past their bedtimes."

"Good point." Jon withdrew his phone and typed. "We should arrange special activities for the children and additional help for the childcare workers." He walked away, still typing, without saying goodbye.

Abby ate the last bite of her chicken wrap. "At least you know you got a hard worker."

Lacey gathered her silverware with her napkin and piled it on top of her now-cold lasagna. "So true."

"Those Shippers do great work." Abby took Lacey's plate and tray and stacked them with her own. "Do they take applications?"

"I have no idea how they choose their victims." Lacey stood.

The petite Abby rose and latched on to Lacey's arm with the strength of a linebacker. "Please let them know I'm available."

"You're volunteering for the chopping block?"

"Why are you still knocking it? Look who you ended up with." Abby sighed. "They could find me someone medium, dark, and dreamy."

"Medium?"

Abby pointed at the top of her head. "When you're as short as me, anything over five foot ten is a pain in the neck. Literally. I dated a basketball player in high school and spent my junior year walking around like I had a nosebleed."

"Have I ever told you you're ridiculous?" Lacey grabbed the stacked trays and headed for the trash cans.

"Not in the last hour." Her friend followed at her heels. "You'll tell the Shippers?"

"Yes. I'll tell them."

Abby squealed and wrapped her arms around Lacey's waist from behind. They waddled together to the cans.

"I wish I could go to the ball." Abby released her and put the silverware in a shallow tub with water while Lacey dumped the food scraps in a trash can. "You chose the right job as a hostess. You'll get to wear a gown and play Cinderella while I'm stuck with all the Hansels and Gretels."

"I never pictured myself as Cinderella." Lacey stacked their trays with the others. "Not even when I was younger."

"Cinderella or not, you found yourself a real Prince Charming." Abby laced her fingers together and squeezed her lids closed. "Please, Lord. Just one more knight in shining armor for me." She opened one eye and peeked. "Don't forget to put in a good word for me with the Shippers."

"I'll remember. You want the four fairy godmothers to hook you up ASAP." Lacey looped her arm around Abby's, and they walked out of the staff mess. "I have high hopes for this ball. It will be great for the public relations department. Who doesn't love a fancy masquerade?"

They made their way down Route 66 and rode the elevator to the seventh floor. As Abby and Lacey exited the car, they met Gerry, Daisy, and Althea.

Lacey's first instinct was to run. Then she reminded herself she was with Jon now. No reason to hide from the Shippers. "Good afternoon, ladies. Where's Emily?"

Gerry shifted from one foot to the other. "She went ashore for . . . something."

"How's your day going?" Abby asked.

Althea crowed. "I am on a roll." She pulled a handful of cash from an envelope and showed it off. "My son-in-law's a pastor in Chicago. He told me he'd be praying for a blessing, and the Good Lawd answered. This is yesterday's winnings. Can hardly wait for bingo today."

Gerry tsk-tsked. "I wonder what your preacher son-in-law would say about your constant gambling."

"How is this gambling?" Althea's eyebrows sloped. "The ship lets seniors play for free. All it costs me is my time."

"She's got you there." Abby pointed at Gerry, who lifted her nose.

Daisy tittered softly.

Althea tucked her envelope in the front pocket of her red sequined fanny pack and zipped it shut. "This is going in my wedding-funeral fund."

Abby's gaze slid to Lacey.

Lacey sighed internally and took the obvious question. "What exactly is a wedding-funeral fund, Mrs. Jones?"

"A little emergency stash of mine. One of the things I like best about these boats is the steady stream of romantic opportunities walking up the gangplank. The love of my life might be in the next group of passengers." Althea paused to pat at the short silver curls around her face. "If he does come, I want to be sure I'm ready. Weddings are a costly business. I speak from experience. I already paid for three of them."

"And where does the funeral part come in?"

"The only thing more expensive than a wedding is a funeral. I want to have everything paid for in case I kick off before I find my next Mr. Right."

Abby gave a breathy giggle.

Lacey hurried to ask another question before the older woman noticed Abby's merriment. "Isn't that a bit morbid, Mrs. Jones?"

"Why, baby? There are two things you can't avoid in life: love and death. Be prepared for whichever one comes first."

"She ought to know." Gerry lowered her nose enough to join the conversation. "With three husbands under her belt, she's the authority."

"Which one was your favorite, Althea?" Abby winced as Lacey kicked the side of her foot.

"Not the first one." The thrice-married expert wrinkled her upper lip until her top row of teeth showed. "He was the opposite of a keeper. But was I happy when I dumped the cheater? I still cried myself to sleep every night for two months." She reached over and put a hand on each of their shoulders. "Take my word. Don't ever put yourself through that pain. Divorce feels like someone gave your heart a bikini wax."

Lacey flinched at the analogy. "Got it, Mrs. Jones. Thanks for the advice."

Abby elbowed her. "You won't need it. You've snagged yourself a major catch."

"So we ascertained." The quiet Daisy finally spoke, giving Lacey a genuine smile.

"I'm tickled pink for you." Althea enveloped Lacey in a soft, teddy-bear hug. "You don't have to worry about Jonny. He's good as twenty-four-karat gold."

Gerry tugged Althea away. "That's enough touchy-feely stuff. Lacey has a job to do. And I want to check my email." She nodded at Lacey and Abby. "We'll chat later, girls."

"Hold on." Lacey jerked forward. "I . . . I should wait and say this when Emily's here, but . . . thank you . . . for . . . pushing me and Jon together. I don't think I'd have had the courage on my own."

"Awww." Althea pressed a fist to her ample bosom. "You're welcome, baby."

"We were happy to help," said Daisy.

Gerry frowned and sniffed loudly. "Don't mention it." Her voice held a suspicious wobble.

Althea threw her arm around the tall, bony woman beside her. "We'd better get her out of here before she starts bawling. You'd never suspect it of her, but she's quite the crybaby."

"Stop being absurd." Gerry raised her nose again and stalked away.

Althea and Daisy snickered at each other and followed.

Lacey nudged Abby. "Are you sure you want to trust your love life to that bunch?"

"You thanked them, didn't you?" Abby held out both hands. "They may be a little unorthodox, but I like their results. If they can match me with a man who looks, talks, and acts as well as your boyfriend, I'd pay any fee."

"Don't get your hopes too high. God broke the mold when he made Jon."

"That's right. Rub it in." She crossed her arms. "It's hard to believe this is the same Lacey Anderson who used to bolt at the first hint of romance. You've come a long way."

Lacey didn't bother to deny it. She hoped to go further still. With a man like Jon, her cynical doubts were dissipating like the foam on an ocean wave. Maybe someday soon, she'd stop shoving away the dreams of forever and family whenever they entered her mind.

Emily's heels burned as she made her way down the never-ending Progreso pier. What had possessed her to hunt for suspicious activity during a port visit? She wasn't forty-two anymore, no matter how young she felt inside. Not to mention her investigation had uncovered exactly nada. Now would be the perfect time for one of those red bicycle taxis, but none appeared. She slid her purse handles around her wrist and bent to tighten the strap on her orthopedic sandal.

"Excuse me." Someone swerved around her, his arms full with a paper grocery bag.

"Ricardo?" She reached to stop him as he passed.

"Yes?" The crease in his forehead disappeared as he recognized her. "Mrs. Windsor. Buenos días!"

"Buenos días." The poor dear. Working so hard that sweat was leaking from every pore, and she was about to make his day worse. But she had to deliver the news about Lacey and Jon. "I wanted to speak to you."

"Yes?" He looked at the bag and backed up. "Will it take long? I need to get these supplies to the kitchen before Chef becomes angry."

"Supplies?"

Ricardo blanched. "I may have burned a large batch of cherry tarts. He worries when I waste the flour that there will not be enough. I bought more today."

"Why not ask the provisions manager? He loads new supplies all the time."

He shook his head. "No. It is fine. My brother, he has a store here. I get it very cheap. No time for paperwork."

"Don't fret." Emily patted his arm. "I can talk while we return to the ship."

He nodded hard enough that the hair flopped over his forehead. They walked together, the pristine white outline of the MS *Buckingham* waiting in the distance.

She cleared her throat. "I know I encouraged you to ask out Lacey Anderson, but—"

"I did." Ricardo hefted the bag in his arms. "We ate a lovely dinner together."

"Yes, that's nice, but I'm afraid it won't . . . you probably don't—"

"Mrs. Windsor." He stopped and faced her. "I decided not to date Lacey. She is cute but not my type."

"You don't say." Emily pursed her lips.

"Yes." The bag sank lower as Ricardo talked. Thick packages of flour peeked from the top. "It was my decision. I suggested we remain friends and . . . and nothing more. If you will please excuse me, this is heavy."

He scuttled away, and Emily shook her head. She never should've encouraged him. The Shippers could find Ricardo someone else. She switched her purse to her other arm and ran through the options in her mind. Perhaps Malaya at the front desk would be a good candidate.

A matchmaker's work was never done.

CHAPTER 38

Jon made a quick hello circuit around the lido deck on the way to his office. A cruise director never lacked for friends. Total strangers called him by name and slapped him on the back as he passed.

His teeth ground together as he observed Collins stretched out on a deck chair. His paunch showed through the gaping holes between his shirt buttons, knobby white knees protruded below his shorts, and a straw hat rested over his face.

Jon approached the man and stood beside the chaise lounge. "Working hard?"

Collins tilted his hat back. "I contacted a friend of mine in the bureau for an update. He says the crew member they arrested on the MS *Royal* is ready to crack. Only a matter of time till they get the names of the ringleaders. All we got to do is wait."

"Even so, do you suppose you might keep an eye on the passengers and crew here?" Jon tapped the top of the chair. "In case we missed someone."

Collins rose with a grunt. He wandered away without a backward glance.

Jon spied Emily on the tier above the swimming pool. Her keen gaze took in the scene below. Her mouth moved, but there was no one beside her.

He took a detour up the stairs and approached the older woman. "Enjoying some alone time?"

"Not at all." She lowered herself to a nearby chair. "I was talking to the Lord."

Jon took the seat beside her. "Did my name come up in the conversation?"

"Naturally. And Lacey's too."

"That's good. We could use some divine assistance." His smile faltered. "I admit, I've been asking God for some extra help in the relationship department."

Her brow crinkled. "Is there a problem?"

"Nope. Things are going well, but"—Jon rubbed a hand against his pants leg—"I thought things were going well two and a half years ago. Then Lacey disappeared without notice. If she did that again . . ." He shook his head.

"Worrying doesn't fix anything, dear." Emily reached over and patted his knee. "Talking to the Lord is the best thing you can do. And the second best is being honest with Lacey about your feelings. If you do that, everything will work out for the good."

He hoped she was right. Since Lacey had introduced him to her parents, he felt a smidgen more secure in their relationship. But the word *love* had never once escaped her lips. A desperate desire for some sort of guarantee wrestled with his patience.

Emily and Jon sat for several seconds without saying anything. The sound of squeals and splashes drifted from the pool area. He studied the little matchmaker beside him. She wore a peaceful, relaxed expression.

"I haven't seen much of you lately," Jon said.

"Probably wouldn't have noticed me anyway with those stars in your eyes." Emily drummed her fingers on the armrest. "Have you made any headway on the drug case?"

"How—" He peered over his shoulder and lowered his voice. "How do you know about that?"

"We have our informants." Emily raised her brows. "I assume you've told Lacey."

"Yes. She's been keeping a lookout for anyone suspicious."

"Good. You can count on help from the Shippers. I visited the port myself to surveil the passengers. If we spot anything unusual, I'll report it to you."

Jon's abdomen trembled from trying not to laugh. He wished Detective Collins had half this lady's gumption. "Thank you, Emily." He managed to say it without even a hint of laughter. "I appreciate your help. But I have to get going. I've got a—"

"Wait." She lifted an authoritative hand. "While I've got you here, allow me to unburden my mind."

"Yes, ma'am." Jon sat a little straighter.

"I'm serious. No one is happier than I am that you and Lacey found each other, but you'd better be careful. She may appear strong and resilient and, yes, a little prickly . . ."

He pinched two fingers close together. "A little."

Emily laid her hand on his. "But her heart is fragile. It doesn't take a lot to chip it."

Jon placed his free hand over hers. "I'll treat it with care."

"Do you love her?" The faded blue eyes studied him.

"Since the moment she told me to pick up a piece of trash that wasn't mine."

"That's my girl." She bent forward. "You hurt Lacey, and there's not a ship in the ocean you can hide on." Her eyebrows climbed higher, and her chin puckered as she stared him down.

Jon leaned over and kissed her tissue-paper-soft cheek. She smelled of hair spray and butterscotch candy.

"You're a marvel, Emily Windsor."

"Pish-tosh." She pushed him back.

Jon stood and winked at her. "I'll save a front pew for the Shippers at the wedding."

He stuck his hands in his pockets and whistled as he walked away.

Emily admired Jon like a doting grandmother might. When he was out of sight, she soaked in the sunshine and the lazy clouds floating overhead. "Lord, you did good work with that one."

"Emily!" Gerry bustled up and dropped onto the chair beside her. "Carl emailed me."

"Hmm?" Emily refocused on her friend. "Who?"

"Carl Paroo, my cousin, the detective." Gerry waved a small stack of papers. "He plugged in the new information we sent him and hit pay dirt."

Emily took the stack from Gerry. A picture of Jon in a graduation cap caught her attention first. Her smile disappeared as she read the words printed underneath. She glanced at Gerry, and her hands clenched. The paper crackled. "Is he sure about this?"

Gerry nodded. "I called him myself when I read his report."

Emily shot to her feet. "This is bad."

The ex-librarian's lips sloped in a frown, and she nodded. "Lacey won't like it. She'll feel betrayed."

"I can understand why." Emily rubbed her fingers against her chest. "It . . . this is . . ." She balled up a fist and thumped it on her leg. "Things were going so well."

Gerry pressed her forehead. "What do we do now?"

Emily dug her walkie-talkie from her purse and pushed the button. "Mayday. Mayday. All Shippers gather at HQ. And, Althea, if you're in the bingo hall, you'd better get your behind to my cabin in five minutes. This is serious!"

Twenty minutes later, she was explaining the urgency of the situation to the cranky Shipper who had to leave her card behind when it was almost complete.

"I don't get what the problem is," Althea said. "The man has a buttload of money. What's wrong with that?"

"The problem is"—Gerry's hand had barely left her head since she learned the news—"he didn't tell Lacey." She massaged her right temple with her fingers. "You know she'll hate it."

"He must have his reasons." Daisy sat on the edge of the couch, her posture ramrod straight. "People with money are still people."

"I wish I could be that kind of people." Althea's gaze rose to the ceiling, and she pressed her palms together. "Give me a try, Lawd. I promise I'll pay my tithes."

"Please focus, Althea." Emily sank onto the chair by the couch and pounded a fist on her rib cage to dislodge the tight sensation that plagued her. This case was giving her indigestion. "Lacey has trust issues. After meeting her father, I don't blame her. But what can be done about it?"

"It appears there's not much we can do," Gerry said. "Number one, Jon's rich. A fact we can't change. Number two, he didn't tell her. We can't change that either."

"Or can we?" Emily beat her chest a little harder. "The biggest problem is, he wasn't honest with her. Our Prince Charming turned out to be an actual prince." She snorted. "Or should I say 'monarch.' If we can convince him to tell Lacey immediately, it might soften the blow."

Althea angled forward. "What do we do?"

Emily pushed herself from the chair. "Divide and conquer. Keep your walkie-talkies handy and scour the ship. Whoever spots Jon first alerts everyone. Between the four of us, we can help him make the right choice."

The Shippers filed from the cabin and headed in four different directions. They had to find Jon before Lacey discovered she didn't even know her boyfriend's real last name.

CHAPTER 39

"He did?" Jon cradled the phone between his ear and shoulder as he typed on his office computer. "Great. Won't be long before this is wrapped up. Collins? He's been . . . keeping an eye on things. Listen, I need to get going. We have a huge masquerade ball in six hours. I appreciate you calling."

A knock sounded at the door as he put the receiver on its cradle.

"Come in." He shoved the masquerade paperwork to the side and began to fill out an accident report for a passenger. What kind of genius decided it was a good idea to take a selfie on a gym elliptical? And what kind of genius was Jon for allowing corporate to add a giant, swanky event on top of his other duties?

"Can I help you?" he asked without looking away from his computer screen.

"Hello, Mr. McMillan."

Jon's fingers stilled on the keyboard. He raised his head to find a battle line of Shippers facing him. They wore four matching expressions. Unhappy. His mind raced through the possibilities.

Denial.

Avoidance.

Retreat.

"No sense running." Emily advanced. "We'd track you down again."

The woman was a mind reader.

He stood and motioned to the two chairs in front of his desk. "I'm sorry I don't have enough seats for everyone."

"We'll stand, thank you," Gerry said.

It was the first time he'd seen her without a book.

Jon's hands twitched, and he folded them in front of him like a chastened schoolboy. Maybe he should bow his head. He surveyed the others. Emily stood slightly in front, grasping a black three-ring binder. Althea and Daisy chose identical positions—arms crossed in front of them with their eyebrows dipping in the middle.

He gulped. "What can I do for you ladies?"

"You can tell us who you really are"—Althea jiggled her head back and forth as she said his name—"Mr. Jonathan King McMillan."

"It seems you already know." He ruffled his hair. "Would you mind telling me how *much* you know?"

Emily marched forward. "We know you belong to the family who owns this cruise line." She took out the binder and opened it. "You went to Harvard. Graduated summa cum laude with a master's degree in business administration. And your father has announced his retirement as CEO for the end of the year. We assume he's been grooming you to take his place."

"Have you considered a career in espionage? The government could use people with your talents."

"Jonathan." The disdain in Daisy's tone lent her an air of offended majesty. "This isn't the time for joking."

"I apologize." He bent his head. "My intention wasn't to deceive you. My father and I thought I could run the business better if I learned it from the ground up. I've spent the last few years absorbing every aspect of cruising from stem to stern. When the drug problems broke out, I determined to investigate them myself, and corporate assigned me as the new cruise director."

"Is Lacey aware of this?" Emily asked.

"She knows about the smugglers. But not my true identity. I plan to tell her soon."

"*Soon* is too late." Gerry stepped beside Emily. "If she hears it from someone else, it will break her. Confess everything now."

"I'm working on it." Jon rose to walk around the desk and held out his hands. "Please, give me one more day. I wanted to tell her in a special way when I propose."

"Propose!" Althea clapped her hands together and squealed.

"Are you crazy?" Gerry's mouth hung open. "It's too soon. There are countless examples of unexpected marriage proposals that went haywire: Mr. Darcy and Elizabeth, Rochester and Jane Eyre—"

"None of those people actually existed." Althea swatted at her. "Besides, I'm sure Jonny is going to tell her all about himself first." She turned to him. "Right?"

"Would I ask her to marry me without explaining who her new in-laws will be?" Jon grinned. "Let me get the ball out of the way tonight. Then we dock in Cozumel tomorrow. Since you introduced us to its romantic lighthouse on our last visit, I arranged for a special surprise."

Daisy uncrossed her arms. "What kind of surprise?"

"The beach covered in candles and orchids. A special chef flown in to prepare the meal. Orchestra playing in the background. The works."

Althea and Daisy made eye contact and cooed in delight.

Gerry shrugged. "Sounds like a decent setting. It might soften her up before you tell her."

But Emily shook her head. "It's too risky. What if she finds out before then? It would crush her."

"No one will tell her. Only the captain is informed of my true identity, and he won't say a word." Jon took her small hands in his. "Trust me, Emily. I never want to hurt Lacey. It's just one more day."

"Did you pray about this?"

"Why do I need to pray about it? Isn't God the one who brought Lacey and me back together? I don't want to miss the chance he's given me."

Emily stared at him. A cross between a groan and a growl left her lips as she withdrew her hands and moved away. "I hope you don't end up regretting this. Let's go, girls."

The other three parted to the sides, and she walked through the middle and out the door. Gerry and Daisy followed without comment. Althea stopped at the threshold. She gave him a wink before closing the door.

Jon let out the breath he was holding. He walked around his desk, hooked his foot under the bottom drawer, and slid it open. A small black box sat inside. He retrieved it and flipped the lid to reveal a delicate engagement ring. After kissing Lacey during their time in Nevis, thoughts of spending the rest of their lives together had flooded his brain. He'd barely waited a day before calling to place an order with a well-known jeweler in Galveston, and then picked up the ring on their last turnaround in home port.

The design reminded him of Lacey in every way. Unpretentious but rare. Jon held it closer to the window behind his desk. The afternoon sunlight hit the diamond and cast tiny rainbows across his office floor.

He sank onto his chair.

Was Gerry correct? Would Lacey also think it was too soon? It took almost three years to get her to officially admit she was dating him. Perhaps this *was* rushing it. But Jon couldn't help it. He needed to be sure Lacey wouldn't run again. More than that, he wanted to stop wasting time. And a life without Lacey was the biggest waste of time he could imagine.

CHAPTER 40

THE STRAINS OF A CLASSIC love song wafted through the double doors to where Lacey stood by the elevators. Past the entrance, gauzy tents, chocolate fountains, and flickering tea lights awaited the guests. The lido deck had been transformed into a romantic wonderland.

Lacey lifted a gloved hand to move a tendril that tickled her chin. Her hair curled in gentle waves and fell around her shoulders. The softer style complimented her turquoise evening gown. The floor-length dress swished around her as she moved.

She held a black basket with the Monarch crown emblem on the front. Red and white long-stemmed roses peeked out of the top. To her left sat a table filled with masks of all shapes and sizes. Guests began to arrive and choose which disguise they preferred before entering the moonlit masquerade. Lacey passed them a rose on their way in.

"Greetings, honored guests," she said to the couple who stood in front of her.

Such over-the-top dialogue would not have been her first choice, but the cruise line was attempting to create a regal atmosphere. She extended them two roses. The woman placed the flower in her teeth and pulled out a phone.

"Lesss take a pictchah," she mouthed around the stem as she dragged her partner down into the shot.

"Allow me to help you." Lacey placed her basket on the ground, took the phone, and counted to three.

The pair posed with the flowers in their mouths. "Cheeth."

She passed the phone back to them and picked up her basket again as they walked outside.

So much for the elegant approach.

If Monarch Cruises was going for a majestic feel, this evening was a total flop. But if their aim was to please the passengers, then chalk up another success. Conversations and laughter hummed.

"There you are." Jon walked through the outside doors. His tailored, single-breasted tuxedo emphasized his height as he stood in front of her. He wore a gold Monarch crown pin on the black satin lapel, and his matching tie gleamed against the pristine white shirt. He took the flower basket from her, placed it on the side table, and twirled a finger. "Could you give me a 360 spin?"

"What do you mean?" Lacey glanced behind her. "What's wrong?"

"Nothing's wrong. I want to get the full picture, so I'll know what to dream about tonight."

Lacey shuddered even as she laughed. "Did you search cheesy pickup lines on the internet?"

"I've got more if you want to listen."

"Pass." Lacey reached to smooth a wrinkle in his tie. One of the elevators dinged, and she retrieved her basket. "Go away now. We've got work to do."

A thin, balding man in a pin-striped suit, bow tie, and horn-rimmed glasses exited the elevator with Reid Collins and walked up behind Jon. Carrying an old-fashioned briefcase, the stranger looked more ready for a boardroom than a ball.

"Hello, Jonathan." He held out a hand in front of him.

Jon turned, and his smile faded. "Hello, Mr. Eliot. You're underdressed for the party." He motioned to Collins, who'd swapped his shorts for a pair of dress slacks but paired them with a different ill-fitting Hawaiian shirt. "Both of you."

"What?" Collins brushed at his outfit.

"Yes, my apologies." The stranger's hand hung awkwardly in midair, and he let it fall to his side. "I flew into Mérida, drove to Progreso, and boarded while the ship was docked there. Since my motive was purely business, I didn't bring any formal attire."

Business?

Lacey studied the gentleman. Who would be allowed to board a cruise in the middle of the voyage? A bigwig from corporate? Had the detective found evidence on the MS *Buckingham* and contacted him?

Mr. Eliot extended his hand to her. "How do you do? I'm—"

"Let's not waste time." Jon's voice rose. "You picked an inconvenient moment for a visit, Mr. Eliot. We're in the middle of an event." He looked at the stranger and then strode to the doorway. "Follow me."

The man's pinstripe-covered legs scampered after Jon as he stalked away. Collins followed at a leisurely pace, hands stuck in his pockets, leaving Lacey alone in the entry. She clutched the basket of roses to her body, wishing she knew what was going on. Did they find the smugglers?

Emily winced as she left the elevator. She should've worn sandals. Her feet wouldn't last long in these tight shoes. She pinched the skirt of the ankle-length lavender dress she'd last worn to her great-niece's wedding.

Lacey stood near the entrance, craning her neck at the crowd beyond the double doors.

Emily hobbled over and patted the distracted girl. "Lacey?"

"What? Oh, Mrs. Windsor." She took a rose from her basket and offered it to Emily. "Greetings, honored guest."

Emily accepted the flower. "A simple 'hello' will do fine. Have you seen my friends?"

"No, ma'am. Not recently."

Emily checked her wristwatch and tapped the pointy toe of her dress pump. Where were the girls?

Passengers in formal attire swarmed the outside deck. A tiny man with a pencil-thin mustache and a tall white paper hat passed the doors. He paused when he saw Emily with Lacey and walked inside.

"Mrs. Windsor!"

"Hello, Chef. I'm anticipating the special dessert tent tonight."

"I baked a delectable praline cheesecake for the festivities." He kissed his fingers. "Care for a sample? I can bring you one."

"I'm sorry, dear. Your creations are wonderful, but I'm not very fond of pralines. I'll stick to the cherry tarts." She laughed. "Unless Ricardo burned them again."

"Again?" The chef scrunched his face. "When did he burn them the first time?"

"Oh . . . I—" Emily bit her lip. Had she ratted out Ricardo to his boss? "That is, I heard he bought extra ingredients from his brother's store at the last port. Perhaps I was mistaken."

"Ricardo doesn't have any brothers," Lacey said. "You must've misunderstood."

"Yes." The chef sneered. "He's the spoiled baby boy of four sisters. And it shows in his performance. I never met a pastry chef who expected more hand-holding."

The sound of his complaining faded into the background as Emily replayed the conversation on the pier. No. Ricardo had mentioned a brother. Did he mean in the friendly, non-blood-related sense?

Lacey looped the basket on one arm. "Maybe he was referring to the time he made too many tarts a few voyages ago. Three thousand was a bit much for the captain's reception."

"Don't remind me," Chef growled. "A hundred people attended that VIP get-together. What possessed him to make three thousand? Did he think each guest would take a doggie bag? Now you tell me he's buying extra ingredients again. I better set him straight." He stormed away, leaving the two women alone.

Emily touched Lacey's elbow. "Jon informed me you were helping him investigate."

"You know about the—"

"Drugs? Yes. I promised him the Shippers would keep an eye out for anyone suspicious. The reason I went ashore today was to do reconnaissance work."

Lacey's lips twitched, but she didn't interrupt.

"None of the passengers seemed fishy, but on the way back, I met Ricardo with a large bag." Emily drew closer and whispered. "Don't you find it odd that a pastry chef purchased replacement supplies from an imaginary brother with his own money?"

"Yes." Lacey's brow wrinkled. "Yes, I do." She dropped the basket, tugged the long silky gloves from her arms, and balled them in her fist. "Excuse me, Mrs. Windsor. I need to make Jon aware of this."

Jon skimmed the press of people and took Mr. Eliot by the elbow. "Let's talk in private." Jon steered him through the festive crowd to a deserted part of the deck, behind the food tent. Cases of bottled water and boxes of assorted gourmet cookies cluttered the area.

Collins tore open one of the wrappings and shoved a gingersnap in his mouth.

Jon released Mr. Eliot. "What are you doing here?"

"Didn't your father call you?"

"I haven't spoken to him in a few weeks."

Mr. Eliot held his briefcase with one hand and opened it with the other. After riffling through the contents, he drew out a file. He closed the case and stuck it under his arm, then flipped through the folder and removed a single sheet of paper. "The employee caught with the drugs on the MS *Royal* divulged the names of his suppliers to the FBI. They're closing in, and your father believes the drug problem is under control. He wants you to conclude your work here and return to Florida."

Collins slipped a fresh piece of gum from his pocket. "Guess I better start looking for a new job. I knew cruise ship detective was too good a gig to last."

Jon ignored him. "Why the rush?"

Mr. Eliot pushed his glasses up the bridge of his nose. "He resolved to entrust the reins to you before the New Year. Mr. McMillan plans to introduce you as the official CEO of Monarch Cruises then. I'll remain in the executive secretary position and assist you during the transition. This is the projected timeline."

He held out the paper, but Jon made no move to take it.

"Don't you have my email address? It wasn't necessary to bring this personally."

Mr. Eliot offered an apologetic head tilt. "Your father wanted me to make sure you came."

Collins laughed. "He sent a babysitter."

"Mr. Collins, please." A crease gathered on the secretary's forehead. "There's no need to be flippant."

Jon loosened the knot of his tie and yanked it down. "Dad told me I had until summer."

Mr. Eliot dropped the paper in the folder. "He feels the stockholders will be more accepting of the change if there is an interim period when you both are at the company. This way, you can run things, but he'll still be around until his official retirement."

"And what if I don't want to leave yet?"

"Surely the assistant cruise director can fill in for the last few days before the ship sails home. You can be replaced here but not at head-quarters. You're the heir to the Monarch legacy."

Collins spit his gum in a nearby trash can and snagged another cookie from the open box. "Must be nice. You get a successful business served to you on a silver platter because you're Jonathan McMillan."

"Jonathan McMillan." A quiet voice repeated the name.

Jon spotted Lacey frozen by the corner of the tent, her hands hanging limp at her sides.

She scanned the three men. "Eavesdropping is always a bad idea."

"Lacey." He stepped toward her and took her by the arm.

She made no move to stop him. On the contrary, she was stone-still. Was that a good or a bad sign?

"Please give me a chance to explain."

She looked around him at the other men. "Does this explanation require three people?"

Jon kept a loose hold on her, afraid she'd run away. He nodded to Mr. Eliot and Collins. "Would you excuse us? I have something urgent to discuss with Miss Anderson."

Collins stretched. "Prime time to check out one of those chocolate fountains."

"Please pack your things," Mr. Eliot said. "I have the company jet waiting at the airport in Cozumel. Your father expects us back by tomorrow evening."

Jon ground out his words through clenched teeth. "We'll discuss it later."

"Yes." The secretary stuffed his file folder into the briefcase. "I'll . . . be going, then." He skittered past them and disappeared around the corner of the tent.

Jon focused on Lacey.

She didn't look angry.

She didn't look happy.

She looked . . . like she was greeting passengers on the first day of a cruise. This was her customer-service face.

CHAPTER 41

THE EVENING BREEZE BLEW HER unraveling curls in front of her nose. Lacey pushed the hair from her vision. She smoothed it down and tried to slow her beating heart with several deep breaths. Monarch's first official masquerade ball was building to a smashing fever pitch.

This was no place to make a scene.

Jon's hand remained on her arm.

She brushed it away. "You said you wanted to explain."

"Yes." Jon unbuttoned his tuxedo jacket. "I'm not sure where to start."

"Why did you call yourself Jonathan King?"

"King is my middle name—after my mother's maiden name. She met Dad when he was a one-ship operation. He was so besotted he christened the cruise line after her."

"King." Lacey's eyes closed as she processed everything. "*Monarch Cruises.*"

"Exactly." Jon pointed at the gold crown logo pin on his tuxedo lapel. "My father's a mushy romantic."

She tapped her fingers on her forehead. It all made sense. The job-hopping. His ability to show up anywhere and at any time without consequences or recrimination. He was the owner's son. "Does that make you a billionaire? Like one of the heroes in those romance novels Gerry reads?"

"Not quite." He grinned. "The last time I checked, I was still in the millions category. It'll take a good thirty years before I reach billionaire status."

Lacey's breath escaped in a short, exasperated puff of air. "Why are you smiling?"

He sobered. "I'm sorry. I know this is a lot to take in."

"You think?" She struggled to keep her voice quiet. "Why didn't you tell me?"

"I was waiting for the right time."

"There were plenty of right times. When we first met, you were Jonathan King McMillan. When we met again, two and a half years later, you were Jonathan King McMillan." Every time she said his name, Lacey bit out the words. "When we officially started dating, you were Jonathan. King. McMillan. Stop me if I'm getting anything wrong."

Red tinged his cheeks. "No. You're correct."

"You lied to me." She said it simply, without any emotion, like she was remarking on the weather.

"You don't have to make it sound so serious, I only—"

Lacey's ball gown billowed as she spun and walked away. She rounded the corner and collided with Emily crouching on the other side.

The little spy straightened and patted her gray hair. "Excuse me, dear. I misplaced my—"

"Don't bother." Lacey veered around, but Jon caught her at the edge of the tent before she walked into the noisy party.

"Lace, wait." He observed Emily hovering nearby, walked in front of Lacey, and lowered his voice. "Please let me—"

"Hey, Jon. What time does the midnight buffet start?" A man in a feathered gold mask that matched his sparkly tank top and spandex biker shorts approached their trio.

Lacey rubbed a hand over her face.

Jon jutted his chin forward, his tone dripping with sarcasm. "Mid. Night."

"Wow." The guy backed up. "Sorry. Didn't mean to bother you." He waggled his head as he walked away.

Lacey gave Jon the eyebrow. "Don't take it out on the passengers. You should behave with professionalism, even if they *can't* fire you for it."

"What does that mean?"

"It means no one is going to risk offending the owner's son."

"Forgive me for being rich." Jon raised his palms and laughed, but the sound carried no real mirth.

"It's not about being rich." Her volume rose. "It's about the fact that you lied to me. Every day. Day after day. Month after month."

"Excuse me, Mr. Cruise Director?"

Lacey and Jon turned again to find a woman with a broken mask.

She held the silver bedazzled piece of plastic by its elastic band. "Do these come in any bigger sizes?"

Emily swerved around them. "I can help you, dear. Follow me." She cast a worried glance their way, then left with the woman.

"Ay! Ay! Ay!" Someone at the ball repeated the cry at lightning speed. A woman in a hot pink gown with a satin bow on her head skated across the polished wooden floor as if it were made of ice.

Lacey stared at the scene that was unfolding like a half-baked sitcom. Was this a practical joke? They must be filming her with a camera. Any minute now, Jon would drop the act, point a couple finger guns at her, and yell, "Gotcha!"

But he didn't.

Jon faced Lacey and crossed his arms. "I didn't think it was necessary to pull out my bank statement and wave it around."

"It's. Not. About. Money," she said. "I don't even know who you are. All those times I thought you were irresponsible and flaky because you didn't like the job. It was the complete opposite. You were working hard, learning about the family business. No wonder I couldn't reconcile your actions with who you seemed to be as a person."

"Isn't this good news?" He moved close and grasped her by the elbows. "I'm not a flake. I'm not irresponsible. And I'm in love with you."

The words she used to treasure stabbed at her wounded heart. The warmth of his hands on her arms confined instead of comforted. She felt stupid and used and betrayed and . . . and stupid.

She shook his grip off. It hurt to acknowledge him, so she focused on the partyers in the background. "This is over."

"What do you mean?" Jon bent forward and tried to capture her gaze.

Lacey looked him squarely in the eye. "I can't be with a liar."

He froze. "You're giving up on us again? Without so much as a discussion? I've waited and watched and tried to win you over a thousand times. But you won't even hear me out once?"

Her stomach tightened. "I spent my whole childhood listening to lame excuses. I've had my fill."

She needed to get out of there. Needed to be alone. Needed somewhere to hide.

Her feet swiveled on autopilot and walked away.

Jon didn't stop her.

Lacey cut across the dance floor and maneuvered through conversations until she pushed through the double doors and reached the elevators. She entered one and rode it down. Past the passenger floors. Past the staff cabins. Down, down, down to deck zero. The doors opened, and she walked the empty hallway to the place she'd once wanted to escape from with a passion—the lost and found. Lacey tried the door. *Open.* She twisted the knob to make sure it didn't lock behind her. She flicked the switch. This time, it flooded the room with light. Once inside, she shut the door.

Lacey leaned her forehead against the wall and breathed. That's all she could handle.

In and out.

In and out.

She lifted her face, and a flash of red-and-white-checkered cloth caught her eye. A lump the size of a sour grapefruit rose in her throat. Lacey clamped her lips shut and crumpled to the ground. The silent tears poured as her lungs heaved.

Love was no picnic.

CHAPTER 42

"THERE'S NO MORE SILVER ONES!" The woman with the broken mask wriggled her shoulders in front of the entryway table.

Emily threaded her fingers together so as not to smack the whining adult. "Choose from whatever's left."

"All the good ones are gone." She held up her original mask. "I wanted one exactly like this but bigger."

"We don't always get what we want in life, dear." Emily took the dangling piece of plastic and spun the lady to the table. "Pick or get over it. Those are your choices."

The woman chose a leopard-print disguise and strapped it on. "What about this one? I love cats."

"Perfect. Go enjoy the party." Emily peered around the kitten.

An elevator bell dinged, and a car on the opposite wall opened. Althea's singing filled the air. "*Oh happy day.*" She boogied out of the elevator.

Gerry stumbled behind her, bunching the train of her own evening dress, and Daisy floated at the end in a pantsuit trimmed in black lace.

"Where have you been?" Emily asked.

Gerry tugged at the bodice of her gown. "Sorry. I was having trouble with my zipper."

"Normally, it's me who can't fit into my clothes." Althea laughed. "It was nice to help someone else for a change."

"Never mind that," Emily said. "We're at code red."

Daisy tucked her black velvet clutch under her arm. "What do you mean?"

"Lacey found out the truth about Jon, and they had a skirmish." Emily herded her friends to the lido deck's entrance. "We have to fix this."

Gerry hiked her skirt to her bony knees. "Where is Lacey now?"

"She sped past me a few minutes ago. She's gone Elvis."

"Gone what?" Althea's head cocked to the side. "Is that more navy lingo?"

"It means she's disappeared."

"How did she—"

"Who told—"

"When did—"

The tardy Shippers tried to talk at once.

Emily held up both hands. "I don't have time to explain. You can hear the details later. This calls for major damage control."

She walked to the doors and scanned the sea of merrymakers. Jon remained in the same spot as before, unmoving. Why didn't he follow Lacey?

"This way, girls."

The Shippers advanced across the deck. Couples swirled on the dance floor. Live music blared from the band. A line of people exited the dessert tent with brimming plates. The ladies excused themselves as they broke through the ravenous passengers and planted themselves in front of Jon. He stood with his hands in his pockets, his face pointed at the floor.

"What are you waiting for, you idiot?" asked Emily. "Go after Lacey."

Jon's dazed stare met hers. "I wouldn't even know what to say."

"Saying anything is better than saying nothing." Althea grabbed the sleeve of his tuxedo and pulled. "Trying is caring."

Daisy took his other arm. "Women prefer a man of action, Jonathan."

His solid frame didn't move. "I should give her space."

"Mm-hmm." Gerry nodded at him. "Remember how well that worked the last time? She switched ships."

Jon's eyes widened.

All four women hollered in unison. "Go!"

He bolted in the direction Lacey had departed, the Shippers close on his heels.

CHAPTER 43

FOUR EXHAUSTED SEPTUAGENARIANS COLLAPSED AROUND a table in one of the small lounges. An hour of searching for Lacey had produced zero results. Emily threw down the battered silver mask, and it bounced off the wood and fell to the floor. She'd been clutching it since they left the party.

"Was this yours, baby?" Althea leaned over and retrieved it. "Why's it so mangled?"

Emily ignored the question and slumped on her chair. "I warned him. But did he listen? No. Lacey wouldn't have been nearly as hurt if she'd learned it from him."

Daisy flipped the French cuff of her lace sleeve. "Who told her?"

"Not me." Althea waggled a hand. "I didn't say a word."

Emily massaged the bridge of her nose. "A man came aboard at the last port. Jon's father sent him to fetch his son ahead of schedule. He was a verbal atomic bomb. Couldn't have dropped more information if he was trying. Lacey walked up behind them while they were talking and heard everything."

"How do you know this?" Gerry asked.

"I just happened to be standing nearby."

"'Just happened,' huh?"

"You tried to tell him." Althea's head shook like an overloaded washing machine. "He should've come clean right away."

251

Daisy folded her hands on the table. "I hope she's not too crushed."

"Do you think she got off the boat?" Althea asked.

"I seriously doubt it," Gerry said. "We're in the middle of the Caribbean Sea."

"If she wants to be alone," Daisy said, "we should respect her wishes. Lacey's not the type to do something foolish. She'll come out when she's ready."

"What about Jon?" Emily shoved her chair back and paced beside the table. "He's leaving for Florida soon. They have to make up before he goes."

"But Lacey's heart must be shredded." Gerry wrung her skirt with twitchy fingers. "How can they reconcile that fast? It took her years to let him in."

Daisy hugged herself. "Poor thing."

"I knew it was going too well." Gerry's melancholy side kicked in. "Things were bound to turn corybantic."

"Cory who?" asked Althea.

"Corybantic." The retired librarian explained. "Crazy, frantic, bonkers. Everything's gone sideways."

Althea grimaced. "Between you and Emily, I'm gonna need a dictionary for this conversation."

"Oh, I could shake that boy." Back and forth Emily marched. "If he'd listened to us, this wouldn't have happened. But he had to make his fancy proposal. Now he's got nothing."

"What do we do?" asked Daisy.

Emily stopped pacing and rubbed her hand against her chest. "I . . . I don't know."

The other three stared.

Althea's mouth sagged. "That's the first time I ever heard you utter those words."

Emily's shoulders slumped. She looked at the ceiling. "Lord, what do we do?"

The Shippers waited for an answer, but quiet reigned in the small common area. Almost everyone was at the ball.

Gerry's chair creaked as she leaned forward. "How about—"

A shrill laugh pierced the silence. Two women in spiky heels and matching fuchsia dresses tottered past. They giggled as they held a cell phone above them, filming a video as they walked.

"Wait." Daisy pointed with a finger. "Over there."

Beyond the videographers, Lacey appeared. Dirt smudges covered the skirt of her ball gown, and her hair was a stringy mess. With long, purposeful strides, she passed the matchy-matchy girls.

"Go," Althea whispered to Emily.

The other Shippers stayed at the table as their leader approached the girl whose cheeks were flushed, eyes swollen and bloodshot.

"Lacey," Emily called.

Lacey stopped.

Emily stood a foot away from her, respecting her space. "Are you all right, dear?"

"No." The bedraggled hostess didn't elaborate.

Emily took a step closer. "You don't have to be. This evening must've been a terrible shock."

"To say the least." Lacey tried to walk around, but Emily blocked her.

"Before you go, you should remember Jon is leaving tomorrow. Technically today, since it's after midnight."

"What?" Lacey's thoughts stuttered at Emily's words.

"He's boarding a plane for Florida when we dock in Cozumel. Do you truly want to let him go like this?" She drew near. "I'm not telling you to take him back, dear. That's your choice. But at least hear him out and then tell him exactly what you think—no matter how hard it is to say. When you get to be my age, you'll lie awake at night and ponder all the times you should have spoken up and didn't. Trust me. Don't let this be one of the times you left things unsaid."

Lacey's resolve melted under the sympathetic blue gaze. She nodded.

"Good girl." Emily took her hand. "He's not at the party. Come with me. I'll show you where he is."

She led Lacey through the ship to the main auditorium. They entered the gold-filigreed doors to the darkened room. Only the lights surrounding the stage were on. Jon sat at the edge with his legs crisscrossed, his shoulders hunched so low they almost touched his knees. His head lifted as they approached. He hopped to the floor and met them at the end of the aisle.

Emily let go of Lacey's hand. "I'll leave you two alone."

Lacey's fingers missed the warmth of Emily's grasp. She tucked her hands in the folds of her dress and focused on Jon, but he didn't say anything.

He stared at her with tortured eyes. They told her how sorry he was. And her hard expression replied it was too little, too late. If anyone walked in the room, they'd swear it was silent. But Jon and Lacey carried on a whole conversation without speaking. The semidarkness offered them sanctuary for their mangled hearts.

"Did I tell you how beautiful you look tonight?" he asked.

"Thank you." She stiffened when he reached for her. "Please don't touch me."

Jon ruffled the hair above his forehead. "I messed up big-time. The truth is, I hurt you—and it's killing me."

"Yes. It hurts." She exhaled slowly. "But we have other things to talk about."

He moved once more to take her hand, but she hid it behind her. His jaw clenched. "What kind of things?"

"Emily caught Ricardo bringing bags of flour aboard in Progreso. He claimed it was because he burned a bunch of tarts, but the chef knows nothing about him buying replacements."

"Wait." Jon shook his head. "What?"

"I remember that on the first cruise you took with us on this ship, Ricardo also arranged for extra supplies. We have shelves of provisions in storage. What difference could one grocery bag make? It doesn't add up. You should check out his story. Just in case."

"Okay." He patted his pockets. "I'll tell Collins . . . but Ricardo's not going anywhere unless he has a jetpack hidden under his bunk. First, let's finish talking about us."

Lacey retreated. "What do you mean? We need to check Ricardo's cabin."

Jon advanced and grabbed her hand. "We will. But this is more important right now. Lacey, I made a lot of excuses earlier. I deceived you and broke your trust. There's no defense for it, but I hope you'll forgive me anyway."

He placed his other hand on hers. Lacey's fingers curled into a fist. She tugged it from his grasp.

"Other women would call me a fool for rejecting a man like you." She held the fist tight against herself. "But I can't help it. My brain hears the words you're saying and tells me to let the hurt go. But my heart tells me I fell for a liar." Lacey pounded her torso. "It feels like an old raisin, all dry and shriveled."

He spread his arms wide. "What can I do?"

"It's not your fault I have . . . issues." Lacey took a step back. "It's not your fault I judged your past actions through the lens of my father's shortcomings." She took another step toward the exit. "Really, this is on me."

"What? No. I should have told you about my real name a long time ago."

"Yes. You should have. But you didn't. And you can't change that. Like I can't change how it triggers my insecurities. The answer to your question is—nothing. There's nothing you can do. Except check out Ricardo's cabin, and . . . and . . . go away."

Jon didn't argue. He stood there, silent and grim. But his eyes pleaded with her.

Lacey turned. Her feet carried her up the aisle and out the auditorium door. She walked without looking where she was going—or caring. She wasn't running from love this time. She was choosing to walk away. But the result was the same.

She left him. Again.

And he didn't follow her. Again.

CHAPTER 44

Jon rapped his knuckles on Ricardo Montoya's door and waited. No answer. He glanced at one of the men behind him and nodded. The security guard withdrew a passkey from his vest pocket. He stuck the card in the electronic reader. It beeped, and he opened the door. The tiny cabin sat empty.

Collins poked his head over Jon's shoulder, smacking away on his gum and pushing Jon's already frayed nerves to the edge. His father had sent Mr. Eliot the nursemaid to escort him home. The love of his life dumped him in no uncertain terms for justifiable reasons that were his own boneheaded fault. And they were seconds away from finding more drugs on a Monarch ship.

A few nights ago, he'd been on Cloud Nine. Literally. Now it felt like Cave Negative Twelve.

The guard, Collins, and Jon entered the room and shut the door behind them.

"Where do we start?" Jon asked.

"I'll take the bathroom," the guard said. "That's where they found the stash on the MS *Versailles*."

Collins plodded around the bedroom, pulling back the drawn curtains on the bunk beds and lifting the mattresses. He pointed a finger at the desk as he rummaged through a stack of laundry. "Check those drawers."

Jon opened them one by one. He found piles of empty candy bar wrappers, a few beer cans, and crumpled magazines. "Nothing here."

The sound of scraping echoed from the bathroom. "Nothing in the toilet," the guard called.

Collins checked the closet and dragged out a gray hard-shell suitcase. He flopped it on the ground and yanked the zipper. "Well, well, well. Lookee here what I found." He held a paper grocery bag and dumped it out. Six packages of flour with a Spanish brand name tumbled out. Collins opened one, dipped a finger inside, and stuck it in his mouth. He spit to the side and smirked. "You better not bake any cakes with this stuff."

Jon joined him and lifted one of the bags.

The guard stuck his head out of the bathroom. "You found it?"

Collins nodded. "We got him."

Laughter sounded from outside. The main door swung open, and Ricardo entered the room while talking to someone in the hallway. "She did. All I said was—"

He froze. His gaze darted around, taking in the three men, the suitcase, and the exposed flour bags.

Ricardo spun and bolted.

Jon dropped the bag and chased after him. The pastry chef pounded down the corridor. He swerved around a group of waiters. A maid with an armload of snacks turned the corner, and Ricardo plowed into her. She yelled. Her food crashed to the floor.

The collision bought Jon a few seconds. He closed the gap and dived for Ricardo's legs, knocking him to the ground. A thick rubber sole connected with Jon's chin, but he held on.

The security guard caught up and hauled the fugitive to his feet.

"Why?" Ricardo panted. "Why are you doing this?"

"You're kidding, right?" Jon stood and brushed off his trousers. "Six bags of cocaine are more than enough reason."

"Those are not mine."

"Then why did you run?"

Ricardo's lips twitched, but he remained sullen.

Heads poked out of cabin doors, and a crowd started to gather. Murmurs abounded. Collins pushed his way to the front and joined Jon, the guard, and Ricardo.

Jon cocked an eyebrow. "Thanks for the help."

"We're on a boat." Collins shrugged. "Where's he gonna go?"

Ricardo pointed at him. "You are—"

"Former FBI agent and current private detective, Reid Collins." He raised two fingers to his brow in a salute. "Never even knew I was on the case, did you?"

"FBI?" Ricardo squinted. "You said—"

"I said I was a passenger who got lost." Collins grabbed the chef's arm and jerked it behind his back. "Do I really look that stupid? I've had my eye on the kitchen staff for a while now. You were dumb enough to be a drug mule. Don't add to it by making a scene. We caught you red-handed."

"We?" Jon scoffed. "If you mean thanks to Lacey and a clever little lady in her seventies, I guess *we* did."

"Po-tay-to, Po-tah-to." Collins twisted Ricardo's arm, and the man yelped. "I'm glad this mystery is solved."

Many emotions assailed Jon. Relief wasn't one of them. Busting Ricardo meant good news for the family business. But his last excuse to stay on the MS *Buckingham* was gone.

CHAPTER 45

THE PROMENADE DECK SAT IN quiet repose as most passengers spent the morning in town. Emily stood by the railing while the last few disembarked. Sunshine warmed the top of her head, but she buttoned her jacket to her neck and pushed her cold hands into her pockets.

"I don't remember Cozumel being this chilly."

The other Shippers sat on lounge chairs behind her.

"Feels great to me." Althea tilted her face to the light. "Should we get another icky pedicure? Or see if they have a full-body fish massage?"

Gerry frowned. "How can you say that after what happened with Lacey and Jon last night?"

"I was only kidding." Althea drooped. "Trying to lighten the mood."

"I know you were." Daisy patted her. "Gerry, quit being ugly. Stop picking on Althea."

"I wasn't picking on her." Gerry crossed her arms.

"Girls"—Emily waved a hand behind her—"no time for squabbling." She leaned out as a familiar form appeared on the gangplank below. "There's Jon."

The other three scampered to her side and peered at the dock. Jon wore a navy-blue suit and expensive leather loafers. His dark hair was slicked back in a boardroom-appropriate style.

"He doesn't look like he's going souvenir shopping," Althea said.

He was joined by a shorter man in a black pin-striped suit carrying a briefcase. Mr. Collins slumped behind them wearing baggy jeans and an oversized sweatshirt with the Monarch Cruises crown on the front, a duffel bag slung on his shoulder. They walked together down the pier and away from the ship. Not once did Jon turn around.

"The detective finally found a shirt that fits," Gerry said.

"I'd hardly say 'fits.'" Daisy pursed her lips. "He must've bought the extra-extra-extra-large to have room left over."

Althea tugged at her fanny pack. "Maybe he ate so much at the buffet none of his clothes fit him anymore. I can relate to that." She squinted. "But who's the other guy?"

"Mr. McMillan's secretary," Emily said. "The one who spilled the beans at the ball."

"Oh," Daisy moaned. "This isn't good."

"He's probably leaving for Florida," Gerry said. "We have to go after him."

"Or find Lacey," Althea said. "She needs to talk to him."

Daisy twisted the ruby ring on one of her slender fingers. "Talking didn't help last night."

"But we can't let him leave." Althea cupped her hands around her mouth and hollered. "Joooooooon!"

People on the pier gawked at them.

"Stop it, Althea." Gerry poked her arm. "Everybody's staring at us."

"We can't just stand here." Althea crowded Emily. "What should we do?"

Emily didn't answer.

Sharp footsteps sounded, and the ladies saw Lacey striding across the deck.

"Thank heaven." Daisy waved at her.

Lacey stopped. She looked as if she'd like to balk, but she smoothed her chignon and joined them at the railing. "Mrs. Windsor, your tip paid off."

"What happened?" Emily eased her hands from her pockets.

"It was the hottest topic on the staff grapevine this morning. Security checked Ricardo's cabin and found flour bags filled with cocaine in his closet."

"Mercy!" Althea clutched at her shirt. "I hope they locked him up."

Lacey nodded. "The Mexican authorities came aboard and arrested him as soon as we docked in Cozumel."

Daisy picked at her manicured fingernails. "Why would he do such a horrible thing?"

"Forget the subplot." Gerry motioned to the pier. "The hero is riding off into the sunset without his true love!"

"Listen, baby." Althea placed a hand on Lacey's face and pointed it to where Jon was in the distance. "He's leaving. You have to go after him."

Lacey gently moved Althea's hand away. "We already hashed out our problems last night. Some things aren't fixable."

"You're going to let him walk off?" Gerry asked. "Forever? That isn't a good ending."

Lacey gave a sad smile. "Life isn't like a romance novel, Ms. Paroo."

"Emily, say something," Gerry urged her friend. "Convince her she can't let it end this way."

Emily said nothing. Her vision tunneled to her fingers, knuckles white as they clutched the metal railing. She plopped on a chair.

"Emily?" Gerry knelt. "Are you okay, honey?"

Emily's breath squeezed out in tiny, shallow bursts. She saw two Gerrys in front of her and closed her eyes. Her chest heaved as she tried to get a decent lungful of air. "I don't . . . I . . ."

Lacey rushed to squat by her side. "Mrs. Windsor—Emily? What's the matter? Should I call a doctor?"

It took every bit of Emily's strength to breathe. She barely managed a nod.

Lacey pulled a phone from her pocket and made the call. "Hello? I have a medical emergency on the promenade deck. Send the doctor right away." She wrapped her free arm around Emily's shoulders. "Don't worry. I'm not going to let anything happen to you."

"Oh, Lawd, please no." Althea whimpered.

The other two Shippers huddled by her.

Lacey stayed at Emily's side, rubbing her back.

The worried faces of her friends wavered in Emily's vision. She wanted to tell them everything would be okay. But she didn't have the air.

CHAPTER 46

"WHEN WAS THE LAST TIME you took your medicine?" The ship's doctor wrote in his chart. His poker face gave nothing away.

He'd conducted a thorough examination of Emily before allowing Lacey inside. She smoothed the curly gray hair from Emily's forehead and spread the blanket over her thin cotton hospital gown. The other Shippers had wanted to come in, but the doctor refused. Too crowded.

Lacey noted the tired lines around Emily's eyes. The pale cheeks. The drooping mouth. Where was the indomitable meddler? She didn't recognize this fragile woman.

"Mrs. Windsor." He asked again. "Your medicine?"

Emily reclined on the clinic bed, pleating the blanket with her fingers. "Was it yesterday? Or the day before? A lot of things were happening."

The doctor pointed an accusing finger at her. "Even if World War III is happening, you take your medicine. On time. Every day. This could've been a lot worse."

She wilted. "Yes, sir."

Lacey grasped a button on her uniform jacket. "Shouldn't we transport her to the hospital in Cozumel?"

He shook his head. "These episodes are scary but not uncommon. When a patient suffers from congestive heart failure, like Emily here, it means the muscle isn't pumping enough blood. Fluid gathered in her lungs. That's why she was short of breath. It might cause her to grow dizzy or lightheaded, but it can all be avoided." The doctor leaned on the edge of the bed and gave the patient a hard look. "If she takes her medicine."

Emily turned away, her lower jaw protruding.

Lacey nodded. "I'll make sure she does."

The doctor tore a sheet off his notepad and held it out. "I'm certain you've heard these things from your physician at home, but I'll say them again. Lessen your salt intake, avoid smoking or alcohol, and get plenty of exercise. Walking is especially good."

Lacey took the paper and pointed at the door. "Doctor, there's a group of ladies out there who must be dying for an update. Could you tell them what you told me? I'm sure they'll hold Emily accountable too."

He stuck his pen in his pocket and tucked the chart under his arm. "Good idea. I'll speak to them."

The doctor exited, and Lacey sank to a stool beside the bed.

"Tattletale," Emily grumbled.

Lacey waved the paper under her nose. "I'm sure I'll need help keeping you in line."

"You might be right." Emily sighed, her eyes closed. "I was petrified they were going to bring one of those meat wagons."

"What kind of wagon?"

"An ambulance. That's what my husband used to call them." She pushed at the pillows behind her back.

Lacey laid the paper on the side table and reached out to help her scoot up in the bed.

"I didn't expect the sick bay to be this fancy. It's nicer than my cabin. Think they'll let me stay here?"

"Don't joke about it." Lacey gulped down the lump in her throat. "I told you not to skip your medicine."

"You'd be surprised how serious I am." Emily brushed at the tape holding the IV needle in her vein. "Nothing like tiptoeing past death's door to make you evaluate your life."

Lacey sniffled. "What did you decide?"

"I decided I can't shuffle off until I make sure you're happy."

Lacey's eyes stung. She lowered her head and tried to thread a hand through her tightly bound hair. "Your health is what matters most. Don't worry about my happiness."

"I can't help it, dear." Emily reached over. With weak fingers, she untangled Lacey's hand from the now-disheveled strands. "I don't have any children of my own, but you certainly nag me like a daughter. I suppose that's why I'm so fond of you."

Lacey's lips quivered. She tried to answer, but the red-hot bowling ball in her throat blocked the words.

"Now don't cry. I'm not going anywhere just yet. I still want to see your life jam-packed with joy, and you won't have true happiness until you make peace with the people you love."

Lacey tugged her hand away and shoved the stool back. "Can't you give it a rest? You refuse to quit your matchmaking schemes even when you're lying on a hospital bed? Jon and I aren't a priority right now."

"I wasn't talking about Jon."

Lacey's brow furrowed. "Then who—"

"I meant you and your father."

She raised her chin. "What makes you assume—"

"I've lived on this earth a long time and witnessed a great many things." Emily traced the woven fabric on her blanket. "I noticed your father was a . . . disappointment to you."

"Disappointment?" Lacey grabbed a tissue from the bedside table. "That's putting it generously. He drained the life out of my mother with his laziness and self-centered refusal to be responsible for anything or anybody—even himself. I'm amazed he didn't ask her to spoon-feed him. He only got off the couch to eat, sleep, or poop." She wadded the tissue in a ball and flung it across the room. "My logical side tells me Jon is nothing like my father. He's smart, hardworking, honest." She half smiled, half snorted. "Except for the whole 'lying about his family' thing."

"A stupid decision." Emily nodded. "I told him to tell you sooner. Men never listen."

Lacey laughed a little too hard. Her stomach vibrated with the force. It rocked her body and shook the tears from wells buried deep inside her core. She covered her face and bent forward. Emily's hand settled on her back. With the tenderness of a grandmother, she patted Lacey like a baby while she cried.

"Let it out," Emily said. "It's been a rough week."

"I kn—" Lacey sucked in a breath and tried again. "I know Jon isn't my father. But my insides feel—gray—and pulled apart—like dryer lint." She sobbed. "It took all the guts I had to let him in—and h-he didn't even tell me his real name."

"He was going to." Emily tapped a steady beat against Lacey's spine. "Jon planned to reveal everything when he proposed."

Lacey's head shot up. "Is that what he told you?" She scrubbed at the tears. "How was that supposed to work? Will you marry me? Oh, and by the way, your last name won't actually be King."

"Men struggle, dear." Emily stopped patting and drew her blanket higher. "That's why they need us."

"So you think I should forget everything and forgive him?"

"No, I don't."

"Don't tell me you've finally given up on us."

"Not in a million years. But you have to forgive the first man in your life before you can let anyone else in."

"Who?"

"The first man in every little girl's life." Emily raised her eyebrows.

Understanding dawned. Lacey's jaw hardened, and she sat straight on the stool. Not a tear remained. "I don't want to talk about him anymore."

Emily reached for her, but Lacey stayed out of touching distance.

"Forgive your father." Emily's fingers splayed on the blanket. "Then you'll be able to forgive Jon and accept him for who he really is."

"My father hasn't asked for forgiveness." Lacey crossed her arms. "Not once. It never even occurred to him. Nothing is his fault."

"You can grant someone forgiveness without them asking for it."

"Why should I?"

"The Bible says God forgave us when we didn't deserve it, and we should do the same with others. Have you prayed about any of this?"

Her arms grew tighter. "I've been really busy lately."

Emily took her measure. "Do you think perhaps you avoid talking to the heavenly Father because you have such a difficult relationship with your earthly one?"

The question hit Lacey between the eyes. Of course she believed in God. Prayed. Read her Bible sometimes. But there weren't many instances where she confided in him.

"Ask God what you should do. I'm positive he'll answer." Emily's gentle gaze embraced her from a distance. "Don't forgive your father for his own sake, Lacey. Forgive him for yours."

Lacey stared out the infirmary window. The blinds were raised, and sunshine streamed into the room, casting a bright-white square across the foot of the bed. Pressure built against the back of her eyeballs, but she refused to cry any more tears for a man who didn't deserve them.

Emily leaned her head on the pillow, and her lids drooped shut. "There's one lesson I had to learn the hard way. Bitterness locks you up inside, but forgiveness sets you free. I hope you learn that truth quicker than I did."

Lacey watched the wrinkled face relax as Emily started to doze. It wasn't enough for her to meddle in other people's love lives. Now she was shaking the skeletons out of someone else's family closet.

But her words had convicted Lacey. She tried to consider the advice objectively. When was the last time she'd experienced true freedom? Without the tight little space in the back of her heart that colored the interactions with every person she met? Was this miraculous forgiveness Emily touted the key?

The infirmary door burst open and slammed against the wall. Emily's head jerked as the Shippers poured into the room in a noisy, tearful pile. The doctor followed behind them.

"Oh, baby." Althea bustled up and grabbed the headboard. "I thought you were a goner."

Daisy maneuvered around Lacey and went to the other side of the bed. "Are you sure she's fully recovered, doctor?"

"Once she rests, she'll be fine." He wagged a finger at Emily. "As long as she follows the doctor's orders."

Gerry brandished a notepad. "Don't you worry. Tell us what we need to do, and we'll sit on her and pour the medicine down her throat if we have to."

"Doctor"—Althea lightly patted the top of Emily's frizzy hair—"is it all right if I give her a hug?"

He nodded. "Please do. It might improve her condition."

Althea hunkered low and placed one soft, pudgy arm around Emily. "I was afraid I'd have to pass the pearly gates before I got to see you again."

Daisy leaned in from the other side and laid her arm on top of Althea's. "You scared the living daylights out of me."

Gerry shoved past the doctor to stand beside Althea and then wrapped her long, thin arms around the group. "Don't you ever do that to us again."

Lacey rose from her seat and tiptoed out of the room. As she closed the door behind her, Emily spoke.

"I'm not going anywhere, girls. I never leave a job half-finished."

Lacey laughed. That statement might've terrified her a few weeks ago. Now she bowed her head and prayed Emily Windsor would live to meddle in many more people's romances.

CHAPTER 47

THE BEDSIDE LAMP CAST A warm glow on the wall of Lacey's window-less cabin. She stared at the keypad on the phone, dialed twice, and hung up both times before the call connected. Her body slid off the bed and onto the floor. Lacey rested her forehead against the rough carpet. It felt comforting to be lower.

"God?" She clasped her hands together and propped them under her chin. "Since I'm on my knees anyway . . . Emily thought you and I should talk." Lacey paused, but no ethereal voice answered. "You're listening, right? I could use some advice. You used to do that kind of thing in those Bible stories, but I imagine a person has to be special to get an angel with a message nowadays."

A picture of a poofy mop of gray hair framing a mischievous face flashed through her mind, and Lacey smiled.

"Yes. Emily Windsor is a kind of angel. I admit it. But did you have to send such an exasperating one?"

Lacey waited, but the Almighty wasn't offering any audible responses. Unless she counted the washing machine tapping on the other side of her bedroom wall. Emily popped into her thoughts again. Maybe God already sent his opinion through a pushy little yenta and didn't feel like repeating himself.

Forgiveness.

Raising her head, Lacey shoved herself up and sat with her back propped against the bed. She dialed again and held the phone to her ear.

It rang twice, and her father answered.

"Lacey, is that you?"

"Hi, Dad."

"This is a treat. First, I get to see you on our cruise, and now we get to talk on the phone." Rustling sounded. "Usually, your mom fills me in."

"I stay pretty busy."

"You're an important person. Those Monarch people better be treating you right."

"They are." Lacey picked at a loose thread on the carpet. "How are you doing?"

Her father moaned. "Same as usual. I have my good days and my bad days." He launched into a lengthy explanation of his latest malady. A volley of complicated health terms rolled off his tongue like he was reading a medical dictionary.

Lacey shifted positions on the hard floor and looked at the clock on her bedside table. "Dad," she interrupted, "I just realized this is when you take your nap. You were probably in bed."

"That's okay. It's worth it to talk to you. I'm glad you got over your little snit."

Lacey jerked forward. She sprang to her feet. The old bitterness jumped inside of her like a dog with its teeth bared. "It wasn't a . . . I didn't." She squeezed her eyes shut and whispered a desperate two-second prayer. "God, help me do this."

She sank to her mattress. "You know what, Dad? I hope you get better soon."

"Me too, Lacey-bell. Me too."

Her pulse calmed. "You'd better go back to bed and rest."

"I should. Thanks for calling."

"Dad . . ." So embarrassing. Could she skip this part?

"Hmm?"

Lacey took a deep breath. "I forgive you." She almost choked on the words.

"For what?" Genuine confusion colored his voice.

"For . . . whatever."

"Thanks, honey . . . I forgive you too."

"Bye." Lacey ended the call.

She stared at the phone in silence. A teardrop fell on the glass screen, and she wiped it away with her thumb.

That was harder than I thought, God. But I'm glad I did it. Thank you for pushing me.

It turned out forgiveness wasn't a one-time thing. She suspected she'd be saying those words again over the years. But she felt . . . better.

As Abby would put it, lighter.

Like someone had opened the blinds in her brain and let the sunshine in.

CHAPTER 48

THE SWIVEL CHAIR CREAKED AS Jon swung left and right. Monarch kept a branch office in Cozumel to handle any problems with the city, port schedules, and passengers who'd been left behind. His foot bumped the side of the desk. If he swung the chair all the way around, he could look out the third-story window and see the MS *Buckingham* docked at the pier. But he didn't.

Lacey was there.

Which meant he wanted to be there. But duty and family obligation called him home. Ever since he was old enough to remember, he'd dreamed of following in his father's footsteps. That was a lot to ignore just so he could be there for a woman who continued to abandon him at the slightest sign of trouble.

Okay. The latest trouble hadn't been slight. It was the biggest screwup of his life.

Jon leaned forward and banged his head twice against the desktop. He stopped at the sound of gum popping, raised his face, and glared at Collins sitting on a brown leather couch with his feet propped up.

"You seemed to be enjoying the cruise." Jon massaged his forehead. "Are you sure you don't want to take the boat home?"

"And miss the chance to fly in a private jet? No way." Collins pushed his sweatshirt sleeves to his elbows and reclined on the cushions.

Jon lowered his head and banged it on the desk again.

The office door rasped on its hinges.

"Do you require help, Jonathan?" Mr. Eliot stood in the doorway, biting his lower lip. He crept into the room and waved at the desk. "Can I fetch you an aspirin?"

Jon shook his head. "No thank you. I don't deserve an aspirin."

Mr. Eliot bit his top lip this time. "I've scheduled one more meeting with a Monarch supplier while I'm here. We'll leave for the airport in two hours. Are you sure you don't want me to get you a hotel room where you can rest?"

"No thanks." Jon leaned back in his seat. "I still have things to think about." He whirled his chair around, pulled the cord to raise the blinds, and stared at the distant MS *Buckingham*. Late-afternoon sunshine streamed through the window.

The couch cushions squeaked as Collins moved. "What kind of things?"

"How do you fix a mistake that's unfixable?"

Mr. Eliot tut-tutted. "Nothing's unfixable. It depends on how much effort the mistake maker is willing to put in."

"Effort?" Jon turned.

"Yes, effort." Mr. Eliot undid the top button of his suit coat. "Take this morning. I bumped into you on the pier, and you dropped your phone in the water. A major mistake." He skirted around the desk and leaned uncomfortably close. "And I beg your permission to say again how profoundly sorry I am."

"I wasn't talking about the phone." Jon waved for him to back up, tired of telling the man to forget it.

Mr. Eliot straightened. "It's impossible to retrieve your cell, and I could choose to accept the bitter truth and do nothing more. But no."

"Please don't tell me you hired divers."

"No, sir. A waterlogged phone wouldn't do you any good. I had corporate email me your information, and I sent one of the people from this office to purchase a new one. Same model, same color, and same number, with all your contacts loaded. This isn't a perfect solution, but it's better than apologizing and leaving you to clean up my mess."

Jon nodded, his gaze unfocused. "Clean up my mess."

Mr. Eliot hovered. "Would you like me to fetch you anything while we wait?"

Collins revived. "How about a sandwich?"

Jon ignored him. "Please get my father on the phone."

Mr. Eliot somehow managed to bite both his top and bottom lip at the same time. "Your new cell isn't here yet."

Jon forced himself to take a breath before he answered. "Any phone will do. I need to talk to my father."

"Yes, sir. Immediately."

The secretary scuttled away, and Jon spun to the window.

Okay, God. I neglected to pray about it the last time I had a brilliant idea. We all know how my proposal turned out. What do you think I should do?

Instead of calculating the risks or worrying about what might go wrong, he sat in silence, waiting for direction from the One who already knew what was going to happen.

In the distance, a white plume of smoke drifted across the sky as the MS *Buckingham* sailed away from the pier.

Lacey stood by the balcony of Cloud Nine and watched the quickly receding shoreline. Cozumel grew smaller by the minute. The giant propeller of the ship revolved in an efficient, uncaring rhythm, taking her farther and farther away from Jon. The churning, tumultuous water in the ship's wake reminded Lacey of her soul.

Disturbed.

Chaotic.

Put through the blender.

"I found you."

Lacey spun around. "Emily, what are you doing here?"

The little woman tapped across the small private deck, leaning on a gray metal cane, and joined Lacey at the wall. "I made a deal with the doctor that I could get out of bed if I carried this confounded stick around with me for a few days."

"You should be resting."

"I should also lose five pounds, eat less candy, and stop meddling in other people's lives, but I don't think any of those things are going to happen."

Lacey smiled. "I'm glad."

"Glad I'm not resting?"

"No." Lacey took the woman's arm and threaded it through hers. "I'm glad you haven't retired from meddling. Stubborn people like me benefit."

Emily stuck a finger in her ear and wiggled it around. "Does the medicine they gave me come with side effects? I could've sworn you said to keep meddling."

"You heard right."

They stood in silence at the balcony. The blue sky glided overhead with an ever-changing vista of wispy white clouds, marred only by a translucent stream of smoke issuing from the ship's stack.

"Isn't that a little what life is like?" Emily pointed a finger. "Mostly sunny skies with an occasional stream of pollution. They're both there. It's up to you which one you focus on."

Lacey side-eyed her. "Getting philosophical on me?"

"I'm old, and I just spent the day in sick bay." Emily laughed. "Bear with me awhile."

Lacey patted the fragile hand in the crook of her arm. She stared at the dark veins lining the top. A piece of gauze was taped where the IV needle had been. "Couldn't you rest another hour or two?"

"A little swooning spell isn't going to keep me down. How can I rest, knowing what you're suffering?" Emily tilted her head. "How are you, dear?"

"I called my father."

She gave a small, approving nod. "How did it go?"

Lacey raised her palms. "He didn't declare a miraculous healing and say he'd return to work." She sighed. "But I told him I forgave him."

Emily leaned her cane against the wall and surrounded her in a wrinkly hug. "I'm proud of you. Not many people have the courage to offer forgiveness when it isn't asked for or deserved. You made a giant stride in your healing journey."

Lacey bent and rested her chin on Emily's shoulder. The woman's loving embrace applied an invisible balm to her wounded heart. She absorbed the comfort and silently thanked God for her pushy guardian angel.

Emily thumped her on the back. "Now what are you going to do about Jon?"

Lacey groaned and pulled away. "You don't give in, do you?"

"Correct me if I'm wrong. Didn't you give me carte blanche to keep meddling in your life?"

"It's too late." Lacey gestured to the speck in the distance that was Cozumel. "He got off the ship. What can I do? Jump overboard and do the butterfly stroke to shore?"

"Have you ever heard of a phone call?"

She covered her face. "I said things that can't be fixed on the phone."

"Then I'll have to finagle a way to get you off this ship." Emily looped her cane on her arm, placed a hand behind Lacey's back, and pushed her toward the door.

Lacey dug in her heels. "Even if you could make that happen, I wouldn't know what to say to him."

Emily stopped pushing and walked in front of her. "Answer me one question. And if you say no, I'll drop it. Do you want to be with him?"

Lacey swallowed. "Yes . . . but I've hurt him. More than once. And . . . he's a millionaire. Jon can do better than me."

Emily smacked her arm hard. "Stop right there. It's a wonder he doesn't trip over all the hearts and flowers shooting out of his eyes. Jon will never find a better girl than you, and I bet he'll agree if you give him a chance."

Lacey blinked through a watery haze at the greatest cheerleader of her life. Hope surged inside of her. Was Emily right? If so . . .

"I've got to get off this boat."

Emily clapped her hands and studied Lacey's white knee-length skirt. "Put your slacks on, dear. You'll need to climb off the ship into something smaller."

Her eyebrows shoved together. "You're not planning on stealing a lifeboat, are you?"

"Too much trouble." She shook her head. "In times like these, old friends are the best."

"What are you talking about?"

"Leave the details to me." Emily was pushing again. "You get ready to reenact one of those romantic airport scenes Gerry loves to write. I'll take care of the rest. It's been far too long since I visited the captain."

"Wait. How are you . . . Forget it. If you can get me back to Cozumel, I'll sign a lifetime contract for full-service meddling." Lacey slipped off her dress pumps and stood there in her stocking feet. "I'd better change my shoes too. I might have to make a run for it."

CHAPTER 49

EMILY ENTERED THE BRIDGE, WHERE a row of large glass windows fronted two raised leather seats commanding a view of the bow of the ship. One chair was empty, and Peter sat on the other. He hopped down as soon as he saw her. The washed-out first mate looked like they never let him see the sunlight. His skinny face rivaled the whitecaps dancing on the ocean behind him.

"Mrs. Windsor." His voice squeaked even though he was well past the age of puberty. "Did you come to visit me?"

"Good afternoon, Peter." She propped her cane against a control panel. "Is the captain away?"

"He went to the mess for a bite to eat. Could I be of help?"

"I came to ask a favor." Emily walked over and gave him a hug.

He squeezed her tight. "Anything you want. Name it."

She eased back and eyed him. "Stop the boat."

His thin lips gaped. He lowered his arms and stepped away. "But, Mrs. Windsor, that's against the rules. We've got to make it to the next port by sunset."

"Pish-tosh. We always arrive an hour early and sit around waiting for an available pier. You know that."

"Even so"—he shook his head—"the captain told me to hold the course. He'll put me on bread and water if I go against him."

"I'd be asking the same favor of the captain if he were here. But it's you, so you'll have to do it."

"But, Mrs. Windsor, there's no brakes on a ship. It's a complicated process. You have to stop the forward momentum. And . . . and achieve thrust reversal . . . the propeller—"

"Peter"—Emily held a finger to his lips—"I don't need a sailing lesson. I need you to Stop. The. Ship."

"But, Mrs. Windsor!"

"Please stop butting me, young man." She reached out, took his hand, and placed it on the control. "And crank that nice lever to the Stop position. This is an emergency."

Peter's eyebrows rose. "Is someone sick? Not one of the Shippers."

"No one is ill, unless you count being heartsick. But it's easily remedied if you'll do what I ask. You remember Lacey Anderson, don't you?"

He nodded.

"We have to get her to Cozumel before Jon McMillan leaves."

"You mean, the new CEO Jonathan McMillan?" Peter paled even more, if that was possible, and backed away from the panel.

"How do you know about that?" Emily asked.

He ducked his head and lowered his voice to a whisper. "The captain entrusted me with the information, but he made me swear I'd keep my mouth shut. Please don't tell him I told you."

"Don't worry, dear." Her tone sweetened. "Stop the boat, and your secret's safe with me. Plus, you'll get on the new CEO's good side. He will forever be in your debt. You'll have a job for life."

"But . . . but, Mrs. Windsor, even if we stopped, there's no way for Lacey to return to shore. She can't use one of the tenders."

Emily took hold of the man's elbow and steered him back to the control panel. "You take care of the stopping. I'll take care of the transportation."

He stood with his mouth opening and closing like a freshly caught sea bass gasping on the beach. She ignored him, took out her cell phone, and scrolled through her saved numbers. After finding the right one,

Emily dialed and waited. Glancing at Peter, she shooed him away. "Go." She pushed his arm as a voice on the other end of the line answered.

"Hello, Fernando?" Emily waved at Peter to hurry. "Do you still own that lovely little motorboat?"

Lacey cringed as the lime-green craft she'd hoped never to ride in again chugged alongside the MS *Buckingham*. She waited on one of the lower openings in the ship used to load passengers onto tender boats. Emily, Gerry, Althea, and Daisy stood behind her.

"No call for nerves." Althea laid a hand on Lacey's shoulder. "He'll throw himself at your feet the moment you come into view."

"Don't be melodramatic," Gerry said. "But I agree with Althea. He'll be overjoyed, Lacey."

Daisy gave her a well-manicured thumbs-up.

"Hurry, now." Emily nudged Lacey. "We have to get going."

"We?" Lacey stared at the four women. "Are you all coming?"

"Of course we are, baby." Althea wrapped a polka-dot scarf around her head. "You can't go without backup."

Lacey tried to reason with them—as if that ever worked. "I might be able to travel faster alone."

Emily motioned to her group. "You have almost three hundred years of experience standing in front of you, which is nothing to sneeze at. Let's go." She tossed her cane in the boat, tottered across the small gap, and grabbed Fernando's waiting hand.

"Hola, Mrs. Emily," he said. "It is good to see you again."

"Likewise, Fernando."

Lacey grasped the railing as she climbed into the motorboat, and the other three ladies clambered in after her. The trip to shore was a Shipper seminar on how to win your man. Emily coached her on being brave, even if Jon was a little cold. Gerry suggested several different apologies Lacey could use. Daisy tried to fix Lacey's hair as the wind tore it to shreds. And Althea clapped her hands at how fast the boat was traveling.

They rattled up to the dock in Cozumel, and Fernando leaped out to help them onto the pier.

Althea patted him on the cheek as she exited. "Baby, that was the best boat ride of my life."

"Thank you, Fernando." Emily passed him a twenty-dollar bill. "Here's a little extra for driving at top speed."

"Gracias." He bowed and waved goodbye.

"Let's go." She raised her cane like a general directing the troops.

Lacey caught her by the hand. "I should go alone from here. It's a long walk down the pier, and I've got to hurry."

"The story's getting good." Gerry frowned. "You're not going to make us miss the big climax, are you?"

"Don't worry." Emily took off her jacket and tied it around her waist. "We won't fall behind. Right, girls?"

"Right!" Althea and Daisy chimed.

Lacey gave up. They hurried along the dock as fast as a group of septuagenarians could and flagged a small white minivan with a Taxi sign on top. The five of them piled inside and headed for the airport.

Daisy and Gerry settled in the back. Lacey sat on the first bench seat in between Althea and Emily. She tried calling Jon's phone for the fourth time and got voicemail. She groaned.

"What do I say? I was awful to him last night."

"He loves you, baby." Althea rubbed Lacey's spine. "That covers a multitude of sins."

Gerry's head bumped the van roof as they hit a deep pothole. "Don't you worry, Lacey." She massaged her scalp. "Any woman who helped track down a ton of cocaine can recapture her man, no problem."

Lacey chuckled. "I'd hardly call six bags a 'ton.'"

"Six bags?" Emily lowered her chin. "Is that all they found?"

"Yes. In a paper grocery bag, like you said."

"But six." Emily held her hands in front of her and moved them from side to side and then vertically.

Gerry slanted forward. "What are you doing?"

She shook her head. "Each of those little bags holds five pounds.

When I met Ricardo on the pier, the paper sack was so full that flour bags were peeking out of the top. There *have* to be more than six."

"What do you mean?" Lacey asked.

Emily crossed her arms in front of her. "I mean, someone must've taken a share of the drugs before Ricardo was busted."

"He had an accomplice!" Gerry pulled out her notebook and scribbled.

"Who?" Althea leaned past Lacey. "His roommate?"

Lacey gave a hysterical laugh and pressed her index fingers to her temples. As if apologizing to the man she'd rejected multiple times wasn't hard enough, now she had to catch another smuggler.

"Driver." Daisy raised her voice to a genteel screech. "Please turn the air conditioner on. It's stuffy back here."

"It is broke." He eyed her in the rearview mirror. "Sorry."

"We're about to solve another mystery." Gerry snapped her notebook shut. "Who cares if it's hotter than blazes?"

"Excellent point, girls." Emily sat up straight.

"What is?"

"It must be eighty-five degrees outside. Why would a man wear thick jeans and a large sweatshirt? A man who hasn't worn a decent-fitting set of clothes since we've known him."

Althea gasped. "You mean—"

"I mean"—Emily tapped her finger on the seat cushion—"this morning, Mr. Collins was wearing a suspicious amount of baggy clothing."

"Wait." Lacey took her hands from her head. "They talked about this in our personnel training. Drug mules wear body suits or even tape packets to their torso under their clothes. And I caught Collins in a staff hallway one day talking to Ricardo. I thought he must be lost."

"He's lost all right." Althea nodded. "Sounds like he needs to find Jesus."

Emily scrolled through her phone. "We should be there soon. The Cozumel airport has a special lot on the east side for private planes. Driver—"

She tapped the man on the shoulder and directed him where to go.

The taxi screeched to a halt at the curb. Everyone spilled out of the back. Daisy opened her wallet to pay, and the others looked around.

"How do we ferret out where he is?" Althea asked. "Have him paged?"

"Too iffy," Gerry said. "What if he's somewhere he can't hear the announcement?"

Emily paced in a small circle beside the group. "I pumped the captain for information before we left. He was the one who arranged ground transportation for them. He told me Mr. McMillan was visiting the cruise office on the way to the airport. He's still in Cozumel."

Lacey lifted her cell and tried calling again. It went to voicemail, and she barely kept herself from chucking the phone across the street. "No answer."

Daisy dabbed the hollow of her neck with her handkerchief. "All this fuss would be unnecessary if the man picked up his phone."

"Says the woman who doesn't own one," Gerry deadpanned.

A shiny black sedan with tinted windows drove by and stopped at a special entrance about a hundred feet away. A man in a gray uniform exited the guard hut, raised the yellow-and-white-striped barrier arm, and waved the vehicle through.

"There." Emily pointed. "That car has the Monarch Cruises decal on the window. It must be him."

Lacey ran to the security checkpoint. A thin metal pole and a young man in his twenties were the only things blocking her from Jon. He tugged his cap on his forehead as she approached.

"Excuse me." She pointed in the direction of the black sedan. "Please let me talk to the man who just drove through."

"Do you have the correct pass?" He held a clipboard with a list of names and pointed to it.

"No." She watched the sedan disappear around the corner of an airplane hangar. "But it's an emergency."

He dropped the board on a shelf by the guard's station and rested his hands on his belt. "I am sorry. It is against the rules. You must go in the main terminal and talk to them."

The Shippers arrived in a noisy, panting herd.

"Young man"—Emily slapped the pole separating them from where the private planes parked—"let us through!"

The guard pulled out his walkie-talkie and motioned at her hand with the antenna. "Please move this. You cannot come back here. If you do not leave, I will call the police to escort you."

Gerry appeared on Emily's right. "Then could you deliver a message for us? We need to contact Jonathan McMillan."

He shook his head. "We cannot disturb our VIPs."

Daisy joined them. "You seem a nice fellow. I promise Mr. McMillan will be very happy. In fact, he'll be a tad put out if you don't admit us. I wouldn't want you to get in trouble."

His face twitched.

Althea shoved to the front. "What's your name, baby?"

"Ed-Eduardo." The guard rubbed his free hand against his pants leg.

"Listen, Eddie." She leaned over the pole and sweetened her tone. "You remind me of my grandson. Both hard workers. Doing your job. But this is a matter of love or death."

"Love or death?" He bent closer.

Althea put her arm around Lacey and urged her into their huddle. "This poor girl might spend the rest of her life with a broken heart if you don't allow her through. Let her talk to the man she loves."

Eduardo's jaw firmed. "This is not a movie. There are regulations. I cannot let her in because she fought with her boyfriend. She can call him."

"He's not answering his phone." Daisy flicked her handkerchief in the air. "That's the trouble."

"Then she calls him tomorrow."

Lacey clasped her hands together. "Please, Eduardo. Just five minutes."

His gaze wavered, but he shook his head. "No. It is a matter of security." He dropped his walkie-talkie in its holster and did an about-face.

"Oh!" Althea grabbed her side. "Oh, my gallbladder." She crumpled into a heap underneath the barrier arm. A breeze whipped her polka-dot scarf over her mouth, and she blew it off. "Pffft. Call the hospital, Eddie!"

The guard pivoted and dropped to his knees. "What is wrong?"

Althea moaned. "It's really the end this time. I'll get to see my husbands again in heaven." She beckoned at the clouds. "Open the pearly gates, boys. I'm coming."

"Oh, Althea." Emily grabbed the guard's arm. "Help her. Do something!"

Gerry and Daisy flanked the group. They made a wall with their bodies, blocking Lacey from the guard's view. Emily stuck her hand behind her back and jerked her thumb at the gate. Lacey hesitated only a second. She ducked under the pole and sprinted, expecting to be tackled at any moment.

"Ohhhhh, it's the end." Althea's voice howled behind her.

Lacey's feet pounded against the concrete. Good thing she'd changed her shoes. But this was insane. Would they think she was trying to hijack a plane and shoot her?

She ran past parked cars and oil drums, traffic cones, and private planes. Not a soul stopped her. Lacey slowed, stopped, and doubled over, gasping for air. She sucked in a lungful of oxygen and took off around the hangar where Jon's car had disappeared. As she rounded the corner, she saw the sedan sitting near a small jet with the Monarch crown logo on it. The door was open and the stairs to the ground remained, but the engines whirred to life.

"Wait!" Lacey bolted forward.

Could she get the pilot's attention? She passed the parked car and ran toward the plane. Footsteps sounded behind her. Had the guard caught up? Lacey tried to dodge, but a hand grabbed her arm and held on. She swatted at the fingers holding her sleeve as someone spun her around.

"Let me go. I have to stop—" Her body swung, and she banged against a familiar torso. She stared up into Jon's face.

"Did you want to see me?" He observed her without a smile or a frown.

"I thought you were on the plane."

Jon dropped her arm but didn't move away. "I was in the car, calling my father."

Lacey grabbed hold of him in a death grip. "You can't go to Florida."

"Why not?"

"Because . . ." She never had figured out the right words to say. "Because I'm still mad that you lied to me about who you are, and . . . and I need you to stay with me until I process it. I mean . . . no matter how angry I feel, it doesn't change the fact that I . . . I—"

A commercial aircraft flew low as it approached a nearby runway. The earsplitting sound of the engines drowned out her words. The ground vibrated as the plane roared past.

Lacey tried again. "I'm sorry for how awful I was last night. You didn't hurt me on purpose. I know that. And I raced here to tell you I—"

Another plane thundered over their heads. Lacey clapped her hands to her ears. Why was this so difficult? As soon as the plane was out of earshot, she removed them and hollered. "I love you!"

Jon's lips parted in a tiny smile. "Whoa. You don't have to shout about it." He placed his hands on her waist. "Are you sure?"

Her chin bobbed. "Before we met, I never realized how happy I could be. The past two and a half years taught me how life looks without you, and I . . . I didn't like it."

"I didn't like life without you either."

Lacey paused and put distance between them. "Will you get in a lot of trouble if you don't go to Florida?"

He shook his head. "I already talked with my father and said I couldn't leave until my current cruise finished. I told him I have a girlfriend who hates it when someone doesn't follow through on the job. That scored you Brownie points. He wants to meet you." Jon took a small step. "I do have a girlfriend again?"

Lacey stumbled forward and wrapped her arms around his waist. "Definitely."

He swallowed. "And you forgive me?"

Embarrassment hit her in an excruciating wave of awkwardness. She hid against his chest and nodded.

"Thank God."

Jon placed a finger under her chin and gently tilted it. He lowered his head, and his eyes focused on Lacey's mouth. A millisecond before he claimed it, she inched back.

"Hold on. If you aren't quitting, then how were you planning to return to the ship?"

He quirked his eyebrows and waved at the plane behind him. "It doesn't only fly to Florida. I was going to have the pilot drop me off at the MS *Buckingham*'s next port of call."

"Oh."

Her lower lip jutted out a little, and Jon bent once again. He pressed his mouth to hers. Lacey rose on her toes and melted into him. His right hand cradled her neck while his thumb traced the outline of her jaw. His other hand pressed against the small of her back, urging her close.

Jon allowed a centimeter between them, his breath hitting her skin hard and fast. "I might as well go for broke. Do you think my girlfriend would consider becoming my wife? When she's ready?"

Lacey laughed. She closed the tiny distance and kissed him again.

He eased away once more. "Is that a yes?"

She didn't finish her first nod before his lips covered her own. They spent several seconds punctuating their agreement. A third plane thundered overhead, and the couple pulled apart.

Lacey glared at the ascending aircraft and groaned. "Why is this tiny airport so busy?"

When she lowered her gaze, Jon was holding a small black box in front of her nose. He flipped the lid to reveal a sparkling diamond ring in a shiny platinum setting.

Her snarky eyebrow lifted. "Why did you have that in your pocket? Up until a few minutes ago, I wasn't speaking to you."

He grinned. "I'm an optimist."

"Are you sure you don't just carry it around to use on anybody?"

"Not a chance." His arm around her waist nudged Lacey tight against him. "I even had our names engraved—Jon and Lacey McMillan."

"Lacey McMillan." She repeated the name. "I like the sound of it."

She held out her left hand, and Jon slid the ring on the correct finger.

He sighed when it settled into place, and pressed a gentle kiss to her knuckles. "I was worried it wouldn't fit. I couldn't exactly ask you what your size was."

The weight of the ring felt unfamiliar on Lacey's finger. She held her hand out and admired the diamond. "You did good, Mr. McMillan."

"Thank you, soon-to-be Mrs. McMillan." He kissed the bridge of her nose. "Come on. My plane will take us to where the ship will be docking next. We'll probably beat it there." He kept his arm around her waist as they walked to the waiting jet. "Am I allowed to tell the Shippers this time?"

"Oh!" Lacey moved away. "I forgot. Where's Collins?"

"Collins? Why?" Jon tried to hold her for more cuddles.

She batted at his arms. "This is serious. The Shippers figured out—"

"Hey, what's the delay?" Reid Collins bulldozed his way out of the plane's narrow entrance and stomped down the stairs. "Let's get going!"

Sirens sounded. He jerked to the side, his shoulders hunched to his ears. Mr. Eliot scurried from the jet as a dark-blue four-door truck with the words *Policia Federal* emblazoned on the side sped up. A man in uniform climbed out and opened the rear door.

The tip of a shiny metal cane hit the ground, followed by Emily. The other Shippers spilled from the back seat.

"Oh, baby." Althea headed for Collins. "You left without giving me a goodbye hug."

"What?" He scrambled back as Althea advanced. "Who are you?"

She wrapped her arms around him and patted him up and down. He squirmed in her grasp, but she held firm.

Emily approached. "No use avoiding it, Mr. Collins. Althea's serious about her hugs."

Althea wrestled with Collins like a grandmother with an unruly child. "One good squeeze before you leave." She stroked his stomach. "You gained a little weight on the cruise. Look at this paunch."

He wriggled away and tugged on the hem of his sweatshirt. "That's none of your business."

Althea released the squirming man. "I frisked him, officer. He's hiding drugs under his clothes. Cuff him."

Collins's gaze darted to the advancing policeman. He hesitated a split second, then dashed between the cars. As he passed the cruiser, Emily stuck out her cane. It tangled in his feet. He went sprawling across the asphalt. Her Shipper companions cheered, and the officer rushed to restrain him.

Jon turned to Lacey, his square jaw sagging. "Did I miss something?"

"Most definitely." She slipped her arm around his. "I'll explain it to you on the way to the ship. I hope your jet has enough seat belts for all of us."

CHAPTER 50

Two Months Later

TALL ARRANGEMENTS OF LAVENDER ORCHIDS lined the walkway leading to the deck of the MS *Buckingham*. The bright-green helipad at the bow of the ship had been covered with special wooden flooring for the event. White folding chairs sat on each side of the aisle. Gauzy, transparent drapes stretched above the seating to form a cloudlike tent.

Emily joined her friends near the back and smoothed the sleeve of her gold jacket.

"Where's your cane?" Gerry asked.

She clicked her tongue. "I don't need that thing. It gets in the way."

"This is lovely." Daisy pulled out her disposable camera to take a picture of the flowers.

Emily shrugged. "I'd prefer a twenty-one-gun salute after everything we went through to make this wedding happen."

Gerry nodded. "I'm thankful we still live here. We might have been rotting in a Mexican prison if you hadn't convinced airport security about Collins."

"Whatever happened to him?" Althea asked around a mouthful of chalky pastel breath mints.

Emily smirked. "Jon told me the man sang like a bird after cutting a deal with the authorities. He discovered Ricardo smuggling the drugs but saw a chance to sweeten his retirement and kept quiet for a piece of the action. Would you believe the man wasn't as stupid as he appeared? He learned enough about the higher-ups in the ring to wrangle himself a plea bargain."

Daisy withdrew a fan from her purse and unfolded it. "Can we please refrain from discussing such tawdry subjects at a wedding? I'm glad Lacey chose the simple tulle. So much more timeless than satin. Don't you think?"

"I think I should've tried on this dress as soon as it came in the mail." Althea tugged at the tight fabric of her own outfit, which was doing its valiant best to contain her hips. "I hope I don't pass out during the ceremony."

"That's what you get for ordering online." Gerry dusted off the front of her regular dinner dress with the hand not holding a book. "It doesn't matter what we wear. Everyone will be staring at the bride."

"I beg to differ, my dearie." An Irish accent intruded from behind.

The four Shippers found Seamus O'Riley standing nearby with an appreciative gleam in his eye.

"Gerry, you're a stunner, and no doubt about it."

She leaned away, her paperback novel held against her like a shield. "Don't tell me this wedding includes a magic show."

"Sadly, no." He bent his head. "I came to sneak a glimpse of the finery, and here you were—the finest of them all."

"Thank you." She squeezed the words from lips pressed in a prim line.

"Would you be busy later this evening?" He sidled close to her. "I'd love to escort you to supper."

Gerry shoved her book in her purse and glowered down at the man. "I don't mean to be rude, Mr. O'Riley, but I value being honest. I prefer to date someone who can look me in the eye."

"Gerry." Daisy pinched her sleeve but received a swat for her trouble.

"No worries, my darlin'." Seamus waved away Daisy's concern with an impish twinkle. "What I lack in height, I make up for in confidence." He took Gerry's long-fingered hand and bowed over it. "Another time, then."

He walked away, and Althea locked her arm with Gerry's. "That kind of gumption is hard to resist."

"Somehow I managed."

"Today," said Althea. "But life is long, and we ain't dead yet."

Gerry humphed, and the two left to pick their seats.

Emily stayed with Daisy while she took a few more pictures.

Lacey's roommate raced up in a Kelly-green sheath dress. Her vibrant red hair exploded in a delightful riot of curls. She resembled a mischievous woodland fairy, except for the tennis shoes on her feet and the backpack swinging from her arm.

Daisy's mouth twisted at the incongruous sight. "Did you forget to change your shoes, Miss O'Brien?"

"Oh, no." Abby laughed. She slipped a pair of sparkly gold heels from her bag and set them on the floor. "I hurried here from the child-care center. It's a turnaround day, and we have to get our station set and ready for the new round of kiddos. I figured I could run easier in these."

She dumped her backpack on the ground, raised her left foot, and hopped a little as she tugged at the sneaker. Daisy held out a hand, and Abby grabbed it. She changed into her heels and hid the other shoes in her bag on the floor.

"I'll stow this under a chair until after the ceremony," Abby said.

"Are you the maid of honor?" asked Emily.

The red curls shook. "Lacey isn't having one. She said she wanted a simple wedding. No muss or fuss."

Daisy nodded. "That sounds like her."

"But I suspect," Abby said, "she didn't want me to suffer through the duties a maid of honor has. I've been crazy busy lately."

"That also sounds like her," Emily said.

Abby admired the profusion of flowers surrounding them and sighed. "I wonder if I'll ever get a chance to plan a wedding of my own."

"Oh?" Emily perked. "Lacey mentioned you were interested in our services. Do you want to get married?"

"Desperately." Abby's eyes sparkled. "If only someone could help me find the right man."

Emily took her by the arm. "Pick up your bag, dear. You should sit with us."

Abby's smile almost stretched to her eyebrows. "I'd love to."

Lacey's insides roiled as she stood alone in the dressing room. All those people waiting outside. She concentrated on breathing.

In and out.

In and out.

A knock interrupted her.

"Who is it?"

Jon poked his head around the door with his eyes shut. "I know I'm not supposed to see the bride before the wedding, but it's a bit difficult since we're walking in together."

"You'd better take a good look, then. I'm not going to lead you down the aisle like a Seeing Eye dog."

Jon peeked through his lashes and whistled. "Wow . . . you . . . wow!"

He gestured at the elegant white dress that skimmed from her shoulders to her ankles. No six-foot train for her. The simple cowl neck highlighted her collarbone. Billowy lace sleeves fell to her wrists. She wore no jewelry except for her engagement ring. Her hair cascaded in soft golden tresses.

Jon crossed the room and took her in his arms. "The day is finally here. I wish we didn't have to fly to Florida after the ceremony. Are you sure you don't want to take a quick honeymoon?"

"Watch the dress." She stepped back a little. "I want to, but your poor father has waited long enough to retire. We'll take a honeymoon in a few months, when you've settled the details."

He hugged her close. "A long one?"

"Deal." Lacey took a shuddery breath.

"Scared?"

"A little." She studied the tips of her open-toed shoes peeking out from the hem of her gown. "Am I not supposed to admit that on our wedding day? I should be confident and free from doubt."

Jon placed his hands on her lace-covered arms. "It's okay. I promise you'll be fully confident by our golden anniversary."

"Fifty years with you?" Lacey reached up and tugged on his tuxedo lapels. "That sounds pretty great to me."

"Hey." He batted at her fingers. "Watch the suit."

Lacey grabbed the silky material and pulled him level to her height. "Don't worry. I'll make it worth the wrinkles."

Jon made one last check to ensure the musicians were ready. The scent of flowers floated on the breeze as he met Lacey in the entryway to the forward deck. The buzz of family and friends drifted through the open double doors. Once the string quartet started, Jon and Lacey would walk out together. He settled his hands on her waist and bent to look into her downturned face.

"Nervous?" he asked.

She shook her head even as she said, "Yes. Is everything going smoothly with the guests?"

"Not exactly." One side of Jon's mouth tilted. "My three nieces are fighting over whose basket has the most petals. I told you we should have chosen one flower girl."

"But it would've hurt the other two's feelings." Lacey grasped her orchid bouquet. "I couldn't start out my job as their aunt that way."

"This is why my sister adores you already." He tweaked her earlobe. "She even said she was sitting on the bride's side of the aisle today." His smile faded. "Are you sure you're okay getting married here? Since your family didn't come."

Her gaze dipped. "I won't pretend it didn't hurt. But Dad was being

Dad. When his so-called chronic fatigue flares, Mom has to be there to wait on him hand and foot." She lifted her chin. "This is par for the course with my family. Your mother and father are in the front row, gloriously normal, ready to treat me like their real daughter. They're my bonus gift for marrying you. But you get a burden from my side."

Jon held a finger to her mouth, not quite touching her lips. "Nothing about you is a burden." His smile appeared. "Except your overly fussy attitude about litter."

Lacey swatted his finger away. He cradled the sides of her head.

"The best day of my life was when you told me to pick up that piece of trash. You captivated me from that first moment with your passion, your beauty, and your wholehearted commitment."

Her cheeks flushed as moisture gathered in her eyes. "And you ensnared me with your humor and kindness and your inability to take no for an answer."

"Ensnared?" Jon's lips twisted. "Makes me sound like a guy wearing head-to-toe camo, setting rabbit traps in the woods."

"I tried to run like a rabbit." Lacey laughed. "More than once."

"Thank you for stopping." He went to wrap his arms around her, but she blocked him with her bouquet.

"The dress," Lacey reminded him.

He groaned, then bent his arm at the elbow and held it out. "Let's get the 'I dos' over with so I can kiss the bride."

Lacey curled her hand around his forearm. "Thank you for escorting me down the aisle. There's no one else I'd rather walk with."

Jon leaned forward and lightly bonked his forehead against hers. "Right back at you."

"I now pronounce you man and wife. You may kiss the bride."

The guests laughed as Jon pumped a fist in the air. He gathered Lacey in his arms and gave all the leading men in Hollywood a run for their money for best kiss scene.

Emily exhaled. "Case closed." She offered a thumbs-up to the other Shippers. "Nice work, girls."

Abby sniffled on the chair at the end.

Daisy opened her clutch purse, located an embroidered handkerchief, and passed it to her.

"Oh, Mrs. Masterson, you keep it," Abby said.

"Don't worry about me." Daisy produced an identical hankie from the bag. "I came prepared."

The two petite women with identical builds sat side by side—Daisy in a black cashmere suit with her silver hair woven into a sophisticated French braid and Abby in her vibrant green dress with her fiery red hair spilling down her back.

Gerry leaned to Emily and whispered. "They bring to mind a before-and-after picture."

Emily chuckled.

The minister dismissed the crowd, and the guests rose from their chairs. They walked to a nearby area, where the reception waited. Twenty-four-inch glass vases with cascading cherry blossoms sat in the center of round tables, and the finest china held the chef's phantasmagorical creations. The ship's jazz combo played live music as the diners settled in for a wedding brunch.

Abby sat with the Shippers, still making use of Daisy's handkerchief. "It's silly to cry, but I'm thrilled for Lacey." She wiped away another tear. "And I admit it, sad for me. Who knows what kind of roommate they'll give me next? No matter who they choose, she could never top Lacey." Abby's voice cracked at the end, and Daisy patted her.

Althea leaned over Daisy to add her support. "Never you mind, baby. We'll make sure you aren't lonely." She twinkled at Gerry and Emily. "Right, girls?"

"Careful, Abby." Lacey's voice came from behind. "Don't let them lock you in any closets."

The group stood to give hugs to the bride and groom. Daisy complimented Lacey on the timeless fashion of her dress. Althea and Abby both begged her to toss the bouquet their way when the time came. And

Gerry scribbled in her notebook as the inspiration hit. Emily stood a little apart, rubbing her chest.

Lacey pushed through the Shippers to stand in front of her. "What's wrong? Is your heart hurting again?"

"No, dear." Emily smiled. "It's bursting with happiness."

Lacey's shoulders relaxed. "Even though I won't be here, you have to take your medicine without fail. I've already made Abby promise to keep an eye on you."

"Oh, pish-tosh."

Lacey hugged the smaller woman and squeezed gently. "Thank you. For being my courage when I didn't have any."

Emily smacked her on the spine. "You had plenty of courage. I only helped you find it."

Jon appeared beside them. "Are we finally forgetting about wrinkling the dress? Because I'd like to get in on this." He wrapped his arms around both women, bent, and placed a kiss on Emily's cheek. "How can I ever repay you?" He looked at the other three Shippers. "All of you."

"That's easy," Althea said. "You can have four daughters and name one after each of us. Although, I suppose you could name a boy after Gerry."

"Hey." Gerry obviously didn't care for the idea.

"Four daughters, then?" Jon said. "We'll get right on it."

Lacey elbowed him as the tips of her ears flushed pink. "Behave yourself."

He let go of Emily, took Lacey's face in his hands, and kissed her just as the master of ceremonies called for the bride and groom's first dance. Jon led his new wife to the floor and dipped her in front of everyone.

Althea sighed. "I remember when that was me."

"I bet Jon's back remembers it too," said Gerry.

After the dancing and speeches and farewells were done, the four Shippers stood on the deck as Lacey and Jon climbed into the waiting town car on the pier below and rode away.

Daisy collapsed on a nearby chair. "Thank heaven that's over. They were the most contrary match we've ever attempted. I thought we'd never see this day."

"Oh ye of little faith." Althea sat beside her and pulled out her phone. "I'm gonna send pictures of Lacey's dress to my granddaughter. She'll love it."

"It was gorgeous." Gerry wrote in her notebook. "I think I'll use it in the scene I'm writing, where the jilted bride sits alone in the church parking lot and weeps."

"Don't you dare." Emily shooed her hands at Gerry. "You aren't permitted to use my girl's dress for any kind of tear-jerking scene. There're only happily-ever-afters connected with this wedding."

"I agree," Althea said. "Lacey and Jon rode off into the sunset, and we mark another successful couple off our list."

"After much struggle," Daisy added.

"Oh, you know it." Althea crossed her legs at the ankles and stretched her arms above her head. "Now the excitement's finished, I'm going to make dodo for a week."

"That sounds dirty," said Gerry.

The New Orleans native blew a raspberry. "It means I'm crawling in bed to sleep for seven days straight."

"No time for naps." Emily reached out and tugged Daisy and Althea to their feet. "I'm calling a strategy meeting."

"What for?" they asked at the same time.

"Our new client. Don't you remember that cute little redheaded Abby practically pleading with us to find her a match?"

"I don't recall her pleading," Gerry said.

"Regardless." Emily waved a hand. "There's not a moment to waste. As Althea likes to point out, the love of Abby's life could be walking up the gangplank in the very next group of passengers."

"She's not allowed to date passengers," Gerry reminded.

Emily put her arms behind the other Shippers and gave them something in between an embrace and a shove. "I'm sure the Lord put her in our path for a reason. We have to create a new folder, gather information for her profile, and compile a list of possible matches. There's so much to do."

Emily unwrapped a piece of butterscotch candy as her feet did a little dance against the deck. "But I'm sure it will be our best match yet. I feel it deep down in my bones."

ACKNOWLEDGMENTS

WILL IT SEEM STRANGE TO begin by acknowledging my fictional characters? Thank you to Emily, Gerry, Althea, and Daisy. The Shippers have brought much-needed laughter to my life with their story, and I'm so thrilled to share it with others now. These feisty women are an inspiration for what my later years can be, and I hope I experience as much romance and adventure when I reach my seventies.

I thank God for the two people who taught me to love traveling from my earliest days. My mom and dad kept the wheels rolling throughout my childhood and bought me plenty of books to read in the back seat. They are my heroes.

All the amazing people on my Kregel team polished this novel until it shone bright. Thank you for being a joy to work with and a constant support. And a special thank-you to Janyre Tromp for listening to my pitch that day at the writer's conference and believing my story was worth telling. You were the first editor to support me through the intensive road to publication. I pray God brings many readers to enjoy your own books.

The Scribes236 writers critique group saw this novel in its earliest stages and helped weed out the inconsistencies and bad grammar. Their encouragement and willingness to laugh at my wacky characters cheered me on.

A big shout-out to my kind and talented agent, Cynthia Ruchti.

ACKNOWLEDGMENTS

Thank you for taking a chance on me. It was like being asked to sit at the popular kids' table by the prettiest girl in high school.

Although I've loved books since my childhood, the dream of creating them came as a delightful surprise. God hid that particular plot twist in my own life story until I was ready. I praise Him for His plans and look forward to the surprises He still has in store for my future. Thank You, Lord. I'm honored to tell Your stories.

ABOUT THE AUTHOR

SHANNON SUE DUNLAP LIVES IN hot and humid Texas where she writes stories with a dose of laughter and a spoonful of God's love. She references Mr. Darcy far too often, enjoys traveling the world, and can sing a surplus of obscure songs from classic movie musicals. She's a die-hard fan of happily-ever-afters and believes our heavenly Father has a tailor-made one for each of us.